STEELE OF
THE NIGHT

A Daggers & Steele Mystery

ALEX P. BERG

BATDOG PRESS
KNOXVILLE, TN

Batdog Press
www.batdogpress.com

Publisher's Note: This is a work of fiction. Names, characters, places, and incidents portrayed in this novel are a product of the author's imagination.

Cover Art: Damon Za
Book Layout: ©2013 BookDesignTemplates.com

Steele of the Night / Alex P. Berg — 1st ed.
ISBN 978-1-942274-23-0

1

Fine frozen flecks filtered through a sea of clouds, slowly drifting onto rooftops and streets and knit cap-covered heads. They gathered on metal gutters and the fine needles of the occasional pine that sprouted from New Welwic's vast expanse of concrete and pavers, but like icy magician's assistants, they disappeared as soon as they met the ground's warm embrace. They tried in vain to bring with them a goosebump-inducing chill, but the air itself opposed them. Given the salt-laden headwinds I'd experienced over the past few days during my cruise through the Wel Sea, today felt balmy by comparison.

Some of the flecks drifted onto my jacket, instantly melting into moist specks thanks to my body heat. Hopefully they wouldn't harm the leather.

I turned the corner from Schumacher onto 5th, looking up at the 5th Street Precinct's imposing façade as I always did. Oftentimes, because of the building's orientation, the sun gleamed off the wide, iron-banded double doors in front and filled the seal of justice overhead with a divine, righteous light, sending shadows dripping from the soaring eagle's claws and providing a gravitas to the scales clutched therein.

Not today. The entire seal appeared flat and lifeless, as if viewed with one eye closed. Perhaps the gods conspired to make the elements reflect my own state. If so, I could only hope the clouds would break soon. I'd already concluded I'd do whatever it took to get my feet back on the sunny path.

I yanked on the doors and stepped foot into the precinct. The officer stationed at the welcome desk gave me a nod, and I returned the favor. Beyond him, in a dark cavernous room made even less appealing by the current solar conditions, stretched a quagmire of portable office partitions, worn wooden desks, and coat racks sourced from the finest government surplus furniture supplier. Despite the fact that smoking was supposed to be limited to the front steps, hints of tobacco lingered in the air, as well as whiffs of roasted coffee beans, the drug of choice for those of us who were law-and-order minded. Both of those scents masked the ever-present muskiness of the pit's interior, a mixture of old stone, packed bodies, and whatever aromas wafted up from the morgue in the basement. Thankfully, the latter was only a problem during the worst days of summer.

I glanced toward the pit's side, where my desk sat empty except for the persistent pile of paperwork that graced its corner. Its condition didn't surprise me, but the barren nature of the desk across from it did.

Steele's workspace had been nearly cleared. All that remained were a small framed portrait of Shay and her parents, a bundle of silk flowers that had replaced the plant she'd once tried to nurture in the pit's too-gloomy interior, and a few stacked books.

As if on cue, a mountain approached the desk and scooped the remaining items into an empty fruit crate. Not a real mountain with crags and snow and leaping goats. More of a metaphorical one, with broad shoulders, tree-trunk legs, crags on his forehead, and a less stony disposition. Folton Quinto, to be exact—all six foot six and three hundred odd pounds of him.

My gray-skinned, part-troll detective friend of a decade hefted the crate the way a smaller man might lift a pillow. He turned and brought it with him into the Captain's office—or at least what used to be the Captain's office. Now it was simply the captain's office, with a small 'c,' or perhaps Captain Steele's office. The latter seemed like the obvious way to refer to her, but it didn't roll off the tongue quite the same way her predecessor's designation did.

I caught sight of her through the office's interior windows, standing at the exterior ones with her back to me and staring at the gloom outside. She hadn't spotted me. Neither had Quinto, unless I was mistaken. I took advantage of the opportunity and headed straight to the break room.

I snuck in there with no one the wiser, working my way to the coffee pot. I snagged a mug off the shelf and filled it with coffee that based on the steam was somewhere in the temperature range of boiling hot to 'removes the entire lining of your mouth.' I set my full mug aside while I filled another with hot water from a simmering pot. As I flipped through the tea box in search of something earthy and strong, a familiar cheery voice sounded behind me.

"Daggers! Hey. I didn't see you come in."

I turned to find Quinto's longtime partner and another of my dyed-in-the-wool friends, Gordon Rodgers, standing behind me. Due to his impeccably shorn sandy blond hair, blue eyes, and youthful charm, Rodgers looked much like one of those cover models for teen romance novels. Of course, the guy was married with a couple of kids, and he'd long since traded in his rakishly disheveled shirts and worn jeans for suits and ties, but I'd bet he could land a job selling perfume to old ladies in a heartbeat if the detective thing stopped working out.

He gave me a nod. "You're in early. I mean, not in the absolute sense, but for you."

I shrugged as I plucked a packet of black breakfast tea from the basket. "I couldn't sleep. Lots on my mind."

Rodgers pursed him lips. "Yeah, I hear you. Say…is that a new jacket?"

I looked down at my black leather torso insulator. "Yeah, I picked it up on my way into work this morning. Lambskin, with a removable fleece lining for cold days. I figured it was time."

"You bought it *this* morning?" Rodgers whistled. "You weren't kidding. Was the sun even up when you left your apartment?"

"Possibly," I said. "Hard to tell with the clouds."

Rodgers blinked. "And all this was *voluntary*? You weren't coerced or blackmailed in any way?"

"What can I say? I'm turning over a new leaf."

"More like uprooting an entire tree." Rodgers eyed me dubiously. "So...I hesitate to ask, but what happened to your old jacket? Did you drag it behind a shed and put it out of its misery?"

"I'll give it a proper burial. Stick a picture of it above my mantle."

"Be sure to send word if you're having a memorial," said Rodgers. "I'll send flowers."

I snickered. Rodgers was getting better at his zingers, as well as keeping a straight face while he delivered them. Maybe there was hope for him, yet.

I tore open the tea packet and plopped the bag in the mug of hot water. "I'll do that. Regrets only."

"So what about Daisy?" asked Rodgers. "How's she adapting to the eviction?"

Daisy was my foot and a half long steel truncheon. I'd christened her years ago, though I'd forgotten why. Probably because I'd been bored and lonely and desperate for human contact. Thankfully my personal situation had improved since then—I hoped.

"She's doing fine," I said, patting my jacket. "This coat's got deep pockets, just like the last. Give her a week, she won't know the difference."

"A week? I figured you'd sweat through the lining in an hour or two, tops."

"Very funny." I tested my coffee and found that it had cooled to a mouth-pleasing scorch. As I took a sip, I peered around the edge of the break room cabinets and hazarded another glance toward the captain's office.

Rodgers noticed my gaze. "So, uh...how are you doing? You know. With everything."

He didn't have to elaborate. I knew precisely what he referred to.

After our jowl-faced bulldog of a Captain had revealed to us last night that he'd chosen to resign in the face of corruption allegations—unfounded to be sure—he'd named Steele to the position of interim captain, in part for her intelligence and overall skill but equally in part for her newness. Having spent only a brief six months on the force, she couldn't in any way, shape, or form be tied to the elements of corruption that had tainted both the Captain and a number of other police officers, including my own former partner, Griggs.

In some ways, it was a smart decision. In other ways, it was utterly terrible. Either way, I hadn't taken it well. Despite the fact that I'd been implicated by association in the corruption scandal, I'd still harbored hopes of becoming captain. Maybe not this soon, to be sure, but some day. To be passed by Steele, who possessed roughly a twentieth of the experience I did, hadn't sat well with me. Still, I should've gone over and embraced her, clapped her on the back, congratulated her, and told her how proud of her I was.

Instead I'd stormed off in a huff.

On any other day in our history, my resentful fit barely would've registered—Steele had forgiven me for far worse behavior—but the situation, *our* situation, had changed dramatically over the past few days. We were no longer mere partners. We'd grown much closer over our three day luxury poker cruise case. We'd shared tender moments. We'd become intimate. And at least *one* of us was falling hopelessly, head over heels for the other—the one with a gruff exterior and a heart of gold. The former owner of a desiccated, cracked leather jacket in need of euthanizing, to be precise.

And that same doofus had mucked everything up.

I plucked the tea bag from Steele's mug and pitched it into the waste bin. "I behaved like a petulant child last night, Gordon. I might've really screwed the pooch. I'm about to head over and apologize, but I figured I'd stop by and get her a peace offering before I did so."

Rodgers eyed the tea. "Well, that sounds like a good call. You did storm off without saying anything. But I'm sure it can't be that bad. Your reaction was natural, given the circumstances."

I gave him a look. "It's more complicated than that."

He raised an eyebrow. "How so?"

"Can't really talk about it here. I'm sure you can connect the dots."

The eyebrow lowered. "Right. Well, I wish you the best of luck. But before you go..."

"Yes?"

This time, Rodgers glanced toward the captain's office. "She needs help, Daggers. It's obvious. Quinto and I are doing what we can, but you're her partner. You're the one in the position to do the most."

He didn't even know the half of it.

I grabbed the mugs and turned toward the door. "Way ahead of you, Rodgers. I just hope she's willing to accept my hand when I offer it. I should've tucked an olive branch into my jacket pocket instead of Daisy."

2

The door to Steele's new office had been propped open. I approached it and knocked on the frame as best I could given the two mugs I held.

Shay turned from the window at the sound. Today she wore an elegant black suit with high-waisted pants and a tightly-tailored jacket that flared out over her hips. A bright ultramarine shirt formed a neat triangle over her torso, framed by her jacket's wide lapels, and a pair of black heels brought her naturally tall, lithe form to a clean six feet. She'd parted her hair simply, letting the long locks fall on either side of her face. Her peaked elf ears poked through the cascade of chocolate brown. She blinked and cast her piercing azure eyes in my direction. My heart thudded in my chest, despite my resolve.

"Daggers?" Her already arched eyebrows lifted in surprise. "What are you doing here so early?"

Quinto, who leaned over the captain's desk arranging the items he'd brought with him in the fruit crate, straightened and took note of me as well. "Whoa. Yeah, what is it? Eight-thirty? I wasn't aware you even knew this portion of the day existed."

I ignored the big guy's barb, delivered with one of his trademark wide, bucktoothed grins. I lifted the mugs. "I brought coffee and tea. Mind if I come in, er...Captain Steele?"

"Oh, come off it. You don't have to call me that. Steele will suffice."

But not Shay, I noticed. Was it a conscious slight or an unconscious one? Or perhaps a result of Quinto's presence?

The big guy gave me a nod. "I only see two cups, and you know I don't drink coffee."

"And I only have two hands," I said. "Besides, this stuff is piping hot. With your surface area to mass ratio, I figured it would make you unnecessarily warm, especially considering all that heavy lifting you're doing."

Quinto glanced at the crate. "The lifting's all done. Steele didn't have much to move, to be honest. I suppose that's a good thing. It'll make the move back easier once her interim status expires."

I crossed over to Steele and extended the mug of tea. "Black. That's the way you like it, right?"

She accepted the offering with gentle hands, but her eyes retained a hint of wariness, like a stray dog unsure of a stranger's intentions. "Thanks."

I took a sip of my brew to calm my nerves, although given the caffeine, I wasn't sure it would provide the desired effect. "So...how are things going so far? You know, with the new position."

"As well as could be expected, I guess," said Shay, testing her tea with her lips. "Quinto's helped me move my things, as you can see. Rodgers has been running interference, which is nice. I've only been approached from officers once with a request for input. Then again, I've only been here for a half hour, so there's plenty of time for disasters to develop."

"You can't approach this promotion with that sort of attitude," I said. "Think positive. I'm sure you and I will encounter smooth sailing as long as we work together."

One of her eyebrows lifted ever so slightly at that last part. Did she doubt our ability to succeed, or had she thought I wouldn't be on board with such a truce? Or more worryingly, did she not want any part of it?

Quinto stepped over to join us. "So, Captain Steele. Now that your personal items are in place, what's on the docket?"

Shay gave him a quick glance. "I told you, belay the captain stuff. When it's you, me, Rodgers, Cairny, or Daggers, Steele is fine. No need for titles among friends, even if I am your superior officer for the time being."

"You got it." Quinto smiled. "Although, to be fair, if you don't want us to think of you as our captain first and foremost, maybe you should stop using verbs like *belay*."

The look on Steele's face said she wasn't much in the mood for nautical humor. "Quinto, perhaps you could grab that mug of tea you were pining after? I'd like to have a word with Daggers."

She didn't specifically say alone, but it was implied.

Quinto's smile disappeared. "Right. Sorry."

The big guy about-faced and headed out the door, closing it behind him as he did so. The latch clacked, and the muted din of the pit faded to a dull hum.

I glanced at my partner. "So...how are you holding up?"

"I've been better," she said, taking another sip of her tea. "I'm tired. I didn't sleep much."

"I guess that makes two of us."

Steele opened her mouth. "Look, Daggers, about last night—"

I held up a hand. "No. Please, let me speak. First and foremost, I'm sorry. Truly. I acted like a complete and total ass last night. I should've come up and congratulated you, told you how proud I am, offered to take you out for a dinner and a drink, or whatever it is that would've appealed to you at the time. Instead I threw a hissy fit and stormed off because...I'm an idiot. And because try as I might, I haven't managed to expel every last demon from within me. I still get jealous, both in relationships and in the workplace, apparently. I still get mean when I drink to excess. And I still have occasional bouts of anger and depression, though they're getting better. But those are my problems, not yours. The point is, I apologize for my behavior, and I want to make it clear that I'm here for you. As a partner. As a friend. And hopefully, as something more than that...assuming I haven't screwed things up beyond repair."

Steele took a moment to respond, letting me soak in the unshed tears that floated in her eyes. "Jake...thank you. It means a lot to hear you say that. But you're wrong about one thing. Those problems? Your jealousy, anger, and lingering depression? Those aren't just *your* problems. They're mine too—as your partner, friend, and *yes*, as something more. You can't shut me out like you did last night. If we're going to make this work, you have to let me in. Let me help you with some of those."

My heart soared upon hearing her words, knowing my actions hadn't fully stretched beyond the pale. I nodded. "Yes. I know."

"Do you? Then why are you still so angry?"

I notched an eyebrow. "*Angry?* What are you talking about?"

"You can't pull the wool over my eyes," said Shay. "I can see it in your face. The creases in your brow, the tension in your jaw. Maybe you *want* to be fine with me being named interim captain in your stead, but you're clearly not."

"Huh?" I blinked. "Oh. I think I understand the confusion. Yes, I'm angry—but not with you."

"No?"

I shook my head. "I'm angry with the Captain. Partly for overlooking me in favor of you, I'll admit. I've dreamed of heading the precinct one day, and given that homicide detectives have a good track record of being elevated to the position, I figured I had as good a shot as any. But more importantly, I'm angry with the Captain for putting you in this situation. I mean, to thrust you into a position of prominence with no warning, without training you or preparing you or vetting you to any degree, without giving you any guidelines and without extending a helping hand—it's eminently unfair. Don't get me wrong. I agree with him that you have the skills needed to make a great captain. You're intelligent, observant, and disciplined. You have natural leadership qualities. You don't take crap from anyone, and you're a top notch detective to boot. But no one inherently understands how to run a police station after six months on the job. The Captain threw you into the fire—a fire he essentially started with all those corruption allegations swirling around the Wyverns. I'm not sure I can forgive him for that."

Shay tilted her head. "Really? *That's* what you're upset about?"

"Absolutely," I said. "But don't fear. I'll do whatever I can to help out. Paperwork? Check. Pre-screening complaints to see what's worth your time? Check. Can't figure out what the procedure is on a certain situation? I'll point you in the right direction, and if I don't know, I'll track down someone who does. And if things get really rocky, I'll channel the spirit of our departed former Captain and become your attack dog. Anyone messes with you, and I'll maul them like a rabid wolverine."

Shay smiled. "Aww... Offering to commit senseless acts of violence in my name? How sweet."

I smiled back. "Better believe it. But seriously, anything you need. Just ask. Or don't. I'll try to keep my eyes open."

Shay's smile widened. "Thank you, Daggers. That means more than you know."

"So we're...okay, then? After last night?"

"You could say that," said Steele. "To be quite honest, I'd like to kiss you."

I leaned in a little. "You could, you know. You're the captain now. Nobody here has the authority to stop you, and I promise not to file a harassment lawsuit."

Steele peered to the side. "I'm not sure it's such a good idea. People are watching, figuratively and literally. Not a good precedent to set for my first day on the job."

I followed her gaze. Activity in the pit appeared normal on first glance, but a more thorough examination showed an increased level of surveillance focused in our general direction. Quinto and Rodgers I could deal with, but it seemed as if a good third of the pit's inhabitants cast furtive glances our way.

I frowned. "Well, if kissing's out, I guess casual groping is, too."

"Don't push your luck," said Shay. "Perhaps we can build our way back up to that—assuming you can answer me a final, burning question."

"With that sort of lead up, how can I say no?"

Shay gave me a nod. "What's with the jacket?"

I snorted and smiled. "I thought you'd notice. I picked it up on the way into the precinct this morning. What do you think? Do I look dashing?"

"Oh, it looks great," said Steele. "But I was more interested in *why* you bought it. Did the mice get fed up with the rents you were charging them on the last one?"

"You sound like Rodgers. No, I just thought it was time for a change. I took your comments about my appearance to heart—which isn't to say I'm about to start wearing suits and ties to work, mind you. But I figured I could upgrade my attire *a little*."

"So now you're *listening* to me?" said Shay. "You do realize this means I'm reconsidering my self-imposed ban on kissing."

"I'm normally a fan of law and order," I said. "But hey, who am I to judge if the captain bends her own rules every now and then?"

My partner leaned in closer. Lilac perfume drifted off her neck, producing a heady aroma that roiled my thoughts and emotions. Her lips puckered, but a knock at the door derailed whatever tender moment might've elapsed.

Shay pulled back and called out. "Come in."

The door opened, and in stepped a blond, clean cut, fresh-faced young man. He reminded me of Rodgers except ten years younger and with the sharp blue uniform of the city's patrol officers in place of our detective's whatever-you-please attire. I recognized him right off the bat.

"Hey, Phillips," I said. "How's the beat treating you?"

"Not too bad, Detective Daggers," he said. "I've yet to be stabbed or beaten while on the job, so that's not too bad."

"But not while off duty?" offered Steele.

"Figure of speech, Detec—I mean, *Captain* Steele," said Phillips. "Congratulations on the promotion, by the way. Much deserved, as far as I'm concerned."

"Thank you," said Shay. "You bring news, I assume?"

"Right you are," he said. "Even though *I'm* fine, not everyone in New Welwic can say the same. There's been a murder. Rucker Park. Cops found the guy about an hour ago."

"Of course there was," said Steele. "What can you tell us about it?"

Phillips pursed his lips. "Well...that's the thing, you see. It's sort of an odd situation. Hard to do it justice with a description."

I lifted a brow. "Well, if nothing else you know how to get a homicide detective's attention. You want me to check this one out, Steele?"

"By yourself?" she said. "You don't really think I'll let you traipse around solving murders while I'm stuck here fending off attacks from would-be bureaucrats? I'm coming with you."

I shrugged. "Fair enough. The Captain was gone most of last week in meetings, and the rest of the 5th's occupants somehow managed to keep the fort from burning down. We'll snag Quinto and Rodgers, too. Phillips? I'm assuming you can show us the way?"

The young man lit up like a lantern. He not-so-secretly aspired to be a detective someday. At first I'd doubted his mental ability, but he'd redeemed himself over the last few cases in which we'd interacted. Like anyone else, he merely lacked seasoning.

"Absolutely, Detective," he said. "Follow me."

I gave him a nod. Steele grabbed an overcoat from a rack in the corner, and out we went.

3

Steele, Rodgers, Quinto, and I followed Phillips along a paved path that meandered through the center of Rucker Park, New Welwic's primary—and some would argue only—attempt at convincing its citizens forests weren't dark, fearful expanses filled with trolls, boggarts, and wart-nosed witches. The city planners had succeeded as far as I was concerned, but only by reinforcing a new stereotype, that of forests as havens for drug addicts, hobos, and peddlers of over-priced knick-knacks and lukewarm sausage rolls. We passed a few of the former and one of the latter as we wandered along under the centenarian trees' boughs, only somewhat shaded from the sky's meager attempts at snow by their leafless branches. After rounding the edge of a marshy pond thick with cattails and lily pads, Phillips led us off the beaten path and into the trees.

Thankfully, I didn't have to employ Daisy's services as a poor man's machete. Even though the city rarely had enough funds to authorize pay raises to its crime solving civil servants, the bean counters in charge still managed to scrape up enough coppers to pay gardeners to keep the brush in line. Of course, it was also winter, so I'm sure mother nature had something to do with it.

After about a hundred and fifty feet of walking, we came to a section of trees that had been cordoned off with thin, red rope. A bluecoat stood outside the barrier, his arms crossed and his eyelids drooping.

"Hey, Franks," Phillips called. "I brought the cavalry."

The aforementioned Franks startled and threw punches at imaginary dragons before he realized what was going on. He settled back against the tree and cleared his throat—sheepishly, if such a thing was possible. "Oh. Phillips. You're back. Head on in. Shouldn't be anyone inside at the moment...I think."

I gave New Welwic's finest a two finger salute as I stepped over the rope barrier. Quinto followed suit while Steele and Rodgers chose to go under.

"Not far now," said Phillips. "There it is."

He held his hand out toward a small clearing in the trees. Rodgers whistled. I would've if I had any whistling ability whatsoever. As it was I settled for a surprised hum.

"Holy harvest, Phillips," I said. "You weren't kidding."

Tied to the trunk of one of the trees bordering the clearing was a man with feathery, straw blond hair, dark eyebrows, and a straight but prominent nose. He seemed the sort who'd have no problem drawing the attention of ladies of all ages—at least in life. Death hadn't treated him kindly, however. A jagged wound tore through the right side of his throat, exposing the muscle and tissues beneath. Blood soaked his frilly, brown suede jacket and otherwise white shirt, though precious little of it remained unstained. Given the placement of the wound and the pallor of the man's skin, it wasn't surprising. In addition to the gash in his neck, the front of the man's shirt had been torn open. The blood marred it, but something black glistened on his chest.

As I neared the man, I noticed a couple more things. For one, the rope that tied him to the tree wasn't a rope at all. It narrowed as it encircled him, coming to a tapered point at one end and having a leather-wrapped handle at the other. A wrangling expert I was not, but even I knew a whip when I saw one. The other factor I took note of was less visual and more olfactory in nature.

"Whew," I said as I sidled up next to him. "I'm not the only who smells that, right? Phillips, how old is this guy?"

"Uh..." Phillips blinked vacantly. "Isn't that where you come in?"

"It's not from the body, Daggers," said Steele as she approached the man from the opposite side. "I mean, it is, but not from decomposition. That's a very distinctive smell. This is...different."

Shay had a point. After a decade on the force, I'd come to know the scent of rotting flesh well. This wasn't it. The man had more of an alcoholic cat's litter box aroma going on, but far more pungent than that of your garden variety drunken, urine-soaked hobo.

Quinto took up a position between Steele and me. He leaned toward the body and pointed a finger at the man's face. "What is *that*?"

Up close, I could see what Quinto referred to. Over the man's now pale skin lay a thin brown film—of what, I had no idea. I lifted a fingernail and scratched at it. A piece flaked off.

"Eww," I said.

"That's not all," said Steele. "Check these out."

She pointed to his jacket and pants, which were dotted by a number of powdery, white stains. On second glance, I noticed them on his shirt as well, though they were hidden by the cloth of the same color and the copious amounts of blood.

Rodgers' voice sounded behind us. "Guys, you mind spreading out so I can get a look?"

Quinto and I mumbled apologies and stepped back, allowing Rodgers to squeeze in between us.

He stared at the guy for a moment, his brow furrowing. "No way..."

"What is it?" said Steele.

Rodgers didn't take his eyes off the body. "I think I know who this is."

"Really?" I said. "Who? A friend of yours?"

Rodgers shook his head. "No, thankfully. But unless I'm mistaken, this is Chaz Willy Wilson."

"Who, now?" said Quinto.

"The lead singer for Yellow Cobra," said Rodgers. "You know...the rock group?"

We all stared at him. I blinked. Steele frowned.

"Oh, don't look at me like that," he said. "My wife Allison's the fan, not me. Or I guess I should say *was* a fan. She hasn't dragged me to a show in years, since before the kids were born. But I'm pretty sure this is him."

"And this band, Yellow Cobra," said Steele. "They're based in New Welwic?"

"I believe so," said Rodgers. "Toured a lot, internationally even, in their heyday. Now I think they stick around locally. The last I'd heard they performed at some rock club downtown. I forget the name."

"The Moxy?" offered Quinto.

"Yeah, that's it." Rodgers' brow furrowed. "You, uh...a fan, too, big guy?"

"I didn't say that," said Quinto. "But I'm familiar with the club. And the band."

"*You* like crooner ballads?" I asked. "I figured the only type of rock music you'd be into was that of *literal* rocks being smashed against each other."

"Just because I look like I can crush rocks doesn't mean I like listening to said activity," said Quinto. "I dabble in all sorts of genres."

"Well, if you're right, Rodgers, that's a heck of a break," said Steele. "Identification is usually half the battle. Phillips? Who found the man?"

The blond-haired eager-beaver popped around the edge of the tree. "A jogger, Captain. One of those freerunner types. Was cutting across from Abalone Avenue, doing flips off trees and stuff when he came across the body."

"Did you get a statement?" I asked.

"I didn't, but one of the other beat cops did. Pretty standard stuff, as I understand it. No reason to suspect the guy. He went out of his way to flag down an officer and report it."

"Did you search him?" I asked.

"The freerunner?" said Phillips. "Why would we?"

"The man tied to the tree, Phillips," said Steele.

The young officer blushed. Despite his increased experience in dealing with murders, apparently he could still get frazzled. "Ah...no, Captain. As far as I know, nobody's touched him."

"A pristine stiff then," I said. "If only Cairny were here."

"She gets tired of the morgue, you know," said Quinto. "We really should invite her into the field more often."

Steele took Phillips' statement as an invitation. She reached a hand into his jacket and started digging. She handed items to us as she extracted them: a brown leather change purse which still contained a number of coins based on its weight and the jingling sound it produced, a key attached to a round wooden keychain with the number '501' stamped onto it, a black matchbox with the words 'Club Midnight' printed upon the top in a difficult to read red ink, and a small, black leather bound book without any text on the cover.

Somehow, I ended up holding the matchbox while Quinto received the book. I opened up my prize, and sure enough, it held matches. Quinto cracked the pocket-sized tome and held it to his face as Steele moved to the stiff's pants.

"Well," I said to the big guy. "What is it?"

He cleared his throat. "It reads, and I quote, 'The Revenant: A Treatise on the Historical Nature and Verified Supernatural Incidents of Magic, Immortality, and the Occult.' Fifth printing, pocket version, according to the copyright page."

"Whoa, back it up there," said Rodgers. "A treatise on what now?"

Steele pulled her hands back from the stiff's pants pockets, this time empty. She lifted her fingers to his shirt, where she peeled back the blood-stuck halves to better reveal his chest. There, under another layer of dried blood, I spied the source of the black gleam I'd noticed earlier. A symbol, imprinted upon his chest—that of an ankh with pointed tips, sharp and cruel in nature.

"Uh oh," I said. "This isn't good."

Steele looked away from the body, brushing her fingers against her pants to clean them. "And why is that, apart from the obvious?"

I looked at Shay, then Rodgers, then Quinto. They all looked back expectantly. "Don't tell me I'm the only one who sees what happened here?"

"That being?" said Quinto.

"Isn't it obvious?" I said. "This man was murdered...by a *vampire*."

Steele waved her hand. "Oh, come off it."

"Look, I know I'm prone to sensationalism," I said, "but consider the evidence. This man's throat is torn open, with blood all over him. He's carrying a matchbox for a place called Club Midnight. If that isn't some sort of gothic nightclub I'll eat my shoe. He also happened to be carrying a tome about the supernatural and occult entitled *The Revenant*. Are you familiar with what *revenant* means?"

"A spirit which comes back after death," said Steele. "A ghost, specifically."

"That's one definition," I said. "But to many cultures, a revenant is *any* being which comes back from the dead, including zombies. Or vampires."

"How do you know so much about vampire mythology?" asked Rodgers.

"I read a lot. Mysteries and horror share the same literary milieu. I take notes. Up here, in the gray matter." I tapped my head.

"And those notes are how you so skillfully determined we were being attacked by *zombies* that one time," said Steele.

"Was I so wrong about that?" I asked. "Zombies. Golems. Walkers. Whatever you want to call them, I was more or less right. And if we've come across them before, why not vampires? Besides, look at his chest. You know what ankhs symbolize, don't you? Eternal life. Why else would someone who *wasn't* attacked by a vampire have that particular symbol materialize upon their chest?"

"Let's keep the crazy magic-based theories to a minimum, why don't we, Daggers?" said Steele. "Let's assume you're right, vampires do exist, and our victim here was attacked by one. Don't you think his neck wound would be a little cleaner? This throat was torn, not pierced. And there's blood all over the guy. A vampire wouldn't have let that tasty life-giving fluid go to waste, would he? Besides, I'm pretty sure that ankh symbol is a tattoo."

I peered at it. I wasn't so sure. It seemed a little too shimmery to be that. "I can't speak as to the former. I've never seen a vampire bite victim before. For all I know, it's a more *orgasmic* experience than the books portray it to be, with more ripping and tearing of flesh at the throat. But consider this—for all the blood that's on him, there should be more. The attack clearly severed his jugular. There should be dried blood on the ground, on the tree. Everywhere. And there isn't."

"Probably because he wasn't murdered here," said Steele.

"Hey, you have a theory. I have a theory."

"Mine's not a theory," said Steele. "There are tracks in the underbrush. Go look for yourself." She pointed toward the clearing.

Rodgers, Quinto, and I all turned and followed her finger. Sure enough, there in the wet leaves and grass were a number of indentations. Leave it to Steele to spot what no one else did.

I approached the nearest one and knelt to get a closer look. The indentation wasn't particularly well formed—I think dirt would've been a better conduit for it than the layer of leaves and organic matter it was imprinted in—but two things were plainly obvious nonetheless. First, the prints weren't human. They were much more rounded in nature. Second, they were HUGE. At least as long as one of Quinto's massive flippers and over twice as wide, with a pair of heavy imprints at the top edge.

I swallowed hard. "So...maybe the vampire has a friend who's a shapeshifter? Because if they're one and the same, I *really* don't want to meet them in a dark alley."

I stood. Rodgers and Quinto eyed me and the footprint. Their countenances had noticeably hardened.

"Oh, stop being a bunch of babies," said Steele. "I'm sure there's a logical explanation for all of this that doesn't involve monsters."

"Easy for you to say," said Quinto. "You're not the one with a lingering werewolf scar on her arm."

I crossed back to my partner who was investigating the whip used to tie the stiff to the tree. The handle, which hung loosely at the man's ribs, had been branded with text that read, 'Tommy Llama's—Exotic Leathers.'

"Quinto's right," I said. "You may not be the psychic prodigy you once claimed to be, but you're more well-versed in the magical and arcane than any of us. Given what you learned in school and over our previous cases, I can't believe you're not even a *little* concerned."

"I don't know, Daggers," said Shay. "I guess I'm more rational at heart. Occam's razor, right? The simplest explanation is usually the correct one. And despite what you might want to believe, monsters aren't what I'd call simple or logic—"

Steele and I both startled as a loud, inhuman cry sounded from within the trees, a cross between a deep throated shout and a woofy bark.

Rodgers looked around and into the trees. "By the gods, what the *hell* was that?"

Steele glanced at the body, her skin tone paler than it had been a moment before. "Then again, Daggers, your theories often contain elements of truth. Phillips? Let's get this body back to the precinct, ASAP. The detectives and I have a rock club to visit."

4

I yanked on the front door to the Moxy and held it open for Steele, Rodgers, and Quinto. As I followed them in, a wave of cigarette smoke and stale beer smell hit me. I tried to wave it away, but unfortunately the smoke wasn't so much an actual cloud as a pervasive entity, radiating out of the floors and walls and upholstery. As my eyes adjusted to the dim gloom within, I slowly took note of my surroundings. A lacquered bar stretched across the wall to my right, its wood marred by numerous knife-hewn carvings and warped by the sweaty bottoms of countless beer bottles and pint glasses. A sign under the stairwell pointed in the direction of the restrooms, and in front of me stretched a wide open space littered with flyers and bottle shards and mysterious stains. Past that sat the club's stage, currently with the curtains drawn open. A couple people milled upon its surface, but no one seemed interested in cleaning the mess on the main floor.

"Well, we're here," said Quinto, wrinkling his nose. "Anybody have a plan of action?"

"Why don't you and Rodgers head to the second level in search of a manager or owner?" I said. "Steele and I will see if those stagehands can help us."

Rodgers nodded. "Got it." He and Quinto turned toward the stairs.

I held my hand in the direction of the main concourse, and Steele followed it. One of the stagehands worked in the back, fiddling with the drums, or at the very least obscuring the set's view from the rest of the establishment. The guy was enormous, with a black skull and crossbones tank top showing off his thick, muscular arms. Perhaps like Quinto not all of his ancestors had been of the human variety, though if so, it wasn't obvious from his skin tone, which was a normal fleshy shade. What little light existed inside the Moxy's dim interior shone off his recently-shaved head.

The other hand sat at the front of the stage with his legs hanging over the edge. His chest length straw blond hair hung over his face as he peered at the guitar in his hands, plucking at strings and tightening or loosening the tuning pegs in accordance with their response.

"Excuse me," said Shay as we approached him. "I'm Steele, and this is Daggers. Do you have a minute?"

The stagehand lifted his head and tossed his hair back. "Steel and Daggers. *Niiiice* names. I'm Diamond. You guys like to rock?"

Good thing I hadn't brought the coffee from the office with me, otherwise I might've sprayed it all over the poor guy's face. As it was I settled for sputtering and blinking. "I...uh...what did you say your name was?"

"Diamond Drummond. I work here. I'm one of the roadies."

The other guy in the skull t-shirt spoke up. "Don't believe him. His name's really Mickey."

"Shut up, *Dennis*," said Diamond.

Big Dennis chuckled, and Diamond smiled. I glanced at Steele. She returned a rather surprised look, confirming what I already knew.

"So, Diamond," I said. "Has anyone ever told you that you look a lot like—"

"Chaz Willy Wilson," he said. "Yeah, brah. I know. He's my half-brother."

Honestly, I'd undersold it. He didn't look a lot like the presumed Chaz, who we'd found tied to a tree in the middle of Rucker Park. He looked *exactly* like him, or at least close enough for the differences to be negligible. Maybe his nose was a little less prominent, or his eyebrows a shade more narrow, but overall, they might as well have been twins.

"So what can I help you with?" said Diamond as he plucked idly on the guitar. "If you're looking for the band, they don't get in until much, *much* later, and they never sign autographs before the show. Even then, you'll be hard pressed to get their attention. Well...*you'd* be hard pressed." He gave me a nod. "You, on the other hand. *Steel.* They might be interested in you."

"I'm not sure the interest would be mutual," said Shay. "But either way, that's not why we're here. We'd like to talk about Chaz."

Diamond snorted. "Yeah, of course y'are. Go join a fan club or something."

"I think you misunderstand," I said. "We're not rock junkies. We're detectives. You know? With the NWPD?"

"Whoa, brah," said Diamond, loosening his grip on the guitar. "Seriously?"

"Aw, man. What happened this time?" Big Dennis abandoned the drums and joined us at the foot of the stage. "Did Chaz go on another of his wild, drunken benders? Get cited for possession?"

"It's, ah...*complicated*," said Shay. "To be honest, we're trying to figure out exactly what happened. We thought you guys might be able to fill in the gaps a bit."

"Well, think again," said Diamond. "We didn't party with them last night. I've no idea what he and the guys got up to. You should probably talk to Chaz himself."

"He wasn't available for comment," I said. "Bit tied up, actually."

Shay gave me a sly smile. At least *she* appreciated my wit.

"But that's neither here nor there," I continued. "Even if you guys weren't hanging out with Chaz last night, you might be able to help shed some light on the situation. Mind answering a few questions about the band for us?"

Dennis shrugged and sat down on the edge of the stage next to his blond pal. "Sure. Why not? Not like we have a whole lot to do. Bar doesn't even open until noon."

"So you guys work here?" asked Steele.

"Sort of," said Diamond. "We work for Benson. He's the Cobra's manager. But we sort of work for Gus, too. He owns the Moxy. It's complicated, brah."

Apparently, women could be 'brahs,' too. Good to know.

I scratched my head. "What do you mean?"

"We work for Benson, but because Yellow Cobra's had a standing gig at the Moxy, we got conscripted to do regular bar work, too," said Dennis. "Cleaning, maintenance, moving crap around, bartending. That sort of stuff. You know like when animals feed off each other and help each other out? What's that called?"

"A...symbiotic relationship?" offered Steele.

"Yeah," said Dennis. "That's us. With the bar."

I wasn't sure I approved of the analogy, but I wasn't about to challenge Dennis on it. "We're getting off topic. Let's talk about the band. Dennis? Big D? Can I call you that?"

"Better than his stage name," said Diamond with a snicker. "It's not fit for *polite company,* if you get my drift, brah." He tilted his head in Steele's direction.

Dennis glared at the Chaz clone. "Man, you don't know when to quit." Eyes back on me. "Shoot."

"Perhaps you could start by telling us about the band," I said. "Like who's in it."

Diamond's eyes widened. "Brah, you don't know?"

"We're detectives," I said. "We don't get out much."

"Four guys, all told," said Big D, who took our ignorance with better grace than Diamond did. "You already know Chaz, right? He's the lead singer. There's B. B. He's on guitar. Good looking dude, man. Real lady killer, probably 'cause he's got that elf blood like your friend Steele here. Likes to...how should I say this? *Party?* Like Chaz, but even more hardcore, if you catch my drift. Then there's Sammy Styles. Long brown braids. Plays the bass guitar. More quiet than the other guys. Some of the ladies like that, though. And finally you've got Ritchie Roth on the drums. He's a wild man—on the skins, I mean. Otherwise, he's pretty similar to the rest of the guys. Which is still pretty wild."

A little too late, I realized I should've been taking notes. I reached into my fresh new jacket and produced a spiral-bound notepad, upon which I furiously began scribbling names. "Styles. Roth. We already got Wilson. Who was that last guy? B. B. what?"

"DuPrat," said Dennis.

"So I'm guessing they had a show last night," said Shay, gesturing toward the space behind us, "otherwise this place wouldn't quite be in this state of disarray. I hope."

"Don't judge us, brah," said Diamond. "There's lots to do around here. But yeah, there was a show. Three times a week. They'll have another tonight."

I glanced at Steele. No need to burst that particular bubble yet. "So what time did the show end?"

"Same as always," said Big D. "About ten o'clock."

"And then what?" I asked.

"What do you mean?"

"Where did the band go?" asked Steele. "What did they do? What were the two of you up to?"

Big D glanced at Diamond. "The band went to Billy's, right? He was having a party after the show. One year anniversary of the Moxy hosting Yellow Cobra, I think."

"Billy?" I asked. "Who's that?"

"Billy Charles," said Dennis. "He was one of Chaz's biggest influences. Not sure how they met, but they've been friends forever. The band goes and parties at his mansion sometimes."

"But not you two?" said Steele.

Big D snorted. "We're not cool enough. Or rich enough. Or big-breasted enough. Take your pick."

"You offer a man a choice between big breasts and anything else, and you know what the answer is going to be," I said.

Steele frowned. "Daggers..."

"Sorry," I said. "So what did you two do after the band left for Billy's?"

"Stayed and helped bartend," said Dennis. "I, uh...maybe helped myself to some free drinks, too. Then partied with some of the Yellow Cobra groupies. Diamond played guitar and waited for his girlfriend to get off work."

On cue, Diamond cut loose with a brief selection of chords. *"Partied with the groupies? Brah, you babysat them while they waited for the Cobras to come back—which they weren't going to do."*

Big D scowled. "Man, why you gotta put me down like that? That chick with the smoky eyes was *into* me."

A big, rumbling voice sounded out behind me. "Steele? Daggers?"

I turned. Quinto had crept up on us, he of the world's lightest three hundred pound feet. "What's up?"

"Found a manager," he said. "Thought you might want to come up and talk to him."

I closed my notepad and slipped it back into my jacket. Diamond continued to strum on his guitar. I wasn't a rock aficionado by any means, but the melody tickled my ears in a way I found compelling.

I gave the Chaz clone a nod. "So you play?"

Dennis snorted. "Every roadie plays. The only question is what instrument."

"You're not half bad," I said. "Did Chaz ever give you a shot at making the band? You know, given you're family and all."

Dennis caught my eye and shook his head, rather seriously.

Diamond's nose wrinkled and he momentarily stopped playing. "Brah, don't even start with me. That's a sore subject. His own half brother, and he won't even give me a tryout. Not like him and B. B. haven't had their problems..."

I lifted an eyebrow. *Problems?*

I felt a light touch on my shoulder, followed by Steele's voice. "Daggers?"

"Right," I said. "Quinto. Lead the way."

5

Quinto led us upstairs, through a narrow hallway lined with faded flyers and posters of long-retired acts, most of them with cheesy names that featured unnecessary slashed os and umlauts, bands like Riøt Squad and The Ündertakers. At the end of the paper advertisement-induced time warp, he cracked a door and ushered us inside.

I'd thought the gloom in the rest of the Moxy had been bad. I'd been wrong.

I squinted and tried to discern the various shapes within. The window—singular—was the first thing to come into focus, drawing my eyes like a moth to a sad, pale facsimile of a flame. Like the walls outside, it too had been covered in posters and flyers, turning the winter morning's already pale sunlight into a feeble, orange- and yellow-tinged glow. Cigarette smoke choked the air, even more intense than in the main room downstairs. Apparently, whatever fresh hell into which we'd entered was a magnification of the rest of the Moxy—except for the stale beer smell. For better or worse, that had been replaced with a sweaty musk.

"Daggers. Steele. There you are."

I recognized the voice: Rodgers', coming from a person-shaped lump in front of me. He, too, slowly coalesced into human form, one with actual facial features and everything, muddy though they might be.

"Hey, buddy," I said, blinking. "Quinto said you found someone we should talk to."

"Yeah. Benson Forsythe. The Yellow Cobra's manager." Rodgers jerked his thumb over his shoulder.

I followed the hand sign. In the back of the room, a few feet shy of the wall, sat a desk, piled high with papers, empty liquor bottles, and ashtrays overflowing with butts, some of which still smoked. A pair of couches lined the walls in front of the desk, each of them occupied by an unconscious, or perhaps semiconscious, young woman. A middle-aged man sat in a chair between the two, hunched over with a burning cigarette in hand. Another ashtray rested before him on a low coffee table. He wore his hair long, even though there wasn't a scrap of it left on the top of his head. It hung limply over his shoulders, falling onto the fur collar of the heavy coat he wore. Given the temperature, he didn't need it indoors, but apparently the man was into completely superfluous fashion choices, otherwise he wouldn't have also been wearing a pair of wide-rimmed sunglasses.

"What did you tell him?" asked Steele in a hushed voice.

"Not much," responded Rodgers in kind. "Just that we're police, here to talk to him about Chaz."

Shay nodded and stepped around Rodgers toward the man. I followed, leaving Quinto and Rodgers by the door.

"Benson Forsythe?" asked Steele crisply.

The man flinched and held up his cigarette hand. "Please. Not so loud."

"I'm...speaking at a normal volume," said Steele.

The man took a drag on his cigarette and let the smoke out slowly. When he spoke, his voice flowed, raspy and unctuous at the same time, seasoned and yet somehow still raw. It grabbed and focused my attention, its unexpected power sending a chill down my spine.

"Well, try and ratchet it *down* a few notches to something *less* than normal. In case you can't tell, I had a bit of a rough night, and having your goons wake me from a pleasant slumber didn't help. I suppose it could be worse. Better a visit from police thugs than my bookie. Still, it wasn't quite how I'd hoped to—"

Benson lifted his head, finally taking note of us—or at least of Steele. *"Hello!* Where were you last night? Hiding in my dreams?"

Even if I hadn't been romantically involved with Steele, my creepazoid alarm would've still sounded. "Cool it, Jack. You're talking to police captain Shay Steele, here."

"Captain?" he said. "What the hell did Chaz get himself involved in anyway?"

"We'll get to that," said Steele. "Why don't you tell us about your star lead singer?"

"What do you want to know?" he asked. "He's a living legend. A troubadour and a balladeer. He's toured in over a dozen countries and a hundred cities, attracting huge crowds wherever he goes. He's penned over fifty songs. Been performing for over a decade. Women love him. Men want to be him. He's the heart and soul of Yellow Cobra."

"We can get the boilerplate from a flyer," said Steele. "I wanted to know about Chaz Willy Wilson the man."

Benson smiled, an unnerving grin with teeth both too sharp and too white. "Oh. In that case... He's an insufferable prima donna who can't keep it in his pants, drinks too much, smokes too much, spends half his time too intoxicated to work, and worst of all, draws crowds a quarter the size he used to. That more your speed?"

"There we go," I said. "He sounds like a blast to work with."

Benson turned the unsettling smile on me, sending another chill down my spine. "You have no idea."

"Any idea what he was up to last night?" asked Steele.

"What do you think?" said Benson. "He played in the show."

"I meant after that."

"How should I know?" he said. "He went out with B. B., Sammy, and Ritchie. Some party. I stayed here with, ah...these lovely young ladies."

I glanced at the nearest couch. On closer inspection, the ladies were neither as young nor as lovely as indicated, and I had my doubts about their general level of sophistication and charm. The one closest to me wore a disheveled halter top and a pair of jeans with intentionally torn knees, her hair sweaty and stuck to her forehead. Her chest rose and fell slowly, and her face seemed pale in the dim light.

Her eyes snapped open as I stared at her, locking onto me for a fraction of a second before glazing. She barely moved during the endeavor, and her breathing changed not one iota. Was she drugged...or perhaps something else?

I glanced at Benson. "Are you sure these women are alright?"

"They're fine," he said, standing. "Now if you don't mind my asking, what the hell is this all about? What happened to Chaz?"

Benson removed his sunglasses, revealing pale eyes the color of ice. Despite the fact that he shared his gaze between Shay and me, I felt myself drawn toward him, drawn toward the impossibly clear pools of bluish white. Compared to them, the room around us seemed that much darker, the cigarette smoke that much thicker, the musky stink that much fouler. Try as I might, I couldn't look away.

"Chaz is dead," said Shay.

The effect broke like a hammer smashing through a mirror. Benson blinked, and so did I.

"*Dead?*" said Benson. "You're kidding, right?"

"I'm afraid not," said Shay. "We found him in Rucker Park. Looks like he died sometime in the early morning hours."

Benson sat down and slipped his sunglasses back on, sparing me the sight of his eerie eyes. "A drug overdose?"

"We're not entirely sure of the cause of death yet," said Shay. "We're working on it."

Benson leaned back, passing his hand across the bald crown of his head and over the stringy hair at the back. He quickly moved from the first stage of grief to the second. "That son-of-a-bitch. How could he do this to me? Leave me in the lurch like that? What am I going to do? I've already sold the tickets to the next show. I can't refund them. I already spent the cash on...things." He glanced at the empty bottles and a spot on the coffee table that seemed oddly chalky.

I waved away whatever fog lingered over me and cleared my throat. "Sorry...a moment ago you were badmouthing Chaz and complaining about him not being able to fill your venues anymore. Now you can't bear to have him gone?"

"Hey, a quarter of our old crowds is better than none," said Benson. "Seriously though, this isn't a joke? Maybe you have the wrong guy?"

"It's a remote possibility," said Shay. "We'll need someone close to him to identify the body. In the meantime, we need to locate the rest of the band. Any idea where we could find them?"

"Yeah, sure," said Benson, suddenly sounding exhausted. "They've been renting a suite at the Banks Hotel downtown. Or we could check the ready room downstairs. It's in the basement, around in back."

Benson didn't move.

Steele lifted an eyebrow. "Perhaps you could show us the way?"

"Oh. Right." Benson glanced around, picked up a black gambler hat with a strip of metal-studded leather trim, and plopped it on his head. He stood. "Follow me."

6

I let Rodgers and Quinto trail Benson closely as he led us out of the office and down to the main level, but I hung back. As we reached the bottom of the stairs, I pinched Steele's sleeve to keep her at my side.

She regarded my fingers with confusion. "What are you doing?"

I answered in a hushed voice. "You felt that right? In Benson's office? When he took his glasses off?"

Steele's eyes narrowed. "What are you talking about?"

"When his sunglasses came off," I said. "When he revealed those piercing, ice blue eyes? It's like the room suddenly became smaller and darker. I couldn't look away. Tell me you didn't feel the same way."

"Look, Daggers, I know where you're going with this," she said. "I'll admit the man is undeniably creepy, that he possesses a strange...animal magnetism. But that doesn't make him a *you know what.*"

"No?" I said. "What about those women? They were so listless. *Strangely* so. Are you familiar with the act of enthrallment?"

"They were drunk, or drugged," said Shay. "Possibly both."

"They seemed too pale of skin for that to be the case," I said. "And if you insist on being contrary, riddle me this. Why is Benson wearing sunglasses, a hat, and a heavy overcoat inside the Moxy, when there's barely enough light to see what's going on even during the day?"

Shay glanced down the hall at our retreating quarry. "Stop it. You're freaking me out. Now let's move before we lose them."

We hustled to catch up with the others, heading to the side of the stage into the Moxy's back corridors, past an emergency exit, and down a set of stairs. We reached Quinto, Rodgers, and Benson as they stopped in front of a door with a large gold star affixed to it in the upper center.

"Well, this is the ready room," said Benson as he cranked on the door handle. "Who knows if they're here or not. Chances are they're passed out in a gutter somewhere, or—"

Benson paused, jamming Quinto and Rodgers in the door frame behind him. "Dear mother of the gods, what happened here? And—*HOLY HELL, what's that?*"

"You've got to be kidding me," said Rodgers.

I couldn't see past Quinto's shoulders. "Guys? What's going on?"

"Calm down," said Quinto in a deep voice. "No sudden movements. You'll scare him."

I ripped Daisy from my coat and dove in, squeezing past Quinto and forcing Benson into the room as he tried to escape. He shrank against a wall as I turned toward the action.

The scene before me unfolded quickly. In many respects, the ready room looked like a carbon copy of Benson's office. Old posters and flyers plastered the walls, empty liquor bottles and cigarette butts littered the floor, and raggedy, stained couches beckoned with all the appeal of a seventy-year old harlot. Unlike Benson's office, however, this place had been trashed. An interloper had smashed the bottles, trampled and torn the couch cushions, and befouled the rugs. In fact, he continued to do so. He stood before us, staring at us with wide-set eyes, buck-naked and crapping all over the place.

Literally. *Crapping.*

Luckily, it could've been worse. The interloper was a camel.

As Benson cowered in fear against the wall, I questioned my thesis about his supernatural abilities. After all, it wasn't as if the camel howled in a blood rage, stomping and rearing and baring its teeth. It just stood there, slowly chewing on a piece of paper and going about its most basic of bodily functions. A nice, fat clump of mostly-digested organic matter dropped from its posterior, splattering across the floor with a wet smack.

Steele weaseled her way between Quinto and me. "Ah. Well, this makes a little more sense."

"*More* sense?" I said. "Have you forgotten what that word means?"

She ignored me and turned to the sleazy band manager. "Benson, you mind explaining what in the world in going on here?"

"*Me?*" he said. "You think I know?"

"You're bound to have a better idea than we do," said Steele. "Were you here all night?"

"Yeah, but up in my office," he said. "With my, ah...female companions. You can check with them. I didn't come down here after the show. It must've been one of the guys who brought this thing in." His head tilted toward the camel. "Wait... Is that Chaz's songbook? That *thing* is eating my lead singer's songbook!"

On cue, the camel bent down, latched onto a few pages from a notebook, tore them free, and started chewing.

"Someone! *Stop it!*" screeched Benson. "Before it eats any more!"

"What's the big deal?" said Rodgers. "It's a songbook, not a stack of cash."

"To you, maybe," said Benson. "But if you're right and Chaz is dead, that notepad is the only remaining scrap of Chaz Willy Wilson's creative efforts. We need to save it! The fate of the band is at stake!"

"Right," I said with rolled eyes. "*The band.*"

"Alright, everyone calm down," said Quinto. "The animal's wearing a bridle. He's clearly domesticated. Let me handle it."

Quinto approached the camel slowly, with his hands at chest level. The beast eyed him and kept chewing, but it didn't shy away. Quinto spoke in a soothing tone as he walked, carefully avoiding the droppings.

"That's it. Good boy. Who's a good camel?"

In another two steps Quinto was at its side. The animal didn't even flinch as Quinto took hold of the bridle with one hand and pet its neck with the other.

I let out a latent breath that had been hanging out in my throat. "Well, that was surprisingly easy."

"Yes, you're a good boy, aren't you?" said Quinto, continuing to massage the beast's neck. "You guys can come over, and you can put that headknocker away, Daggers. He's not going to bite. He's obviously used to people."

I wandered over, taking the same path as Quinto to avoid unwelcome additions to my shoes. The camel continued to stand there, oblivious to our presence and interested only in the succulent flavor of Chaz's handwritten notes. The bridle which Quinto held in his hand was constructed of faded red and yellow leather. I noticed a few words printed on the top of the crownpiece.

"World Famous Minestrone Brothers," I read. "You think they're the owners?"

"Sounds like a circus," said Quinto. "Never heard of them."

Shay and Rodgers joined us by the seven foot tall animal, as did Benson, the latter only closing to within snatching range. With a quick swipe of his arm, he stole back Chaz's notepad from the coffee table on which it rested—or at least what was left of it.

"Damn beast," he said. "As if I didn't have enough problems to deal with right now..."

It might've been my imagination, but I think the camel narrowed an eye in Benson's direction.

"Hey, did you guys see this?" Rodgers pointed at the camel's hump.

In the dim lighting of the Moxy's basement suite, I hadn't initially noticed anything concerning about our new camel friend's backside, but upon closer look, the fur was matted and dark. "Is that...*blood*? Holy harvest, is this big brute okay?"

"He's fine," said Shay. "It's not his."

I glanced at my partner. "And you know this *because*?"

"It's why I said things made more sense now," said Steele. "Think about it. You were concerned about the lack of blood at the crime scene. I said Chaz being murdered elsewhere and transported to Rucker Park would account for that. Did you happen to take a gander at the camel's feet?"

I did upon her suggestion. They were enormous. Rounded, longer than my own and at least twice as wide, with two toes per foot and a large claw at the tip of each toe—or whatever passed for one.

"Right," I said. "Well, I'd say I feel sheepish, but I'm afraid the pun doesn't fit. Regardless, as glad as I am to see we most likely aren't dealing with a hulking, twelve foot man-were-beast roaming the shrubbery of New Welwic's central-most park, the discovery of this camel raises more questions than it answers. Apart from what's on the camel's back, I don't see any pools of blood on the floor or upholstery. And let's not forget we have no idea how this beast got here. It goes without saying there's no one else here."

Shay turned to Benson Forsythe. "Who would've had access to this room overnight?"

"You saw me turn the door handle," he said. "Any-one. *Everyone*. Seriously. You ever party with a rock band?"

"No comment," said Shay. "You think anyone here might've seen who brought this animal in?"

"Maybe one of the guys upstairs?" offered Benson. "I don't know. Moving this beast in here would've been hard to escape notice."

"*You* missed it," said Rodgers.

Benson scowled.

Shay gave Quinto a nod. "You mind taking this animal back to the station? I'm not entirely sure where to hold it, but we can't leave it here."

"Oh, I see how this works," said Quinto. "I have to babysit the beast because I'm the big burly one?"

"Not especially," said Steele. "More because you've already developed a nurturing relationship with it. I think he likes you."

"Steele's right, Quinto," I said. "This animal could be a witness to murder. Someone needs to squeeze a statement out of him."

Quinto's brow furrowed as he looked at me. "I can't tell if you're joking or not."

"Neither can I," I said. "But think of the accolades you'll get if you succeed."

"Fine," said Quinto. "I'll take him back to HQ. Stick him in a holding pen or something—but I expect to rejoin you guys on this case. Given how this one's un-folding, I don't want to miss more than I have to."

"Fair enough," said Steele.

With bridle in hand, Quinto began the process of leading the camel toward the door and up the stairs.

Luckily, the beast mostly played along. Shay scanned the room, likely looking for more clues. Rodgers followed suit.

I glanced at Benson, who'd retreated toward the door and was in the process of flipping through the mangled remains of the notebook. Emboldened by his response to the camel, or perhaps sufficiently distanced from the events that had transpired in his office, I approached him.

"Can I ask you a question?" I said.

"Do I have a choice?"

I ignored his snark. "Did Chaz have any fascination with...how should I put this? *The occult?*"

The manager lifted his head from the notebook, but thankfully he didn't remove his sunglasses. "Are you kidding? Have you listened to any of his songs?"

"I'm not much of a fan."

Benson snorted and waved the notebook in my face. "People think he was all about the romantic ballads. They didn't bother to listen to the actual lyrics. *Of course he was into the occult.* I mean, honestly. His famous song, "Creatures of the Night?" Fans thought it was an allegory about two lovers meeting after nightfall. Please. If so, it was the most thinly veiled allegory ever. They didn't want to admit Chaz was a dark, brooding weirdo."

"I don't suppose you've got the lyrics to that song available?" I said. "In that notebook, perhaps?"

"Here? Nah. This is all new stuff. Even darker and more depressing than the old if what I've seen is any indication. At least "Creatures of the Night" was nuanced. Catchy. And people liked it. Can't believe he's not going to be playing that to crowds anymore..."

Benson paused and glanced toward the stairs.

"What is it?" I said.

"Nothing. Just an idea. Come with me."

He headed for the door. I gave Steele a glance, but she wasn't caught unawares. She motioned that she and Rodgers would follow.

7

We backtracked to the stage, where Forsythe flagged down the two stagehands Steele and I had already met. "Mickey. Dennis. Come here for a sec."

The pair did as requested, though Mickey didn't seem excited about the prospect of being summoned by Benson at such an early hour—either that or he was miffed about being called by his real name rather than his gemstone-inspired nickname.

"Yeah, boss," said Big D as he approached the front of the stage. "What's up?"

Benson jerked a thumb at me. "This here police officer—he talked to you, right? He's interested in hearing "Creatures of the Night." Think you two knuckleheads could play it?"

"You want us to play a song for you, brah?" said Diamond.

"I'm not your *brah*," said Benson. "And yes, that's exactly what I want. Or what the officer wants. Same difference. That a problem?"

I opened my mouth to argue that I'd never actually asked to hear it, but Diamond drowned me out before I had a chance.

"Yeah, brah," he said excitedly. "I mean, boss. Of course. Uh...let me grab a guitar. Dennis. Give me a beat?"

Big D nodded. "You got it."

The big bruiser headed back to the drums and plucked a pair of drumsticks from a pouch that hung in their midst. Meanwhile, Diamond ran over and grabbed the guitar he'd been noodling on earlier from a stand at the stage's side. He looped it over his chest as he jogged back toward us. He looked back at Big D and gave him a nod.

The big man nodded back, struck his sticks together three times, and went to work on the drums. He played out a steady, thumping beat, mostly from the snare and high-hat with a bit of bass drum action thrown in. Shortly thereafter, Diamond chimed in on the guitar, producing a catchy, enigmatic melody.

He started singing.

In the cool of the night
Under stars shining bright
We meet once again, baby
In the cool of the night
My heart takes flight
To be joined with yours, maybe

Your body grows closer
Your scent an elixir
Making me go crazy, baby

I don't want to be the enforcer
But I can't help but wonder
What you have in store for me, maybe

Now I can taste you on my lips
Your skin so tender and sweet
But you know I want more
Not just your kiss I adore
So lets make sure to be discreet

Creatures of the night
Creatures of the night
Oh yeah

Diamond's guitar playing intensified during the chorus, his fingers strumming hard against the strings, all while Big D punctuated each cry of 'Creatures of the night' with a trio of cymbal crashes. After a brief melodic respite, Diamond kept going with the next verse.

With the moon up high
And a cry in the sky
I feel my body ache for you
Deep down in my bones
For a curse I atone
I feel my body change for you

You draw me in with your eyes
But I can see you despise
The secret I can't bear to keep
But I can share it with you
Give a part to you

So together let's take this leap

Now baby you're changing, too
Feeling the rush of love in you
Filling you like you never thought it could
I bet you never knew
Having it inside you
Would feel this wild and feel this good

Creatures of the night
Creatures of the night
Oh yeah

Creatures of the night
Creatures of the night
Changing me, changing you, through and through

Creatures of the night
Creatures of the night
Alive, and real and oh so true

As the song came to a close and Diamond repeated the refrain, he started to wail on the guitar, his fingers blurring over the strings. Big D took his lead, beating on the drums with a renewed vigor, using his big arms to great effect on the toms and cymbals. Diamond closed his eyes and started rocking back and forth, his head banging forward and back as the music flowed through him. A huge grin spread across Big D's face.

"Alright, that's enough," said Benson, waving his arms to try and get Diamond's attention. "Hey! Are you listening? ENOUGH, I SAID!"

Diamond stopped abruptly and opened his eyes. "Right. Sorry, boss. I get caught up in that one. It's a really good song."

"It is, isn't it..." Benson stared in Diamond's general direction, stroking his chin. He kept it up for a few long seconds.

"Uh...boss?" said Diamond. "You okay?"

Bensons startled, his sunglasses slipping ever so slightly on his nose. He pushed them back up quickly. "Huh? Yeah. Peachy. Hey, why don't you and Dennis take a break from cleanup and spend the morning practicing some of the old Cobra classics. You know, "I'll Never Forget You," "My Baby Wore Black," "Hard Rockin' Afterlife," and "Tears of Blood." All the hits."

"Boss, you serious?" said Diamond. "Are you saying what I think you're saying?"

Benson didn't hear him. He'd already turned and started to walk toward the stairs, apparently oblivious to our continued presence.

Steele didn't let him off the hook that easy. She joined me and called out to him. "Benson! You know we're going to need you to pop by the station. Someone needs to identify the body."

The manager paused in midstride, refusing to turn his head to look at us. "That's, ah...not going to work for me. Not at the moment. Too much to do. Too much to think about. I'll send someone in my stead."

The man didn't ask for our permission to continue leaving. Steele stared at his back as he approached the stairwell, as did I. *Not going to work at the moment?* Did that mean what I think it meant?

Diamond dropped the guitar and hopped off the stage, rushing to our side. "Whoa. Brahs. *Body?* What the heck happened to Chaz?"

"Sorry we weren't more forthcoming earlier," said Steele, turning to face him. "But unfortunately it looks as if Chaz is dead. My condolences."

Diamond stared at us blankly. "Wait? Are you serious? So...when Benson said to practice. Does that mean...?"

Big D ran up, hopped off the stage, and clapped Diamond on the back. "Dude! This is it! Your big break!" He glanced at us. "I mean...that's terrible. Chaz was a good guy. What happened?"

"Your concern is touching," said Steele, her tone of voice indicating she thought the opposite. "But we're not at liberty to talk about it. It's an active investigation."

"Look, I know this is a lot to process," I said. "But since you're both here, I need to ask you the same thing I asked Benson. What can you tell me about Chaz's fascination with the occult?"

Shay sighed. "Daggers...*really?*"

Diamond answered despite my partner's attitude. "I mean, he was into it, for sure. Zombies. Werewolves. Vampires. Especially vampires. All of it, really."

I gave Steele a knowing glance. "Is that so? Ever heard of a place called Club Midnight?"

"That's the one club Chaz liked to go to, isn't it?" said Dennis. "South side of town, I think. Lots of dark, brooding types there. Not really our scene."

"So you've never been?" I asked.

"Look, brah," said Diamond. "Normally I'd be super down with talking to you about vampires and goth clubs and stuff, but if Benson said what I think he did...I need to practice. Big time. Dennis? You got me on the drums?"

The big stagehand smiled. "You got it, dude. Sorry, detectives. Another time?"

The pair of roadies climbed back onstage and retreated to their instruments. Shay and I turned and headed toward the door, joining Rodgers who'd been hanging back, keeping an eye on the action.

He shook his head as we neared him. "You just won't quit, will you, Daggers?"

"Quit on what?" I said. "The fact that Chaz looks to have been murdered by a vampire? No way. Especially not after what we learned here, what with Chaz's interests and Benson's...well, *Benson*. And don't act holier than thou. You were right there alongside me emotionally when we found those tracks in the park."

"Tracks which turned out to be from a camel," said Rodgers. "Which, you have to admit, isn't the most macabre of beasts."

"Suffice to say there are a number of odd things going on in this case," I said. "But who's to say what qualifies as a creature of the night and what doesn't? I'll bet camels have loads of blood in them. Maybe they're not a vampire's first choice, but you know...in a pinch."

Shay furrowed her brows and pursed her lips.

"Don't give me that look," I said. "Deep down inside, you know I'm making good points. So...where to? Club Midnight?"

"We'll get there," said Steele. "But we need to go after the obvious targets first. Remember, we still don't know where the rest of Yellow Cobra's members are, or even if they're okay. That's our first priority."

"Right," I said. "Where did Benson say they were staying? The Banks Hotel?"

Shay nodded. "A suite, supposedly." She slipped a hand into her jacket, producing the key we'd found at the crime scene. "What do you want to bet it's room five oh one?"

8

The entrance to the Banks Hotel stood across the street from us, its teal sign with the hotel's name in a stylish white script partially obscured by an array of tall pines. The trees followed a path that curved inward to the hotel proper, shading the tall pastel pink building within and protecting it from the unwashed gazes of plebeians on the street. Rickshaws clattered past on the cobblestones outside, their drivers yelling at one another in less than civil tones. Chances were the trees protected the hotel from unwanted verbal assaults as well.

"Can I help you?"

I turned toward the owner of the mobile beverage cart in front of me. Apparently, the person before me in line had been served while I'd gaped at the hotel. "Yeah, I'll take a couple coffees. And...do you have any tea? Steele, you want tea?"

Shay stood at Rodgers' shoulder, next to a dull brick building at the side of the street. She shook her head. "No. Give me the coffee."

"Really?" I said. "It's not cappuccino. It's not, is it?"

The vendor, a tusk-faced orc of dubious mental ability, looked at me blankly. "A cappu-what?"

"I told you, I didn't sleep well," said Steele. "Just get it. I'll suffer through the taste and be better off for it."

"If you insist," I said. "Three coffees, then. And do you have any kolaches, or donuts, or fritters? Anything made out of fried dough?"

"I thought you stopped eating those," said Rodgers. "I remember hearing something about a diet."

"Old habits are hard to break."

Of course, said habits were easier to break when fate conspired against me. The vendor continued to stare at me blankly.

"Fine. Just the coffees, then."

He produced what I wanted, so I paid him, handed the drinks to my crew, and set foot on the path to the Banks Hotel. The pines loomed over me, but seeing as I'd never joined the military and taken part in one of our nation's numerous bugbear uprising campaigns, the stroll didn't induce in me a sense of PTSD. Instead, I found the pine's thick boughs and healthy green needles soothing. If ever I met the Banks Hotel's landscape architect, I'd have to commend him or her on designing an environment both functional, beautiful, and that kept New Welwic's winter extremes in mind.

The hotel's front came into view, an elegant façade set under a broad awning of alternating black and white stripes. A red carpet stretched from the edge of the gilded doors to the foot of the path. A doorman held the gates open for us as we approached.

Once inside, I took a sip of my brew and looked around the lobby for the stairs. "Room five oh one, was it?"

"Yes," said Shay. "But given the locale, I'd feel more comfortable with an escort. Wouldn't want to ruffle any feathers. Follow my lead."

She veered to the side, toward the front desk. A charming young woman, dark of skin, wearing bright red lipstick and a sharp gray suit, smiled as we approached.

"Welcome to the Banks," she said. "Checking in?"

Shay shook her head. "I'm Detective...er, Captain Steele, of the 5th Street Precinct. These are detectives Daggers and Rodgers." She flashed her badge. "Is this yours?" She produced the key in question from her jacket.

"Ah, why yes, it appears to be," said the young woman. "Did one of our guests lose it?"

"Do you have a manager I could speak to?"

The young woman nodded. "Of course. One moment please."

She left, leaving us to ourselves. Shay took a sip of her coffee and made a face. "Ugh. Just as terrible as I remembered."

"I warned you," I said. "That cappuccino foam makes a world of difference."

"It's caffeinated," she said. "That's all that matters at the moment."

I took the opportunity to survey the lobby interior. A few curved sectional pieces, upholstered in a mustard yellow fabric, made a rough circle in the center of the room, surrounding a low, wide table the same teal color as the sign outside. Though the furnishings screamed swank, I noticed a few chinks in the armor. Cracked tiles, chips in the paint, a missing button on one of the sofa chairs' cushions.

I heard the clop of heels, followed shortly by the arrival of another woman, this one slightly older than the first but no less charming. She held her hair back in a long ponytail, and a pastel pink ascot tie gave some color to the sharp grey suit she also wore.

"Sorry for the delay," she said. "Traci Gilmore, maître d'. How can I help you?"

Shay gave our introductions again and held up the key. "We found this on one Chaz Willy Wilson, a member of the rock group Yellow Cobra. We understand he's staying here with his band mates?"

Traci sighed. "Yes, that's right."

"You don't sound too happy about it," I said. "Have they been giving you problems?"

Traci took a moment to respond. "We value the business of all our guests, especially those long-term residents like Mr. Wilson and his associates. But it's precisely because of our guest policies that Mr. Wilson and his *Cobras,* if you will, have made themselves more well-known than they should've. There've been a few...*incidents* with other guests. Accusations of vulgarity and impropriety of varying degrees. I'm assuming you're here because of another one?"

"Not precisely," said Shay. "On the bright side for you, Mr. Wilson is now in our custody. You won't have to worry about him again. But we do need to locate the rest of his band members. Perhaps you could show us to their room?"

"Of course," said Traci. "Follow me."

She headed around the side of the desk and toward the stairs. Rodgers, Steele, and I hustled after her. Her heels clacked on the polished stone steps, as did Steele's.

"So, Ms. Gilmore," I said as we climbed. "If you don't mind my asking—if the Yellow Cobras have been such difficult guests, why haven't you asked them to leave? As far as I understand it, they've been in New Welwic on a permanent basis for what...a year now?"

She sighed again. "I couldn't answer that question, but they haven't been at our hotel for that long. To be honest, having them stay here started as a misbegotten promotional stunt. Mr. Fillgary-Banks, who owns this hotel, is a fan of their earlier work, and he thought having them stay with us could help spruce up business for the winter months. We already have a reputation as a retreat for some of New Welwic's more exotic and eclectic personalities, you see. Regardless, they've been far more trouble than they've been worth. The events the Cobras committed to playing for us in exchange for reduced room fees were a total flop, we've received numerous complaints about them with regards to noise, and even for our clientele, their sobriety—or lack thereof—is sometimes hard to justify. And that's not even counting the more egregious stuff."

We reached the fifth floor landing and hung a left. More of the hotel's distinctive teal paint covered the walls, interspersed by sections dressed in the more flamboyant pastel pink.

"What sort of egregious stuff?" I asked.

"Well, there was the incident where Mr. DuPrat exposed himself to one of our other guests," continued Traci. "And of course the continued infighting between Mr. DuPrat and Mr. Wilson."

"That's B. B. DuPrat," I said. "The guitarist?"

"Correct," she said. "Some of their disagreements could get rather vocal. Anyway. Here we are. Could I see the key?"

We paused at the end of the hall in front of room 501. Shay gave Traci the key. The manager placed it in the lock and turned it.

"Shouldn't we knock?" said Rodgers.

"It's before noon," said Traci. "I think you're giving these gentlemen too much credit."

She pushed open the door, took two steps in and paused. Her jaw dropped. "Holy..."

Only through years of dedicated practice did I manage to keep my own jaw muscles in line. The scene wasn't quite as wild as the one we'd found at the Moxy's ready room—but it didn't lag far behind.

9

I walked forward into the living room, stepping carefully to avoid the broken glass and jagged, lacquered wood splinters—the sad remnants of a guitar if the fractured neck strung with frayed strings was any indication. A hole gaped in the ceiling; the chandelier which had hovered there lay shattered and spread across the floor, its crystalline shards sparkling in the morning light. The balcony windows' drapes had been thrown open, and outside, a wicker chair hung precariously from the edge of the railing. Inside, an industrious creative type had turned a stretch of the living room wall into a piece of modern art using spaghetti and meatballs in lieu of paint. Someone else had taken to playing a game of rock music-inspired darts on the opposite wall. At least that was my explanation for why numerous drumsticks protruded from the lath and plaster.

"Well," said Shay. "At least we found the rest of the band."

So it appeared. The living room contained a pair of couches. On one of them sprawled a man with a pair of long brown braids spilling from the red paisley bandanna that covered his head. He wore a pair of elaborate leather chaps, and though he'd misplaced his shirt, thankfully he still wore pants underneath the leg protectors. Based off Diamond's descriptions, he'd be Sammy Styles, the bassist.

On the other couch, face down and sunken deep into the cushions, lay a slender guy wearing tight white pants and a puffy white shirt, though the latter had seen better days. Numerous scrapes and tears marred the cloth, and someone appeared to have spilt one or more drinks on it. A shock of platinum blond hair topped the guy's head, but despite its volume, I still caught sight of a pair of pointed ears peeking out. An elf. Therefore, the man was B. B. DuPrat, the guitarist.

By process of elimination, that made the lean, wiry guy on the floor Ritchie Roth—or so I assumed. His puffy, voluminous black hair certainly seemed fitting for the drummer of a rock band, as did the plain black t-shirt and torn jeans he wore. Of course, who knew why his clothes were covered in mud, or why a fresh black eye glistened on the right side of his face.

"Uh...I *think* they're alive," said Rodgers.

"They are," said Shay. "I can see their chests moving. Not *vigorously,* mind you."

Traci found her voice. "*My room!* What the hell did these morons do?"

"It doesn't look too good, does it?" I said. "Hopefully you collected a hefty deposit before you allowed them to stay."

"That's *it*," said Traci. "I don't care what Mr. Fillgary-Banks says. They're gone. *Finished*. Out of here. Effective immediately."

"That might be easier said than done," I said. "I'm not sure how amenable any of these guys are to waking. We probably shouldn't have sent Quinto away. I bet he could carry two of them by himself. Although...do you have smelling salts?"

Traci closed her eyes, took a deep breath, and let it out slowly. When she reopened her eyes, she'd regained a sense of calm. "Yes, actually. I do. Believe it or not, this sort of...*thing* isn't completely unheard of at the Banks. Rockers aren't the only ones prone to excess. Give me a moment."

Traci left, leaving us detectives to our investigation. Steele moved further into the room, while Rodgers joined me in the middle.

"You've seen Yellow Cobra in concert, right Rodgers?" I pointed the trio out with my free hand. "Sammy Styles? B. B. DuPrat? And Ritchie Roth?"

"I think so," said Rodgers. "I'm sure we can get someone else to confirm. Or ask them—if we can get them to wake."

I snapped my fingers a few times in B. B.'s direction as I sipped my coffee. He didn't even flinch.

"Hopefully the smelling salts will be enough," said Shay. "Looks like we're dealing with more than booze."

She bent over a coffee table and picked up a collection of miniature cardstock envelopes, the kind drug dealers used to distribute their product.

"Anything left?" I asked.

Shay shook the envelopes. "Maybe a pill or two. I'll pocket them for analysis. Same with this." She dragged her finger through a pile of white powder that had been scraped together in the middle of the coffee table. She used one of the now empty baggies to scoop up the remainder.

Shay stood, slipping the envelopes into her jacket before wiping her fingers on a protruding couch cushion.

"So," she said, joining us by the Cobras. "Either one of you notice anything unusual I might've missed?"

"Now what kind of question is that?" I said. "First of all, how are we supposed to know what you may or may not have overlooked? You're usually the most observant one in our group. And second of all, *everything* about this case is unusual. I mean, there are drumsticks protruding from a wall, for crying out loud."

"Well, I'll tell you what I *don't* see," said Rodgers. "Camels."

I pressed my lips together and nodded sagely. "You know...now that you mention it, I hadn't noticed the lack of camels."

"Like your jokes are any better," said Rodgers with a frown. "But on a more serious note, there's something else I don't see. Blood."

Rodgers had a point. Though the camel's back had been matted with the stuff, there didn't appear to be any in the apartment—though the spaghetti and meatball wall art provided a serviceable analogue.

The clip clop of heels announced Traci's return. "Got it," she said, holding up the smelling salts.

"Good," I said. "Let's start with this one." I shot a finger at Sammy.

Traci uncorked the bottle, leaned over the couch, and waved the salts under Sammy's nose. The man startled. His eyes shot open, his arms flailing as he bolted upright.

"What the...? Whose it...? I..." He blinked several times, peering left and right.

"Sammy Styles?" I said.

"Huh? Yeah. Is this our room? What the hell happened...?"

I pointed out the other prone forms. "Are those your band mates, Ritchie Roth and B. B. DuPrat?"

"What? Yeah... Who are you?" He shifted his glance from me to Rodgers to Steele.

I gave Traci a nod. "Let's get the others. Sammy, I'm Detective Jake Daggers with the NWPD. We need to ask you some questions about last night."

Traci waved the salts under Ritchie's nose. He bounced off the floor, flopping around and behaving in a similar fashion to his pal Sammy. "Whaza! What? Where? I... I mean...huh?"

"Welcome to the party," I told the guy. "Sammy. About last night? What can you tell me? Start at the beginning."

"Dude...what?" he said, pressing a hand against his head. "Seriously, what's going on? How did I get here?"

Traci waved the salts under B. B.'s nose. All the platinum-haired elf did was groan. The hotel manager looked to us for guidance.

"Give him another sniff," said Steele. "Ritchie. You mind telling us what happened to you?"

Ritchie sat up from the floor, brushing chandelier shards from his clothes and holding his neck. "Happened? I don't understand."

"You're covered in mud," said Rodgers. "You have a black eye. And you were taking a nap in a pile of broken glass."

"Was I?" said Ritchie. "Aww, man. *Again?*"

Rodgers eyed me. "Are these guys for real?"

B. B. groaned, louder this time, as Traci placed the smelling salts near his nostrils. He turned his head and cracked an eye. "Ugh...what happened? I feel like death."

"But you're alive," I said. "And awake. Everyone is, now. So maybe my partners and I can finally get some answers. What happened last night?"

"Seriously, dude. Detective. Whatever," said Sammy. "You asking over and over isn't going to change anything."

"Pardon?" I said.

"I don't remember anything, man," he said. "It's like...*a blur.*"

"Ritchie?" I said.

The drummer blinked and cracked his neck. "I...uh...think we went to Billy's. After that? I couldn't really say."

"Wonderful," said Shay with a roll of her eyes. "B. B.? You have anything to add to the discussion?"

The elven guitarist let out a pained sigh. "Do we really need to do this right now? My head is killing me, and I feel like I got worked over by an angry ogre."

B. B. peeled himself off the couch, sat up, and leaned back against the cushions.

Traci jumped and screeched. "Gods! What...?"

Sammy's eyes widened. "Dude...*what happened to you?*"

Blood covered B. B.'s chest from his collarbone to the bottom of his ribs. His shirt had been torn open, revealing gashes in the flesh beneath—at least three or four. More blood soaked the couch cushions upon which he'd been laying. It was only because of the man's prone position that we hadn't noticed earlier. He must've come in and immediately collapsed on the sofa, otherwise surely the blood would've spread.

The sight threw me for a loop, too, but I played it off. "So much for your observation, Rodgers."

Steele closed on B. B. "Multiple lacerations. Not too deep, based on coagulation. Looks like they're stable. B. B., what the heck happened?"

He looked at Shay blankly. "Uh..."

"We need to get this man to a doctor," said Rodgers.

"No, it's okay," said B. B. "Just some scrapes...I think. Some rest, a little bourbon. I'll be fine."

"I think Detective Rodgers is more right than you are," said Shay. "We need to get this man some medical attention, but we also need to get all these knuckle-heads to the station for statements. Ms. Gilmore? Could you send a runner to the 5th Street Precinct? Tell them to have a medic ready. The rest of you, come with us. Time to have a chat."

"Hold up," I said. "Traci? Could you spare a couple security guards? Have them help Detective Rodgers escort the Cobras back to the station? Steele and I have another pressing matter to attend to."

Shay lifted a brow. "We do?"

"Yes," I said. "Club Midnight. That place could blow this case wide open."

"Seriously, Daggers," said Shay. "We need to get these musicians back to the precinct for questioning."

"And you don't think Rodgers and Quinto can handle that?" I said. "Come on. We need to visit that club sooner or later."

Shay eyed Rodgers.

He shrugged. "Quinto and I'll handle it. You two go on ahead. I'll meet you back at the station."

Shay sighed. "Fine. Daggers?"

I smiled. "You won't regret this." And I hoped she wouldn't—but she might if Club Midnight really was everything I feared it could be. Hopefully the vampires only frequented the place after hours.

10

The receptionist at the Banks Hotel's front desk was able to give us directions to Club Midnight, but even with an address in hand, finding the actual locale was no small feat. We walked up and down the street in question three times looking for a sign before eventually stopping and asking for directions at a shoe shine stand. As it turned out, the entrance to Club Midnight lay in the middle of an alley, buttressed on one side by stacks of discarded wooden crates and on the other by overflowing trashcans, to which I added our now empty coffee cups. Even the club's door was unmarked.

I swallowed hard as I stood before it. Needless to say, its location didn't inspire in me a sense of ease.

I pulled on the door, which turned out to be un-locked, and held it open for Shay. "Ladies first."

She gave me a knowing glance. "Mmm-hmm."

"What?" I said. "I'm a gentleman."

"One who's scared of things that go bump in the night, maybe."

She entered, and I followed. The place didn't have any windows to speak of, but thankfully someone had left a couple lanterns burning, bathing the interior in a flickering, orange glow.

Unfortunately, the ambience did nothing to dispel my growing concern. A pair of crimson velvet-upholstered divans flanked a curved archway, the latter of which opened up into an expanse as black as the deepest pits of a subterranean reservoir. End tables sidled up next to the divans, their wood dark and gleaming and their legs finely wrought, featuring carved roses and clawed feet. Black-framed paintings covered the walls, depicting scenes of men and women in loin cloths reaching towards lone rays of light as hordes of diseased, skeletal masses pushed toward them. Heavy, black drapes covered the entrances to hallways to our left and right.

I cleared my throat. "Well, this is cheery. Um...*hello?*"

My call died in the hanging folds of fabric and couch cushions. I waited a few moments for a response, but none came.

"I don't like this," I said. "Not one bit."

Shay smiled and snickered.

"You think this is funny?"

"A little, honestly," said Shay. "I'm not sure I've ever seen you so on edge."

"And I'm surprised you're not taking this more seriously," I said. "Perhaps you were right about the camel and his abnormally large feet, but there are numerous elements of this case that point to nefarious supernatural goings-on. Not just the manner of Chaz's death, mind you, but his belongings. His manager, Benson

Forsythe. I assume you noticed how he didn't want to travel to the station to identify Chaz's body. You know—because it's daylight."

"I'm giving you the benefit of the doubt for now, Daggers," said Shay. "But keep in mind, there have never been reports of vampire activity in the city, at least not during my time on the force, and we've never had a murder of this kind before. Besides, if vampires do exist, you don't think they'd congregate in as stereotypical a location as this, do you?"

"Why wouldn't they?" I said. "Stereotypes are based in fact. That's why they're so useful. If I were a creature of the night, this is precisely where I'd hang out." I peered into a corner. "Is that a spider web?"

"Looks like a decoration," said Shay. "Regardless, I guess I'm of the opinion our beliefs about supernatural creatures are more based in myth than reality."

I chewed on my lip. "I don't know about that. Like I said, stereotypes are pretty accurate in my experience. Don't want to get shivved? Don't go into the slums at night. Don't want to get your pockets picked? Stay away from street urchins and gnomes with leather-soled shoes. Don't want to get your blood forcibly removed by vampires? Avoid creepy gothic nightclubs without windows."

Shay crossed her arms. "Well, we're here, at your insistence. Even though I didn't rank this place particularly high on our list of investigative options, I agree we should, in fact, check it out. So—" She held a hand toward one of the drapes. "After you."

"Who's the gentleman, now?" I said.

"The term you're looking for is *lady*."

I swallowed back my fear and swiped at the nearest drape, drawing it across the door frame. A dark if otherwise unspectacular hallway beckoned.

"Hello? Anyone there?" I called again.

Shay's foot *tap-tap-tapped* as I waited. "Well?"

"Fine. I'm moving."

I set off down the hall, trying to keep my eyes sharp but finding it difficult to do so in the gloom. The starving, desperate folks in the paintings shook their heads at me, telling me to turn back while I still had a chance. I ignored their sage advice.

After turning a corner, I found myself at the back of a wide open lounge. More couches and loveseats, all of them upholstered in black or deep red, spread out across the floor. A bar stretched to my right, while somewhere deep in the darkness, the gleam of an elevated stage shone through.

"See?" said Shay. "It's a club. Nothing else."

I peered toward the far corner. I'd noticed movement.

"I think I saw someone. Hey! Hello?"

Again, no response.

"Go on," said Shay.

My hand itched, and I debated hanging onto Daisy for safekeeping. Nonetheless, I moved, crossing the room to the far corner. Of course, once I'd arrived, I found nothing. The hairs on my arms rose, and I felt a chill run down my spine.

"I *really* don't like this," I said, looking around.

"I guess no one's here." Shay turned and glanced back the way we'd came. "Seems odd they'd leave the front door open. This is a decent neighborhood, but still..."

"Unless whoever owns this place isn't worried about theft," I said. "For obvious reasons. Not all thieves are dumb. There could be rumors about this place. Rumors that—"

I felt a chill touch on my shoulder. I turned and screamed.

A tall, wiry man with immaculately moussed black hair and pale skin stood behind me, a black-as-night jacket draped over his shoulders. He held his thin lips parted by a hair and his hand at shoulder level, perfectly still.

He didn't seem inclined to kill me. Not right away. I stopped screaming.

"My apologies," he said in a cool, measured voice. "I didn't mean to startle you. My name is Vance. Can I help you?"

"I... Uh... I mean...that is—"

Shay bailed me out. "I'm Captain Steele from the NWPD. This is my partner, Detective Daggers. Are you in charge here?"

"I'm the owner and operator of this establishment, yes," he said. "Is there a problem?"

Shay produced the matchbook from her jacket. "Is this from your club?"

He nodded. "It is."

"An individual was found with it in his possession this morning. Chaz Willy Wilson. Are you familiar with the man?"

"Chaz. Yes, of course," said Vance. "An excellent creative mind. Bit of a troubled soul, but who amongst us isn't. I consider him a friend. But when you say he was *found...?*"

"There's no easy way to say this, Vance," said Shay. "Our officers found him dead. In Rucker Park. He passed away early this morning."

Vance drew air in sharply through his teeth. "So he's passed on, then. I have to admit, I...wasn't expecting to hear that."

"You said you consider him a friend," said Shay. "Do you mind if we ask you a few questions about him?"

"Yes, of course," said Vance. "I'll show you to my office. Please, come with me."

11

Vance paced back and forth across his office, his hands clasped behind his back. Unlike the rest of his club, the room possessed that most elusive of structural elements—a window. Of course, it too had been covered with thick black velvet that drowned out the sun's light. Instead, a single candle illuminated the space, one placed within a bleached-white sculpture of a human skull that sat on the man's desk. At least, I *hoped* it was a sculpture.

"I can't believe he's dead," said Vance. "His image remains fresh in my mind. He was such a vibrant individual. Moody and morose at times, yes, but clever. Creative. So full of vim and vigor."

"So he was here last night, I take it?" asked Shay.

She sat in one of the padded chairs before Vance's desk, though she'd rotated it to face the center of the room. I'd chosen to stick to the margins, near the bookshelves overflowing with old tomes and packed with black leather, crystal, and polished stone curios. There, I could distance myself from the oddly pale Vance—or at least I would've if the man stopped pacing and retreated behind his desk like he should.

"Chaz stopped by the club last night," said Vance. "I didn't get a chance to talk to him, but I made eye contact. He waved at me as he arrived."

"Would you describe him as a regular?"

Vance nodded. "To an extent. He didn't visit with *great* frequency, but I believe his regularity had more to do with his schedule than his desire. He performed often, after all. But perhaps I'm injecting my thoughts and emotions into matters where they're not insightful."

"How would you characterize your relationship with the man?" asked Steele.

"As I said, I considered him a friend," replied Vance. "As a connoisseur of musical acts, I recognized him when he first arrived many months ago. I introduced myself, and we struck up a conversation. Surprisingly, he and I shared many interests. His knowledge in certain subject matters was impressive given his public persona. I admit I'll miss our, how should I say...*philosophical discussions* regarding theology, life, death, and the afterlife. I hope the latter treats him well."

I snorted. *Philosophical discussions?* Was that a vampire euphemism for suffering the cold embrace of a pair of sharp incisors around one's neck?

Vance's voice sounded close behind me. "Is everything alright? You seem withdrawn."

"Huh? Me?" I turned from the bookshelf to face him. "I'm fine. Just...preoccupied. With the details of the case."

"Are you sure?" said Vance. "You appear to be on edge. Not that I've spent time with you personally, but compared to other men of your age and body type, your breathing appears to be elevated."

I blinked. "Excuse me?"

"I'm a student of physiology," said Vance. "Not strictly speaking, but it's a hobby of mine."

Of course it was. How else would he locate the body's foremost veins?

"Don't mind Detective Daggers," said Shay. "He's convinced Chaz's murderer hails from supernatural origins."

The man's eyes widened. "Truly? Please, tell me more."

"Steele," I said in a strained voice. "What are you doing? *Ixnay the ampire-vay alk-tay.*"

"Killed by a *vampire?*" said Vance. "Are you serious?"

I sighed. The cat had fled the bag. Might as well go with it, at least until Vance decided to savage my neck to bury the secrets of our knowledge with him. "It's a possibility given the state of Chaz's body. Why? You wouldn't...*know any,* would you?"

"Vampires?" said Vance. "Well...it's not that simple."

Now it was Shay's turn to do a double take. "Hold on. Say what?"

"As you might've surmised from my establishment's décor," said Vance, "I'm extremely interested in all aspects of the occult. So was Chaz. That was the common interest which drew us together. You're familiar with his song, "Creatures of the Night?" I'm not a fan of his particular musical stylings, more of the subject matter.

The man wrote it about his undying belief in the existence of the undead—no pun intended."

"We're familiar with the song," I said. "One of his roadies played it for us this morning."

"Well did you know fate inspired him to write the song following what he considered to be a supernatural encounter with a *real vampire*?" said Vance. "It occurred years ago, here in the city. Said he woke up dazed after a night on the town, pale and weak and with the scent of his lover's breath heavy over his neck."

"And you believed him?" I asked.

"I don't know," said Vance. "Who's to say if revenants are real? I've long suspected many visit my club, but I have no way of knowing for sure."

"Alright," said Shay. "I think we've ventured sufficiently off topic. Back to Chaz. You said he was here last night. When did he arrive?"

Vance, who'd blossomed at the mention of vampires, now cooled and settled back into his original groove. "Let's see...around two o'clock, I believe. Perhaps quarter till."

"And was he alone?" asked Shay.

"No," said Vance. "He arrived with his band mates."

That was news. "All of them?"

"No. One was missing. His guitarist. B. B., I believe."

"But the others, Sammy and Ritchie were with him?" asked Steele.

Vance nodded.

"Was Ritchie covered in mud, or Sammy shirtless, by any chance?" asked Steele.

"No," said Vance. "They seemed quite normal by my recollection. Although for one of them to be shirtless wouldn't be particularly *abnormal*, per se."

"What could you tell us about their visit?" asked Steele.

"Well, as I mentioned, I didn't converse with Chaz last night," said Vance, "so I couldn't give you insight into their plans for later in the evening. But I can tell you they didn't stay long. After consuming a few drinks, they left about a half hour later with one of my regulars."

My mind assailed me with thoughts of a seductress shrouded in shadows, a black widow of the highest degree. "A woman?"

"A man," said Vance. "Another enthusiast of the occult. Jefferson Torment."

I lifted an eyebrow. *"Seriously?* You're kidding, right?"

"I don't think it's his real name, but it's the moniker I'm familiar with."

"Any idea where they went?" asked Shay.

"None. My apologies."

"And what about this Jefferson character?" I said. "Any idea where we could find him?"

"Not off the top of my head," said Vance. "But I'll ask around. I can send word to your station once I have an address."

"We'd appreciate that," said Shay as she stood. "Daggers, could you jot down Chaz's arrival and departure times? I have a feeling this case involves a lot of moving parts. I don't want to confuse anything."

I pulled my notepad from my jacket and took notes. "Quarter till two arrival. Left a half hour later. Got it."

I glanced at Vance. Despite his appearance, aura, and our discussions of the occult, he'd yet to bare his fangs. Perhaps he'd recently fed. Either way, I figured one last question couldn't hurt.

I slipped the pad back home. "Vance, are you familiar with the ankh?"

"A symbol of eternal life, common to many different religious sects," said Vance. "It's synonymous with vampires and their culture for obvious reasons. Why do you ask?"

"You've said you didn't spend any one on one time with Chaz last night, but did you manage to get a look at his chest?"

Vance narrowed an eye. "Where are you going with this?"

"A symbol of an ankh was found imprinted upon Chaz's chest," said Shay. "We're not sure how long it's been there."

Vance stood straighter and inhaled sharply. "No..."

"Does that mean something?" I asked.

"Perhaps, perhaps not," said Vance. "But I can tell you that though I didn't lay eyes on the man's midsection last night, I've seen it before. Recently. And it was bare. Chaz wasn't a fan of body modification. Said it clashed with his public persona. To have a symbol like that appear, and potentially overnight, could be a mark of acceptance. Or it could mean he was specifically...*targeted*."

"By who?" said Shay.

Vance lifted an arched eyebrow. "I think you already know."

A trace of a sharp smile escaped Vance's lips, sending a shiver through my body. I took Shay by the hand and made a quick exit lest Vance change his mind and decide to introduce me to the hereafter.

12

Our rickshaw rattled forward as we approached the precinct, its wheels clacking and clattering off the cobblestones and its axle crying out for grease. The ruckus would've made conversation difficult if there were any. As it was, Shay hadn't said much of anything since leaving the club, leaning to the side and staring at the sides of brick buildings we passed along the way.

"Did I do something wrong?" I asked.

"Huh?" Shay blinked and brought her attention inside the rickshaw. "No. You're fine."

"Then what's wrong? Are you worried about the cost of the rickshaw? You're the captain now. You can take them as often as you want. You think the old bulldog walked anywhere?"

"It's not that," said Shay.

"What then?" I asked. "Is it Vance's statement? It's disturbing, for sure. That guy gave me four different types of the willies."

"Vance?" said Shay. "No. Well, not really. I'll agree he was odd. I'm...more concerned about Chaz's death than I was, let's put it that way. But that's still not it."

I gave her a moment to elaborate, but she didn't. "You can talk to me, you know. We're partners, remember?"

And more, I thought, but I didn't want to press the issue at the moment.

The rickshaw driver turned onto 5th. Shay made eye contact with me. "I don't want to return to the precinct. I'm not ready to be captain yet."

"It was your idea to head back," I said.

Shay looked at me over her invisible glasses.

"Well, we can tell the driver to keep going," I said. "Do a drive by."

Shay sighed. "Just because I don't welcome my new responsibilities doesn't mean I can shirk them. Things are what they are. All I can hope for is a quick resolution to my interim status."

I assume she meant a demotion, but she left the ending open. The rickshaw driver came to a stop at the base of the precinct's stairs. I paid him and hopped out after Steele.

"I'm not sure what you're worried about," I said as I pulled on the front door. "You're doing great. Besides, this place basically runs itself."

We took a right past the information desk and headed toward Shay's new office. A quartet of officers and detectives stood outside her door, papers in hand and frowns set deep into their jowls.

"You were saying..." said Shay.

I didn't get a chance to respond as the leader of the bunch, a gray-mustachioed fraud detective by the name of Brown, intercepted us en route.

"Listen here, Steele—Captain," he said, waving his clutched papers in front of him. "This is outrageous! A single paddy wagon? Only four men assigned to the scene? What am I supposed to do with this?"

"Ah...*pardon?*" said Steele.

Brown smacked the papers. "The requisition for supplies and officers for my sting operation. I put the paperwork in a week ago. A week! Now we're less than forty-eight hours from game time and I find out I've been granted half—half!—of what I asked for. How am I supposed to cover all the exits with only four officers on duty?"

"Uh, did you talk to accounting?" said Steele.

A young clean-cut man in brown slacks and a crisp white shirt stepped forward. "He came to me first, ma'am. I tried to explain it's not merely a matter of balancing the books. We have other officers who've made requests in that time window. We simply don't have enough to spare."

"Enough to spare?" Brown snorted. "*Please.* This is about nothing *other* than the books. You're telling me we can't bring off-duty officers in to help? You understand how close I am to nabbing this guy, don't you?"

"Off-duty officers demand overtime pay," said the young man. "So you're right. In that sense, it *is* about the books."

Brown huffed. "See? An admission. We can pull this off, but we need the authorization for more men. Tell him, captain. Tell him how important this is."

Steele pushed toward her door and cranked on the handle. "Well, honestly I'm not particularly familiar with the case. If you could fill me in..."

One of the other assembled bluecoats pushed his way through as Shay stepped into her office. "Captain, look. I'm sure whatever Detective Brown is up in arms about is *very* important, but over here in the real world we've got a five thirty-nine in progress. I'm going to need some backup, *now.*"

Steele retreated toward her desk, her brow furrowed. "A five thirty-nine?"

"Yes, ma'am," said the officer. "You know? An active hostage situation. Fifteenth and Kline. Some sort of domestic dispute between a dwarf and his live-in girlfriend."

"And what do you propose we do about it?" said Shay.

"That's why I'm here, ma'am," said the officer. "I'm not sure what the protocol is. An officer reported seeing the dwarf with a knife, which would make this a five forty-five, but a neighbor says this is a usual occurrence, in which case we could downgrade the whole thing to a two twenty-seven."

"Five forty-five?" said Steele. "Two twenty-seven?"

Brown pushed his way back to the front. "Captain! I demand an answer on my requisition! Would you please talk to this pencil pusher? We're talking about letting a serial con man off the hook here."

"*Pencil pusher?*" said the accountant.

Everyone started to yell and make demands. Steele retreated, but she'd run out of room, bumping into the wall behind her desk. He face lacked color, and her nostrils flared.

"Alright, *that's it*," I yelled, holding my hands up. "Brown, are you kidding me right now? The budget's fixed, you know that. If everybody got what they wanted, the rest of us would be out on the street. And you, accountant. Whatever your name is. Work with him. Compromise. Cut costs elsewhere. Maybe you can't get him eight men, but you can probably squeeze out six. Or move the timing on the sting. Just figure something out."

"And you," I said, pointing at the bluecoat. "Cut it out with the numerical designations, will you? Congratulations on memorizing the beat officer's handbook, but just because we have a code for a gnome groping an elven stripper while eating a ham sandwich on a Tuesday doesn't mean we need to use it. So there's a hostage situation? Great. Get a mediator. Defuse the situation. And if that doesn't work, break in through the back and subdue the perp before anyone gets hurt? Are we all clear?"

Brown grumbled. The accountant looked sheepish. The officer and his partner nodded.

"Good," I said. "Now get the hell to work. Seriously, you know better than to bug the captain with this crap. And close the door behind you!"

The mob left, closing the door with a clack. Silence reigned once more.

I took a deep breath and turned to Shay. "Sorry about that. I wasn't trying to undermine your authority. You just seemed to be getting frazzled, and I figured I could help. Those idiots really should've been able to sort through these problems by themselves."

She stepped away from the wall. "It's alright, Daggers. I, ah...appreciate you stepping in with the assist."

"Because it's a fine line I'm trying to toe," I continued. "With you being the captain now but me still being your partner. And friend. And...you know. Everything else. Plus with my career aspirations. It's difficult. Tricky. Maybe a little of both. Dricky, if you will."

Shay smiled. "I'm serious. You did great. I *was* getting overwhelmed. I *let myself* get overwhelmed. It's to be expected, given how I got here. But I need to do better. The Captain put me in this position for a reason, and I need to step up. Next time, I will."

I nodded.

"But...be sure to stand close behind me," said Shay. "In case I stumble and need help getting up."

"Always."

I met her eyes. They said 'kiss me,' and I would've if Shay hadn't already made herself clear about prying eyes. Undermining her authority with forceful displays was one thing. Compounding the problem with amorous ones was another.

"So, what now?" I said.

"Honestly?" said Shay. "I could go for some lunch. I'm getting hungry."

Someone knocked on the door, and I heard the clack of the latch.

"Seriously?" I said as I turned. "How is it you bunch can't handle—oh. Hey, Rodgers."

Our cheery detective pal stood in the doorway. "Hey, Daggers. The petitioners driving you crazy yet, Steele?"

"Crazy's not the right word," she said. "More like a combination between restless and angst-ridden."

"I bet there's a word for that in one of the lower tongues," I said. "Seems like a very goblinesque sort of emotion."

Shay gave Rodgers a nod. "Did you make it back okay with the Cobras?"

"Sure did," he said. "I just moved the lot from the interrogation rooms to the holding cells. Well, except for B. B. He's with a medic."

"How's he doing?" I asked.

"Pretty good," said Rodgers. "Whoever or whatever attacked him had their efforts thwarted by his ribs. Though I suspect he'll be in a lot of pain once the lingering effects of his drug overdose wear off."

"So you got their statements?" said Steele.

Rodgers sighed. "Yeah, for all the good it'll do."

"It went that well, huh?"

"Those guys are less than useless," said Rodgers. "They all told the same story. Said they headed to this Billy Charles guy's place after the show, took drugs, and don't remember a thing until we roused them. So either they're really well coordinated in their lies, or more likely, they're all telling the truth. I'm leaning toward the latter given that they didn't have time to hash out their stories before we found them."

"Not unless they did it before passing out," said Shay.

Rodgers nodded.

"And what about the camel?" I asked.

"He's holding firm in his resolve," said Rodgers. "Refuses to give a statement."

"What a jerk," I said. "Threaten him with charges of resisting arrest."

Shay smiled. "I don't think that's going to work, Daggers."

"You're right," I said. "He did come along peacefully. Maybe obstruction of justice?"

"How about Quinto?" asked Shay. "How's he doing?"

"Oh, dandy," said Rodgers. "He's still down in another of the holding cells with the aforementioned dromedary. Claims the beast is 'traumatized' and needs special attention. Sounds like an excuse to get out of interrogations and paperwork if you ask me."

"Thanks," said Steele. "Keep us posted if anything changes."

"With the camel's vow of silence?" said Rodgers. "You bet. What about the Yellow Cobras? Should we release them?"

Shay nodded. "We have to, I think. At this point, despite not knowing what they were up to last night, we don't have any reason to suspect any of them, nor do we have the evidence to support it. Cut them free once B. B. gets stitched up."

"You got it." Rodgers started to turn but paused. "Oh, wait! I almost forgot why I popped by in the first place. A woman stopped by while I was chatting with the Cobras. Said she needed to talk to the two of you. I had the officer at the door stash her in the waiting room until you showed up."

I looked through the office windows toward the wait-ing area in question. I spotted a puff of blond hair peek-ing over the backs of one of the leather couches.

"Did you get her name?" I asked.

"Sure did," said Rodgers. "Heather Cleary-Wilson. Take that as you may."

13

Shay knocked on the doorframe to the waiting room. "Excuse me? Ms. Cleary-Wilson?"

The woman on the couch looked up. Wavy, blonde hair framed her face, similar in length and style to Chaz's own locks but with traces of a darker color at the roots. She wore a faded denim jacket over a black crop top that emphasized her considerable assets, paired with a set of black leather pants that hugged her lower body. Garish makeup covered her face: bright lipstick, heavy eyeliner, eye shadow, and blush. It all worked in concert to create a very specific look, but I wondered if there wasn't perhaps *another* reason for the quantity. Under the concealer and blush, her right cheek seemed puffier and darker than the rest of her face.

"Yes, that's me," she said. "But you can call me Heather. Everyone else does."

"Heather, then," said Shay, entering the waiting room. "I'm Captain Steele. This is my partner, Detective Daggers. We understand you asked for us?"

"Yeah," she said. "Benson—Benson Forsythe?—he sent word that I needed to come down here. Something about Chaz?"

Apparently, Benson had found a way to avoid making a trip through town during daylight hours. *Surprise, surprise...*

"So...he didn't tell you *why* we needed you to come down here?" I asked.

"No," said Heather. "Why?"

What a guy, that Benson. Shay sat down on the couch across from Heather, and I joined her.

"What's your relation to Chaz Willy Wilson, Heather?" asked Steele.

She played with her fingers and rolled her eyes. "He's my...*husband*. Sort of. We're separated."

"And how long have you been apart?" asked Shay.

"I don't know," said Heather. "A year. Year and a half. What's this about? Is Chaz in trouble again? I didn't bring bail money."

Shay looked at me. I gave her a slight nod. She was better at this stuff than I was.

Shay leaned in. "Heather, I can't believe Benson didn't tell you, but the reason we needed you to come down is that we need someone to...positively identify Chaz."

"What?" she said. "Like from a lineup? Did he commit a crime?"

Shay shook her head. "He's dead, Heather."

"*What?*" The woman's eyes widened. "What are you talking about?"

"Our officers found him in Rucker Park this morning," said Shay. "He'd passed several hours earlier. I'm sorry."

Heather leaned back into her cushions, took a deep breath, and let it out slowly. I gazed into her eyes, but she seemed to have left the mortal coil.

"Heather?" I said. "Are you still with us?"

"What?" She blinked. "Yeah. I guess I'm...having a hard time taking it in, is all. I saw him last night."

"You did?" I said. "Do you remember at what time?"

"I'm not sure." She moved her head slowly, as if in a daze. "Around one o'clock. Maybe one fifteen."

That would've been before Chaz's foray into Club Midnight. "Where was this?"

"At my apartment."

"Would you mind telling us what happened?" asked Shay.

"Uh...sure. He dropped by," said Heather. "With Sammy and Ritchie."

"But not B. B.?" asked Shay.

"No."

I made a mental note of that, then realized I'd promptly forget my mental note, so I tore my pad out of my jacket and started furiously scribbling. "What happened after they arrived?"

"They were all wasted," said Heather. "Like, high out of their minds. I don't know if I'd ever seen Chaz quite that bad. Whatever drugs they took messed with them something fierce. Anyway, they knocked on the door. I was still up, so I opened it, and they helped themselves right on in. I hadn't seen Chaz in at least a month, so I asked him what he wanted. He started babbling about *us* and *our bond* and how I was the only one who could ever really make him happy, but he was drunk and I could barely understand two-thirds of what he was saying. I told him to go home. He kept going though, telling me he loved me and trying to touch me and getting handsy. I think in his mind he could just pop over and apologize and suddenly I'd get wet for him, like none of the last year and a half ever happened. *As if...*"

Heather drifted off. Shay gave her a moment before pressing her. "And? What happened then?"

The young woman didn't respond, but I noticed a sparkly shimmer form in the corner of her eyes. She turned her head to hide it, but—whether consciously or unconsciously—she also turned her head so as to hide her bruised cheek.

"It's okay, Heather," I said. "He's gone. He can't hurt you anymore."

She took another deep breath, but when she spoke, her voice broke. "He got angry when I told him no, but he kept going. Trying to grab me. Force himself on me. I screamed and bit him on the arm. That's when he punched me. Knocked me right to the ground. Thank the gods Sammy and Ritchie were there. They pulled him off me. Dragged him out of my apartment and slammed the door shut behind them."

"Was that the end of it?" asked Shay.

Heather nodded. "I cried myself to sleep. Woke up late. That's when I got Benson's message."

I tucked my notepad away. The case had taken a dark turn—though to be fair, it had already started on a shadowy path, albeit a different sort of one. "Had Chaz ever been abusive in the past?"

Heather shook her head. "No. Never." She gazed toward the floor. Her voice caught. "And you know the crazy thing? Despite everything he'd done, and everything I'd said? Part of me did still love him—until that moment when he hit me. It...broke me. Inside, I mean."

Heather trailed off. I got the impression she'd said about all she intended to on that subject.

"I know this is a difficult thing to ask of you in this situation," said Shay, "but as we mentioned at the start, we need someone close to Chaz to identify him. We have his band mates here, though, so if you don't feel up to the task..."

"No," said Heather. "It's fine. I'll do it. Maybe it'll give me some sort of...closure."

Shay started to rise, but I stuck out a finger. "Excuse me. One more question, if I may Heather."

She looked up. "Yes?"

"What can you tell us about Chaz's obsession with vampires?"

Shay leveled me with a gaze to match her last name. "Really? Daggers, this is so not the time."

I considered her statement for about a fraction of a second before coming to the conclusion that she was right. Even if she wasn't, I realized I'd better listen to her unless I wanted to find out if our old Captain had ever splurged on a police issue dog house.

"My apologies," I said. "Mrs. Cleary-Wilson? Perhaps you could follow Captain Steele and I downstairs."

14

I led Heather down into the dungeon, which really wasn't as horrific a place as it sounded. Rather than a damp, dark, dreary coffin of stone for the living, it was a clammy, dim, bleak coffin of stone for those who were already dead. To my knowledge, its moisture-slicked granite halls had never been used for torture or imprisonment—at least not during my lifetime. Given New Welwic's long history and penchant for using buildings far past their expiration date, who knew what sorts of uses the 5th Street Precinct had been put to hundreds of years ago?

I shivered as I reached the bottom of the stone steps, more from the persistent aura of death than the temperature. At least in the winter, the subterranean morgue tended to be a bit milder than outdoors. It never stopped being creepy, though.

I spotted our coroner, Cairny Moonshadow, on the far side of the morgue's main room. She stood next to the wall of cadaver vaults, their shiny steel faces and handles gleaming in the room's muted, artificial lighting. A half dozen examination tables dotted the floor between us, most of them bare except for stacks of folded white linens, collections of neatly arranged surgical instruments, and the occasional clipboard. A human-shaped protrusion sprouted from underneath one table's white cloth.

I wrinkled my nose as I walked into the space, not from any unpleasant aroma but rather the overpowering scent of the lemon cleaner the janitor used to sanitize the floors. He often went overboard in the morgue, probably based on unempirical assumptions about the rate of decomposition of human bodies and their effect on air quality. I'm sure Cairny, with her extensive scientific knowledge, could put him on the straight and narrow. Of course, that would require her to talk to the man, and given her absentminded nature, chances were she'd never even noticed him.

My shoes clacked off the tiles, as did Heather's and Steele's behind me. Apparently it wasn't enough to announce our presence. I cleared my throat. "Hey, Cairny."

She turned and gazed at me with her big moon eyes, the only physical characteristic that gave away her part fairy, or fae, heritage. Long, midnight black hair fell on either side of her face, contrasting sharply against her pale, ivory skin. For as long as I'd known her, she'd always employed a monochromatic clothing style, which is why I didn't bother to ask who'd died upon seeing her black trousers, held up by her black belt, partially covering her black shoes, and paired with an airy blouse of purest black. I did, however, gape a little at the pink scarf around her neck.

"Oh," she said, blinking as she focused on me. "Hello, Daggers."

I gave her a nod. "Nice scarf."

She pushed past me, noticing who stood behind my shoulder. "Steele! Oh my goodness, congratulations! I heard the news when I got in this morning. This is so exciting!"

"For you maybe," said Shay. "For me, not so much."

"Nice to see you, too..." I mumbled.

Cairny glanced at me with narrowed eyes before turning back to Steele. "No? Why not?"

"It's...complicated," said Shay. "Look, can we talk about this later? We have other business to attend to first." She tilted her head at Heather.

"Oh. Of course." Cairny stuck her hand out in the glam rock woman's direction. "Cairny Moonshadow, 5th Street Precinct coroner. Pleased to meet you."

Heather took note of her hand but neglected to take it, instead eyeing the surroundings with revulsion. "Uh...likewise."

"Heather's here to identify Mr. Wilson," said Shay. "He's here, I assume?"

Cairny nodded. "Officer Phillips delivered him a few hours ago. Right over here."

She led us to the exam table covered with the white sheet, grabbed the sheet's corner, and flipped it up, revealing Chaz's still form, torn throat and all. "Here you go. One body, ready for identification."

"Way to showcase your empathy," I said.

"Pardon?" said Cairny.

"This is Mr. Wilson's wife, Heather," I said.

"Oh. Sorry."

I glanced at the woman in question, but despite the shedding of a single tear upstairs, she'd reverted back into a state of shock. She stared at Chaz's lifeless body, her face a mask, devoid of emotion.

We all gave her a moment, but eventually Shay prodded her. "Heather?"

"What?" she said. "Right. Sorry. It's Chaz. Without a doubt."

She continued to stare, especially at the wound in Chaz's neck. Was it my imagination, or had she started to pale?

I stepped in front of her, blocking her view of Chaz and hopefully keeping her from passing out. "Thank you, Heather. That's all we needed. You're free to go."

She looked up and swallowed. It wasn't my imagination. Blood had definitely drained from her face. "What happened to him?"

"We're working on it," said Steele. "But you can be sure we'll let you know as soon as we've sorted out the details."

Heather nodded. I held my hand toward the stairs. She started to move, her heels clicking on the tile. She paused halfway to the exit.

"Wait," she said, turning. "So, if Chaz is dead...what happens to all his stuff? And his money?"

She made the remark in such a casual, offhand way, her tone almost innocent enough to prevent suspicion.

"You're still married, correct?" I said.

She nodded.

"Then I imagine you'll inherit the entirety of his estate. Whatever's left, anyway," I said. "Unless he made other legal arrangements, but that's for the lawyers to decide. You can leave your address upstairs with the officer at the front desk. If we hear anything, we'll be sure to keep in touch."

"Right. Thanks." Heather started once again, this time making to the stairs without interruption. As the sound of her heels faded, I turned back toward the action, important questions at the forefront of my mind.

"Seriously," I said. "What's with the pink scarf?"

Cairny shrugged. "Quinto thinks I should experiment with color more. What do you think?"

I pursed my lips. "He might be right, but *pink*? It's not you."

"Well, I like it," said Shay. "It makes your eyes pop."

"Thanks," said Cairny. "But for once I think I agree with Daggers. Still, I'd rather talk about you. You're not excited about the promotion?"

"It's too much responsibility," said Shay. "I'm not prepared for it. Seriously, let's talk about it later. What can you tell us about Chaz?"

"And before you apply the caveat that you've only performed a preliminary investigation and that your analysis is subject to change as you perform more tests, yes we know," I said. "But with that all said—how'd he die?"

"Well," said Cairny. "You noticed the gaping wound in his neck, right?"

"Was that sarcasm?" With her, it was hard to tell. "Of course we noticed. But you always ingrain in us the need not to make assumptions."

"It wasn't sarcasm," said Cairny. "I'm always puzzled by the things you miss. I figured I should ask. But to make sure we're all on the same page, that's almost certainly what killed him. The enormous neck wound."

"And what time did he die?" asked Shay.

"If I had to guess, based on lividity—sometime between four and six AM."

I reached up and pulled the white sheet down to Chaz's midsection. Cairny had removed his shirt. I pointed a finger at his chest. "And this?"

"You mean the tattoo?" said Cairny. "What of it?"

Shay smiled. "Told you."

I snorted, unwilling to accept as gospel any explanations lacking supernatural origins. "What makes you think it's a tattoo?"

"And you're concerned about *my* sarcasm?" said Cairny. "Do you understand how confusing these questions are to me? It's a tattoo based on the damage to the epidermis. Fresh, too."

"How fresh?" asked Shay.

"I'd guess he got it sometime last night," said Cairny. "Pre-mortem, based on blood coagulation."

"So if Vance was right," said Shay, "then Chaz got this tattoo sometime after his exit from Club Midnight but before his death. Between two and six, then."

I snorted, dissatisfied with the conversation's direction. "Enough about the presumed tattoo. Let's talk about the death wound. What caused it?"

"Well, I'm still working on that," said Cairny. "But based on the jagged edges? It must've been something that applied a substantial force but through a pointed instrument versus a sharpened one. Based on the size, it could've been...teeth."

"Aha!" I cried, turning to Shay. "See?"

Cairny furrowed her brow. "I feel like I'm missing something."

"Don't mind Daggers," said Shay. "What else can you tell us?"

"Quite a bit, depending on what sort of information you're after." Cairny plucked a scalpel from the edge of the examination table and began using it as a pointer. "For one thing, this man lost a lot of blood very fast, which is undoubtedly what led to his death. His left internal and external jugular veins are severed, as is his common carotid artery on this side. Honestly, I'm surprised the man didn't have more blood on his person given the highly vascular nature of the injury. Rather, instead of blood, his face and neck are covered with what I can only describe as an *organic film*." Cairny prodded a spot on his neck covered with the light brown, translucent substance. It flaked off in response to the touch.

"We noticed that," said Shay. "Any idea what it is?"

"I have some guesses, but only that," said Cairny. "Nothing I'd be willing to share at the moment. I was, however, able to isolate the source of the foul odor attached to this man as he was brought in."

I'd almost forgotten about that. I took a quick sniff, but the pungent litter box smell was almost completely absent, or at least hidden behind the janitor's zeal for lemon scents. His clothes, which Cairny had removed, must've harbored the stink.

"So," said Shay. "What was it?"

"Fecal matter," said Cairny.

I grimaced. "Eww. And to think I touched him. But to be honest, I thought he smelled more like the proverbial number one than the number two."

"And you'd be right about that," said Cairny, "because this particular fecal matter is quite high in urate."

Cairny possessed dual degrees in chemistry and biology. I tempted fate by asking a follow-up question. "What does that have to do with the smell?"

"Urate, or uric acid, creates ammonia gas upon chemical breakdown. Urea, which is present in human urine, undergoes the same transformation upon reaction with water in the presence of certain enzymes. The ammonia gas creates the smell you're referring to."

I tried to wrap my head around the implications. I failed. "So...you're saying Chaz was covered in poop, but a special kind of poop?"

"Precisely," said Cairny. "Guano. It was obvious given its white color."

"*Guano?*" I said. "Like from bats? Steele, did you hear that?"

"Or seagulls." Cairny's brow furrowed again. "And I'm not imagining it. I'm definitely missing something."

Shay sighed. "Daggers is under the impression Mr. Wilson was murdered by a vampire."

Cairny cupped her chin. "Hmm."

"You actually agree with him?" said Steele.

"I didn't say that," said Cairny. "I'm simply considering the possibility."

"What's there to consider?" I said. "Chaz had his throat torn out, by *teeth* in all likelihood. He lost all his blood, and he's covered in bat droppings."

"Or seagull droppings," said Cairny. "I'm not experienced enough to distinguish between the two. The fact that he lost all his blood is immaterial. Of course he did, given the state of his throat. And as far as teeth are concerned...I'm not entirely convinced. I'll need to give it some thought."

"And the ankh tattoo?" I said. "He was also found with a book of the occult in his possession, and he frequented a known vampire hangout."

"*Known vampire hangout?*" said Steele.

"Close enough," I said.

Cairny eyed me dubiously. "I *said* I'll give it thought."

I snorted. "You two and your facts. Those never carried as much weight as my intuition in the old days."

Shay brushed me off. "Anything else, Cairny?"

She shrugged. "I found some bruising on his backside, as well as unidentified hair fragments in his clothing. Well...unidentified until I heard about the camel—which doesn't fit into the vampire narrative, I must say."

"It'll fit," I said. "I'll find a way for it to fit."

Once again, my partner ignored me. "Cairny, what are you doing for lunch? I'm starving."

Her eyes widened. "Is that an invitation? Give me five minutes to free Quinto from his new two-toed friend and I'll meet you at the door."

"We'll do you one better," said Steele. "We'll head out and you can meet us there. Thoroughly Bread, just down the street."

Cairny nodded, but I eyed Shay with concern. If she couldn't even wait five minutes for her best friend then her hunger situation had become dire indeed. Better we move quickly else she bite my head off, either figuratively or literally.

15

"How about that booth over there?" I pointed. "It should fit five."

We stood inside the aforementioned Thoroughly Bread, a new eatery a few blocks down the street from the precinct. A sign depicting a racehorse chowing down on a sandwich hung over the entrance, but the owners hadn't been content to set the metaphor aside at the door. Horseshoes, riding crops, and paintings of racing stallions adorned the walls. Even the fixtures for the booths had been styled to look like animal stalls.

At least the interior didn't also harbor that distinctive stable smell.

Shay shrugged. "The booth would fit five *normal* individuals. Might be tight with Quinto. Still, not like I see a better option."

Folks packed the interior, filling most of the chairs. I wasn't sure if the crowds were due to the quality of food or the place's novelty, but either way, it seemed like a good sign.

The door opened, setting off the chimes. In walked Cairny, Rodgers, and Quinto.

"Ah, good," I said. "Guys? Booth in the far corner. Looks like our only option."

We shuffled between the tables, thankfully reaching the booth in question before any interlopers beat us to the punch. Shay and I shuffled in on one side, Rodgers and Cairny on the other, while Quinto pulled up a free chair and positioned it on the end.

Quinto sighed, his chair creaking as he settled his bulk into it. "Whew! Tell you what, I'm glad you guys suggested lunch. Wrangling a thousand pound beast really takes it out of you, even for a guy my size."

"Mmm-hmm," I said. "It's a real drag, I'm sure."

Quinto gave me a lips pressed together sort of look. "And what's that supposed to mean?"

"We all saw you sweet-talk that camel at the Moxy," I said. "Well, not Cairny, but everyone else. By all accounts your relationship with the beast has only grown stronger."

Quinto shifted his gaze to Rodgers. He knew where the unspecified accounts had originated.

"What?" said Rodgers. "It's true. You've been hanging out with that camel all morning. Don't act like it's been a miserable experience."

"For your information," said Quinto, "I've been hard at work. Soothing that animal. Making sure he doesn't damage the holding cells. Collecting evidence, including blood and fur samples. Looking into that Minestrone Brothers circus—no leads yet, in case you were wondering. Not to mention cleaning up after the beast.

Good gods, does that thing poop a lot. And before you ask, yes, I washed my hands before coming over."

"Don't worry, dear," said Cairny. "You've found a new best friend, relegating me to a second banana. I understand."

Quinto frowned and shook his head. "I can tell when I'm being ganged up on. Did you two order yet?" He shot a finger toward the service counter.

"Sure did. For all of us." I held a numbered placard in my hand. I flicked it Quinto's way for him to place at the edge of the table.

"Uh-oh," said Rodgers. "That sounds ominous."

"You don't trust my judgment?" I said.

"With food?" said Rodgers. "Not by a long shot."

"Don't worry," said Steele. "I made the culinary decisions."

"Well, lay it on us then," said Cairny. "What are we having?"

Steele began ticking off the choices on her fingers. "For Quinto, to satisfy his love of bold flavors, we got him a salami sandwich with pickled peppers, spiced cabbage slaw, and goat cheese. For you, Cairny, a blackened catfish po' boy—"

"Blackened catfish?" said Cairny. "Is that a statement about my fashion choices?"

"Daggers thought it would be funny," said Shay. "But ultimately I felt the flavor profile would be up your alley, so I allowed it. Rodgers, we got you a smoked turkey, ham, tomato, and sage-scented cheese club."

Rodgers gave a thumbs up. "Perfect."

"Daggers ordered a pulled pork with cole slaw and swiss on an onion roll, and I opted for poached chicken with a house-made aioli and locally sourced cheddar on a baguette."

"Fancy," said Rodgers. "Daggers, a year ago, could you have imagined yourself eating like this?"

"A year ago I didn't even know what aioli was," I said. "So no. But I do think I would've given this place a shot. I mean, *sandwiches?* Within minutes of the precinct? Come on."

"Please," said Shay. "You would've been thrown off by the crowds, trendy sign, and too-clean interior."

I shrugged. "You're probably right. With no bar to speak of, I would've about-faced and found the nearest dank hole to eat in by myself. In other news, have I mentioned how much I prefer having friends?"

I made the statement in jest, but as with all jokes, mine was only amusing because of the truth at its core. Shay gave me a silent, warm smile, but her intent was clear. *You don't have to be alone anymore, Daggers,* her bright blue eyes told me, *and you're better off for it. We all are.*

"Hey, you know what we're missing?" said Quinto. "Drinks."

"I told the cashier at the front to bring coffee and tea with the meal," I said.

"Not that," said Quinto. "The alcoholic kind. Steele's captain now. We should celebrate!"

Shay's smile faded. "Um...no thanks, Quinto. I appreciate the sentiment, but I'd rather not."

The big guy blinked. "Why not? Don't tell me you're going to be as big a hard ass as the old Captain when it comes to drinking on the job."

"That's not it," said Shay. "I just don't feel like I'm...worthy of the position."

Cairny nodded. "Impostor syndrome. Very common in people who are in positions of power, even for those who are highly educated and experienced. Don't worry about it."

"But that's the thing," said Shay. "I'm *not* experienced. I don't have any idea what I'm doing, or supposed to be doing. If not for all of you, I'd be lost."

Quinto gave a dismissive wave. "Please. Anyone thrust into your position would be—except for a captain transferred from a different precinct, which is probably what the higher-ups will do when they've decided to award someone the position permanently, but that's different. Anyone else, even long time detectives, wouldn't handle the change any better than you have."

Shay lifted a brow. "You can't be serious."

"He is," said Rodgers. "You're far more intelligent than most folks in the precinct. You're probably the smartest one among the bunch of us, except for maybe Cairny. Experience be damned, that's huge. And you've already figured out the most important part of being a captain, which is that you can't do everything yourself. Let other people handle the dirty work. That's what we're here for. Don't worry. We won't let you down."

Shay glanced at me.

I gave her a nod. "That's exactly what I said earlier—or tried to. I'm not always the most eloquent individual when I'm nervous. But they're absolutely right. We're here for you."

It took a moment for our collective support to buoy her, but eventually it did. Shay smiled. "Alright. Well...thanks, guys. I appreciate it."

"Thirty-five?" a voice rasped.

We all looked up—then down. A burly goblin server balanced a tray laden with our sandwiches and drinks on his back.

"That's us," I said. "Quinto, let's help him out."

We distributed the foodstuffs, allowing the goblin to return to the kitchen with his tray and back intact. Apparently, Shay wasn't the only one whose hunger had taken control of their senses, as we all attacked our sandwiches with a ferocious intensity. Their delectable smells probably had something to do with it. The sweet, smoky scent of my pulled pork told me I'd made the right choice before I sunk my teeth into the first bite.

Moans, slurps, and belches served as the only conversation during the meal, but as soon as we'd finished, Shay revealed what sort of captain really lurked under her fashionable pantsuit.

"Alright," she said, wiping her mouth on a napkin. "Now that we're recharged and refreshed, let's get back to work. Daggers, you've been taking detailed notes, right? Let's talk timeline. Where are the gaps?"

In her desperation, Shay had somehow eaten quicker than me. I popped the last bite of pork roll into my mouth, sucked the barbecue sauce off my fingers, and went digging for my notebook.

"Ah, let's see here," I said, pulling the pad from my jacket with my clean hand. "Well, we know Chaz was alive and well with his band mates when they finished their show at the Moxy at around ten PM. After that, the Yellow Cobra foursome apparently visited the house of this Billy Charles, who we still haven't met. Probably should do that. From there, we're in the dark until about one or one fifteen, at which point Chaz, Sammy, and Ritchie all stopped by Chaz's estranged wife, Heather's, apartment. We're still not sure what happened to B. B., but clearly the band lost contact with him in that period.

"We don't know for sure if Chaz and company headed straight from Heather's apartment to Club Midnight, but the timing suggests that's the case, seeing as they arrived at the goth club by a quarter to two. They only stayed for a half hour, leaving with some weirdo by the name of Jefferson Torment, who then separated Chaz from the group, branded him with the mark of eternal life, savaged his neck, and left his corpse in the middle of Rucker Park after feasting on his life force."

"*Daggers...*" said Shay.

"Right. Sorry," I said. "What I meant to say is that we're not sure what happened after Chaz, Sammy, and Ritchie left with this Jefferson character. That's our last point of reference until Chaz's death, which Cairny estimates occurred between four and six. We also don't know when Chaz received his ankh tattoo, but based on the testimony of Club Midnight's manager, Vance, it was after he left the club. Assuming Chaz did, in fact, get a tattoo and wasn't marked for slaughter like I previously suggested."

Shay pursed her lips. "And you said the Cobras didn't provide any additional useful testimony, right Rodgers?

The cheery blond detective shook his head. "None. Claimed they don't remember a thing."

"So, basically, we're left with a lot of gaps," said Quinto.

"And we need to fill them in," said Shay. "Cairny, I'll need you to hang back at the precinct and do what you do best. Keep investigating Chaz's death. I'm not sure if there's any way for you to match the blood from the camel's back to him, but if you can, that would be helpful. And if word arrives from Vance regarding Jefferson Torment's address, forward it to the rest of us."

"What'll we be up to?" asked Quinto.

"I'd like for you and Rodgers to head back to the Moxy," said Steele. "In addition to Chaz, we need to build a more concrete timeline for those two Cobra roadies, Diamond and Dennis. I'm not entirely sure I trust their motives, or lack thereof."

"And look into that band manager, too," I said. "Benson. See if he's been outside at all today."

Shay sighed. "Yes, him too, if not necessarily for the reasons Daggers has in mind. His motive for wanting Chaz dead is suspect, but there might be some deeper connections we haven't uncovered yet."

"And you and Daggers?" asked Rodgers. "Where are you headed?"

"To the home of Billy Charles," said Shay. "We need to figure out what happened to the Cobras between ten and one."

16

It didn't surprise me that Billy Charles lived in Brentford. Big D had mentioned the man's mansion, and Brentford provided the crème-de-la-crème of fancy New Welwic living, at least for those who preferred lavish, sprawling estates over penthouse high-rises. Admittedly, the exclusive neighborhood was situated farther away from the luxury shopping, shows, and soirées of the city's famous downtown Pearl district, but when rickshaws stood at attention, ready to shuttle wealthy tycoons at a moment's notice, who needed that level of immediacy?

I personally preferred the artfully crafted Brentford homes, surrounded by tall trees and neatly trimmed hedges, to the Pearl's condos. As a small boy, I'd often dreamed about becoming wealthy enough to buy a home in the district. Of course, I'd also fantasized about coming into possession of a harem containing a hundred beautiful, nubile women or of turning into a fifty-foot supercolossus with the strength of a thousand men, skin of stone, and with lightning bolts shooting from my fingertips. All three outcomes seemed equally likely now.

Shay and I abandoned our rickshaw at the foot of Charles' estate, following a gravel path bordered by manicured grass toward the front door. Though I'd long since admitted defeat to Shay in the eagle-eyed observation department, it didn't take her level of prowess to pick out the red flags that separated Charles' place from other Brentwood mansions. The empty liquor bottles half-sunken into the bushes, for example, or the lipstick-covered toga hanging from an oak branch, or the lone mattress, abandoned in the grass to the right of the door—which, speaking of the devil, had been left ajar.

I took stock of it as Shay and I mounted the front steps. "I guess the Yellow Cobra gents weren't the only ones who partied to their fullest extent last night."

"It would appear so, wouldn't it?" Shay knocked on the front door, which creaked and swung in upon her touch. "Hello? Mind if we come in?"

No one answered. Shay turned to me. "Think this qualifies as an exigent circumstance?"

"Oh, ho," I said. "Someone's been brushing up on their police lingo. And you claimed not to be ready to be captain."

"If you must know, yes, I've been trying to broaden my horizons. And not simply last night...when I slept about two winks out of the available thousands. Answer the question."

"Exigent circumstance allows us entry without a warrant or approval in the events of imminent danger to individuals, evidence destruction, or a suspect's escape.

The last two I think we can eliminate as ongoing. The first however... We found Chaz dead. He was clearly wasted when he died. The party started here. I sure hope Billy Charles is okay."

"So you're saying we should go in?"

I shrugged. "You're the captain."

"Way to ease the burden from my shoulders." Shay pushed the door open the rest of the way and walked in. I followed her.

The home immediately opened into a brightly-lit atrium. Colored light streamed in through stained glass windows set high in the walls, illuminating a majestic grand piano, odd geometrically-shaped sculptures, and more discarded booze bottles. Of people, however, we saw none. Nor did we find any in the adjacent living rooms and common spaces. It wasn't until we popped outside to the patio that we found a living, breathing being.

A shirtless elf sprawled across a lawn chair, his chin length silvery-blue hair disguising much of his face. Cigarette butts and broken bottle shards surrounded him, but then again, they littered the patio pavers and grass as far as the eye could see. So did discarded items of clothing—many of them female undergarments, though there were a decent collection of mismatched socks, shoes, and earrings on display, too. Many of the pieces of patio furniture had been overturned and mistreated, leading to a number of broken wooden legs and torn scraps of upholstery among the detritus.

I approached the elf. I'd started to wonder if he was alive, but a slow rise and fall of his chest kept me from having to expand my investigation into a multiple homicide.

I poked him in the ribs. "Hello? Billy Charles?"

The elf muttered something indiscriminate, but he didn't move or even flutter his eyes.

"See this?" asked Shay.

I followed her finger to a table—miraculously upright and intact—not far from the incapacitated elf. On its surface I noticed a trio of razor blades, each of them not far from a stack of mysterious white powder. A selection of pills and dried herbs, probably not of the culinary kind, had also joined the party.

"Are those the same substances we found at the Cobra's suite at the Banks Hotel?" I asked.

"There's no way to know without doing chemical analysis," said Shay, "but I'm sure Cairny could perform it for us. I should've left the samples I gathered at the Banks with her. Of course, since I didn't, it means I still have the baggies."

"Might as well put them to good use."

Shay reached into her jacket and produced the miniature envelopes with the samples collected from the Cobra's suite. She knelt by the table and opened the first of the bunch.

I glanced at the elf. His breathing progressed at a slow, steady pace, but his skin color resembled that of his hair. "I wonder if I should drag this guy indoors. I know it's not *that* cold today, but I'd hate to have a negligent hypothermia death on my hands."

"Probably not a bad idea," said Shay as she scooped a small pile of pills into one of the envelopes. "If Billy Charles dies, we'll never figure out what the heck the

Cobras were up to—among other negative conse-
quences."

Glass crunched behind us, and someone spoke in a
gravelly voice. "Who said anything about dying? Now
get your grubby mitts off my stash."

17

I turned to find an old man standing behind me—or at least, I assumed he was old. Crags and crevices covered his face, and not just big ones. The man had at least three times the density of wrinkles as anyone I'd ever met, but at the same time, he stood fairly straight, and I didn't spy a liver spot anywhere on his person. He wore a paisley blue vest over an unbuttoned shirt that looked as if it had been left in a pile of laundry for a few months, and he'd wrapped a length of bright red fabric around his temples, allowing his finger length grey hair to curl out around it. He held a cigarette in his hand. He dragged on it as he stared at us.

"Excuse me," I said. "You are?"

"Billy Charles," he said around a puff of smoke. "Who the hell are you? The party ended hours ago."

"I'm Detective Jake Daggers of the NWPD," I said. "This is Captain Shay Steele."

"Oh," said Charles. "Well, in that case, help yourselves to whatever you please. Share and share alike,

I've always said, especially for my friends down at the police department."

Shay stood and pocketed the envelopes. "Are you offering us drugs?"

"Are you against that sort of thing?" asked Charles. "If so, why are you taking my pills? Speaking of which, that's a party foul. Only take what you're planning on using, don't you know?"

"You're taking a surprisingly cavalier attitude toward the possession of illegal narcotics, Mr. Charles," said Shay.

"Oh, give me a break," said Charles, waving his cigarette around. "Don't tell me you're one of *those* cops. Where the hell do my generous donations go if not to cut me some slack? And don't make me point out you're on my property collecting evidence illegally. I sure as hell didn't invite you in."

"Ever heard of exigent circumstance?" I said.

"Give me a break, kid," said Charles. "I wasn't born yesterday. You think that's going to fly? Not with *my* lawyers."

"Alright, relax," said Shay. "We're not here to bust you on possession charges. We're merely here to ask a few questions about your party guests last night."

"Right. Like who the hell this guy is and why he's shirtless." I pointed out the elf, in case my pronoun was indistinct enough.

"Him?" said Charles. "I don't know. I think his name was...*Guido*? Maybe Geronimo. I don't know where his shirt went. What does it matter?"

"Don't mind my partner," said Shay. "He's easily distracted. We're not concerned with Guido, or Geronimo, or whoever he is—although you might want to put a blanket over him if you're not going to bring him inside. Rather, we're interested in the Yellow Cobras. Chaz Willy Wilson, B. B. DuPrat, Sammy Styles, and Ritchie Roth. You know them?"

Charles took another drag from his cigarette. "Of course I do. Known B. B. and Chaz forever. Why? What did they get into this time? Your typical, dumbass drunken antics?"

"More or less," I said. "Except this time Chaz died."

Charles blew the smoke out slowly, keeping his eyes steady on me. "You're serious, aren't you?"

"We're homicide detectives," I said. "Want to see my badge?"

"So Chaz didn't just die then," said Charles. "You think someone killed him."

"Maybe, maybe not," said Shay. "We're still in the process of investigating what happened—which is where you come in. We understand the Cobras came by your house last night?"

Charles nodded. "I was hosting a party—for them, ostensibly. One year anniversary of their gig at the Moxy. Not really sure all of them considered that something worth celebrating, to be honest. Chaz in particular wasn't too happy about not touring any more, but there's a lot to be said for staying in one place, know what I mean?"

"Why wasn't he happy about not touring?" asked Shay.

"It wasn't the act itself," said Charles. "It was his waning popularity. Yellow Cobra's from here, you know. More fans in New Welwic than anywhere else.

That's the only reason the city could support them with regular shows. But it wasn't just Chaz. All of them were upset with their fading popularity. But hey, it happens. Even to me."

"You were a musician yourself back in the day?" I asked.

Charles plunged his cigarette-free hand into his chest. "Dagger to my heart, kid. I'm still a musician. I just don't perform anymore. Seriously, you've never heard of me?"

"Not until today."

Charles puffed on his cigarette again. "This world's going to hell. I'm the best damn rock star who ever lived."

I turned to Steele. "He's modest, too."

Shay ignored me. "What's your relationship with Chaz?"

Charles shrugged. "I've known him a long time. B. B. introduced him to me back when they were getting the band together. Really talented guy, very charismatic. Had some personal problems, but who among us doesn't?"

"Like what?" asked Shay.

"Depression. Substance abuse issues. Delusions. The usual."

"And you said you've known B. B. even longer?" said Shay.

"I'm a guitarist, first and foremost, girl," said Charles. "B. B.'s my boy. Shame about Chaz, but maybe this'll be the kick in the pants he needs to finally strike out and start his own band."

I felt my brow furrow. Was Charles unintentionally providing us with motive?

"So let's talk about last night, again," said Steele. "You said the band members came over after their show. All of them? At what time?"

"All of them, yeah." Charles finished his cigarette and flicked the dying butt to the ground. "They came right after the show. Must've arrived about a quarter after ten."

Shay glanced at me. "Daggers?"

I blinked, trying to figure out what I'd missed. Then it hit me. "Oh. Right."

I pulled the pad from my jacket and took note of the time.

"Then what?" asked Shay.

"What do you mean, *then what?*" asked Charles. "Look around, baby girl. We partied! Booze. Pills. A little smoke. We did it right!"

"Pills?" said Shay. "Like the ones I found on that table over there?"

"Probably," said Charles, squinting. "What's over there? My eyes aren't as good as they used to be."

Shay produced a pair of envelopes from her jacket, the first containing the drugs she'd snagged from the table. She poured them onto her hand. "These."

"Right," said Charles, surveying them. "Some stims. Some tranqs. Pump you up and mellow you out at the same time. A perfect combination."

"Since you seem to be an expert, maybe you can help us identify the drugs we found in the rest of the Cobras' possession." Steele returned the drugs to her jacket and emptied the envelope from the Banks into her palm. "Are these the same?"

"Sure. Stims and..." Charles paused, glancing at the collection of pills. "Hold on a sec. Those aren't 'ludes."

"*Ludes?*" I said.

"Yeah, 'ludes. Tranqs," said Charles. "Those are different. Benzos. Anxiety meds. Who had those?"

"We found them at the Banks Hotel," said Shay. "Not sure who took them. None of the band members claimed to remember much of anything from last night."

Charles snorted. "Well, there's your answer. They all took them? Benzos and hard liquor? *Plus stims?* That's a recipe for a walking blackout if I ever heard one."

"Did you supply these to them?" asked Shay.

"Hey, now," said Charles, lifting a finger. "Don't try to pin this on me. My parties are a free for all. I let people take what they want. If they mix things they shouldn't, that's on them, not me."

"From a legal standpoint, that's arguable," I said. "But again, we're not here to bust you, we simply want to know what happened to Chaz. You said they arrived at ten fifteen. How long did they stay?"

"Well, that's the thing." Charles rummaged in his pocket and produced another cigarette. "The guys didn't hang around for more than forty-five minutes, an hour tops. And after I invited them into my home, planned this entire shindig for them. Can you believe that? Anyone got a light?" He held his cigarette out.

"Fresh out," I said, even though I had the Club Midnight matchbox in my pocket. "So where did they go?"

"You're useless you know that?" Charles returned the cigarette to his pocket. "I don't know. Someone mentioned Leopard Jane's, but why in the world would those idiots head there when I was offering free booze and drugs at my place? Of course, if they were hopped up on benzos, that might explain things."

"Who's Leopard Jane?" asked Shay.

"Proprietor of a dive bar down on Wheatley," said Charles. "Beats me why B. B., Chaz, and the others keep going there. Actually, scratch that. It's because of the waitresses."

"And did the whole band leave together?" I asked.

"As far as I know," said Charles. "Why?"

"We're still trying to account for everyone's where-abouts," said Shay. "B. B. in particular. Don't worry. He's fine."

"Of course he is," said Charles, pulling the cigarette back from his pocket and looking at it wistfully. "He's a horse. Can't bring him down."

Given B. B.'s chest wound, I wondered if the guy might know more than he let on. Still, as of now, we had no reason to suspect Charles was more involved in any of the Cobra's antics than he claimed to be.

I turned to Steele. "So...ready to hit a dive bar? I hear they're lovely in the middle of the day."

18

"Is it just me, or have we visited a cornucopia of bars today?"

Shay and I stood inside Leopard Jane's. Unlike the Moxy and Club Midnight, the place didn't suffer any delusions of grandeur. It didn't open up into a concert hall or dance floor, nor did it fill its halls with tables or chairs or fancy booths. The place was a bar only, and it knew it.

At least the bar itself had some flair. An enormous mirror stretched behind its lacquered wood, probably fifty feet from end to end, reflecting the light of hundreds of liquor bottles of every shape and color. An enormous sign with the words 'Leopard Jane's' hung over the mirror, the font big and bold and covered in a leopard print fabric.

Shay shrugged in response to my question. "Every establishment that can sell alcohol does. The markup on it is huge. I'd bet the Moxy makes more on booze than it does on ticket sales. A lot more. With that said, though, I think the number of bars we've visited says more about Chaz and his band mates than it does about society."

I glanced into the rafters, where a number of female undergarments hung from taut strings. "I'm guessing this place makes multiple statements about our society."

Steele nodded toward the bar, where a trio of mopey gents sat at stools. A lone bartender worked the far end. "Let's go see if she can tell us anything useful."

Shay led the way, and I followed. As we approached her, the bartender looked up. "Hi, folks! What can I get you?"

The young lady behind the bar wore a cowboy hat with the sides upturned, out from which spilled her mildly-curled auburn hair, but it was her tight black sleeveless shirt that caught my attention. Initially it had contained the bar's moniker, but a deep, *deep* slit down the middle now cut the name in half. The young lady's natural assets pushed the halves even further apart.

I found it hard to keep my eyes off her breasts. I think that was the point.

"Nothing, thanks," said Shay. "I'm Steele, this is Detective Daggers. Any chance you were in last night, around eleven o'clock?"

"I wish," said the young lady. "I've got the shit shift, noon to eight. Why? What do you need?"

A voice, a little deeper and more seasoned, drifted around from behind a bead curtain to our right, tucked away behind a cash register. "I heard that, Kari."

The beads rattled as a hand pushed them aside. Through them stepped a woman, probably in her mid forties, with shoulder length light brown hair kept clear of her face by a leopard spotted bandana. She car-

ried more weight in her arms, shoulders, and midsection than did the aforementioned Kari, but her propor-
tions remained appealing thanks to her cartoonishly
large chest. She wore the same company shirt as did
the younger bartender, but despite a smaller slit, the
cloth seemed on the verge of tearing, the bar's logo
stretched and difficult to read.

I started to detect a pattern among the bar staff.

The woman nodded toward the patrons. "Kari, go see
if those gentleman need any refills. You two, come
with me."

She headed off to the end of the bar. Once Shay and
I'd arrived, she leaned in and lowered her voice. "Sorry.
Couldn't help but overhear something about a detective.
You're cops?"

I swallowed hard. I knew the woman had lowered
her voice to avoid startling the bar flies, but goodness,
did she really have to lean over so much? Between the
angle of her torso as she rested against the bar, my
height, and the strategically placed cut down the middle
of her shirt, the chasm of her breasts created an ines-
capable, eye-sucking vortex. And of course I happened
to be standing next to Shay, who I wasn't completely
convinced had fully forgiven me for my actions the
night before, and who had the eyes of a hawk. Oh, why
must the gods test me so?

I cleared my throat and tried to focus on the bandana. "That's right. Daggers and Steele. NWPD." I gave
each of us the thumb treatment. "You are?"

The woman pointed at the sign. "Call me Jane. The
whole leopard shtick was always just a way to drum up
business. How can I help you?"

"Any chance you were here last night?" asked Shay. "Around eleven to twelve?"

Jane waved her hand nonchalantly. "I'm here every night, sweetheart. It's the joys of entrepreneurship. Why? Looking for someone?"

"Sort of," said Shay. "Are you familiar with the band Yellow Cobra?"

She shorted. "Of course. They were here last night, too. Rolled in probably...well, right around eleven, like you said. Why?"

"We're trying to piece together their movements from last night," I said, eyeing a scratch on the counter for safety purposes. "With Chaz, specifically, though also for B. B. Was he here, do you recall?"

"Sure was," said Jane. "That cotton ball platinum hairdo of his is hard to miss."

"And what were they up to?" asked Shay.

"Drinking, same as everyone else," said Jane. "Came in already hammered from the looks of it. Got the Leopard Jane signature treatment and left about an hour later."

"*Signature treatment?*" I said.

"Come on, you're not really that dumb are you?" Jane said to me, forcing me to make eye contact. "We get up close. Act real nice. Stick our boobs in your face and get a nice tip for our troubles. Sometimes we climb on the bar and dance, take shots, and get rowdy, though I encourage the girls to spit the liquor out behind the bar when no one's looking. I've found there's an inverse correlation between earnings and a bartender's level of intoxication."

Shay glanced down the bar toward Kari, who was busy cleaning glasses. "Most of your girls like working here?"

"The ones who work the night shift do," said Jane. "It's not the most mentally stimulating of jobs, but the pay's good."

"How good?" asked Shay.

"Depends on the individual. How come? You looking for work? You're a little light on top, but you've got the face for it. You'd probably do pretty well for yourself if you showed some midriff."

"You realize you're talking to the captain of the Fifth Street Precinct, don't you?" I said.

Jane's eyebrows shot up. "Damn, girl! Good for you. Go get yours!"

"Um...thanks," said Shay. "But back to Chaz and the Cobras. You said they came in together. Do you remember if they left together? Around midnight, you mentioned?"

Jane nodded. "Yeah, midnight, give or take ten minutes. No idea if they left together or not, to be honest. I'm more focused on keeping my girls in line and making sure none of the patrons get too grabby, if you know what I mean."

"So you wouldn't know where they headed afterwards, would you?"

"Sorry," said Jane with a shake of her head. "But Crystal should know. She was their bartender. Usually is."

"And is Crystal here?" asked Shay.

"No. She's on the evening shift," said Jane. "But I can give you her flat number. She lives down at the Fae Arms Apartments."

"And is the housing choice circumstantial or intentional?" I asked.

"Oh, she's fae, if that's what you're asking," said Jane. "Biggest damn eyes you've ever seen. Only girl I've ever had on my staff who gets more looks above the neck than below, but she does well for herself. Hold on and I'll snag that address."

Jane leveraged herself off the bar, pulled on her shirt to make sure the slit was positioned properly, and headed back behind the beads. I watched her walk away. When I turned back to Shay, it was to find her smirking at me.

"You just can't help yourself, can you?"

"What? *Me?*" I said. "What are you talking about?"

"Oh, don't worry. I don't blame you. It must be an evolutionary thing. Men of all the sentient species suffer the same problem. But it's amusing. It's like there's a magnetic force that only occurs between them and male eyeballs, and once they reach a certain size, you pass an event horizon and there's no way to look away."

"Look, Shay," I said. "I tried not to stare. Really. But...come on."

"Relax," she said with a smile. "I'm pulling your leg. I'm not trying to be intentionally hard on you. I'm just shooting for a rise. Though you should really firm up your resolve."

There was no way that collection of thinly veiled sexual metaphors was in any way unintentional. As we waited for Jane to return, I contemplated whether it was a good thing that I'd fallen for a woman who was able to make light of my straying eyes or a bad thing that I'd fallen for one who noticed in the first place.

I think it was the former.

19

With a name like the Fae Arms, I'd pictured an idyllic residence, rustic and quaint, surrounded by moss-covered trees, blackberry bushes, and toadstool patches, serenaded by the melodies of rustling streams and cascading waterfalls and bathed in the multicolored glow of a mist-sparkled rainbow.

I live in New Welwic. I should've known better.

What I found was a two-story, centuries old hunk of stone and mortar, surrounded by piles of trash, lean-tos, and shifty-eyed hucksters, serenaded by the not-so-melodic cursing of drunks and mendicants and bathed in their golden showers. But at least the apartment complex had a courtyard with some trees in it, so there was that.

Shay and I headed up the stairs to the second floor. I glanced at the numbers on the doors. "Which one did Jane say it was? Two twenty-five?"

"Two thirty-five," said Shay. "Didn't you make a note of it in your spiral bound pad?"

"I've been saving that for my detailed timeline of the Yellow Cobras and the places they've visited. No room for anything else."

"So basically, Jane told us and you promptly forgot. I wonder what could've distracted you?" Shay put a finger on her chin and peered upward.

"Enough with that already," I said. "I'm constantly addle-brained. This particular instance is no different."

"I'm sure. Either way, here we are."

Shay stopped in front of Crystal's supposed apartment and knocked on the door. We waited.

The Fae Arms was constructed in the form of a hollow square, with the apartments all facing the courtyard and open to the elements. I rested my hip against the railing and gazed into the central greenery. Toward the middle, half-hidden under a leafy green holly shrub that stubbornly resisted the winter's onslaught, I spotted a small statue. If I squinted, it almost resembled a leprechaun. Somehow, I doubted I'd find a pot of gold nearby.

"You think they only let fairies live here?" I asked.

Shay turned from the door. "What kind of question is that? It's illegal to deny someone housing access based on race."

"Which doesn't mean it doesn't happen," I said. "New Welwic has a long history of housing discrimination. Maybe it's not as common as it used to be, but before some of the legal reforms the city council passed, it was quite a problem. I'm surprised your parents never talked to you about it."

"And what were they going to tell me?" said Shay. "Hey kid, you're mixed race, which means you'll come across the occasional douchebag who thinks they're better than you based on that fact alone?"

"Well, not in those words specifically, but yes," I said. "It's a harsh lesson to learn but a valuable one."

"It's also an easy one to learn on your own," said Shay. "Anyone who pays attention figures it out sooner or later. Not that I've ever been discriminated against based on my race, mind you. Humans and elves share the hilltop as far as privilege is concerned, dark elves not withstanding. Now, discrimination based on my *sex* is another thing entirely."

"Yeah, sorry about that," I said. "I was a pretty big jerk when we first met, wasn't I?"

"You weren't the worst. Far from it. And I think your standoffishness was rooted in emotional issues far stronger than casual sexism."

"I'd like to think so," I said. "I'd also like to think the lot of those are behind me. Either way, it has to feel good for you to have broken that glass ceiling. As far as I know, you're the first female captain the Fifth's ever had."

Shay rolled her eyes. "Oh, wonderful. As if I needed any more pressure." She knocked on the door again.

"Seriously, you should be proud," I said. "It's a big deal, interim label or not."

"*Hey!*"

The cry cut through the air, raspy and deep. I swiveled my head to find a bulky, unfortunate mixed breed shambling down the hall toward us—unfortunate in the sense that he'd inherited the worst elements of whatever heritage he possessed. His skin glistened with a pale grayish-green hue, and his shock of red hair stuck out wildly. His eyes pointed different directions, and his lower jaw protruded about an inch farther than it should've. I should've smelled him coming, but it never registered that the approaching wave of garlic and stale gym odor was humanoid in origin.

"*You there!*" he shouted as he approached. "You here to see Crystal? Well, you need to tell her to get her shit together, because I'm tired of it. Tired, *you hear me?*"

"Excuse me?" I said.

"Crystal, knucklehead," he rumbled. "You think I'm playing around? Because I'm not. I'm not above harassing her friends if that's what it takes to get her to pay rent."

Dawn broke over my confusion. "Oh. Sorry, pal, but we're not her friends. We're with the NWPD." I snagged my badge from my jacket and flashed it.

Hunched and Ugly—Hugly?—threw his hands up in the air. "Oh, great. So not only is that little tramp behind on her rent, but she's in trouble with the police, too. *Fantastic!*"

"Let's keep the sexist, disparaging remarks to a minimum unless you know something we don't," said Shay. "Now, based on your attitude, I'm guessing Crystal's not in right now?"

Hugly crossed his arms and grumbled. "Hell, what do I know. That little bi—er, I mean...she's never around when I check. Keeps the oddest hours. Locks herself up tight in her apartment when she's here and sneaks off quick as a cockroach when she isn't. Not to mention she's gone at least half the time, anyway. Maybe I should kick her out. I'll never get what she owes me out of her stuff if I do, though..."

I pursed my lips. Crystal wasn't paying her rent? Jane had mentioned she fared well for herself, and she worked the prime shift at the bar.

"We need to ask her a few questions about one of the patrons who visited the bar where she works," said Shay. "I don't suppose you'd know where we might find her?"

"Oh, I know *exactly* where you'll find her," said Hugly. "Probably at her boyfriend's apartment, wherever that is. Or at that rock club they're always hanging out at. What's the name? The Moxy? Not that it matters. I can't harass her on someone else's property."

I'd argue that from a legal perspective, he couldn't harass Crystal even on his own property, but that wasn't the most pertinent portion of his statement. "Wait...the Moxy? Who's Crystal's boyfriend?"

"I don't know," said Hugly. "Some rocker idiot. Feathery blond hair, dark eyebrows, big nose. Always wearing something with leather on it or with the shirtsleeves missing. I've seen him hanging around here more times than I can count."

Hopefully that last bit wasn't a commentary on his math skills. I turned to Steele. "That sounds like Chaz. Hugly—I mean, er...you. Landlord. Whatever your name is. I don't suppose this boyfriend dropped by last night—maybe with the rest of his band mates in tow? An elf with platinum blond hair, a guy with long brown braids, and another wiry, lean one with black locks?"

Hugly eyed me curiously but shook his head. "Nobody that I know of. Then again, I'm one of those weirdoes who actually likes to *sleep* during the night, so what the hell do I know?"

"Thanks, pal. Steele?" I nodded toward the stairwell.

We left. Once we'd exited earshot, Shay asked the obvious question. "So, if Chaz was dating Crystal, did his wife Heather know? Because if she did, that throws her entire testimony into question—and gives her a potential motive for murder."

"You're getting better at this gig," I said. "But I'm also curious about her rent situation. Jane made it sound like she was a top earner. Why the discrepancy?"

"Only one way to find out," said Shay.

I tapped the side of my head. "Great minds think alike. Let's see if anyone back at the Moxy has a bead on her."

20

Shay and I entered through the Moxy's backdoor, skirting the Yellow Cobra's ready room en route to the music hall. As we passed through the backstage portions of the club, we noticed Dennis resting on a couch a few feet off the main stage, nestled among the bunched curtains, pulleys, levers, and other controls. He spun a drumstick idly in one of his massive hands, humming a tune as he stared at the rafters.

"Big D," I said as we approached. "What's happening?"

He flicked his eyes down upon hearing my voice, but he didn't register any surprise. "Oh. You're back. Steele and...what was it? Daggers?"

"That's right." I glanced at the stage, upon which rested the drum set and guitar from earlier. "Where's Diamond? You two decided you'd practiced enough for one day?"

"Benson makes that choice, not us," said Big D. "And if it was up to him, we would be. But you've had a little something to say about that, haven't you?"

I blinked. I didn't think Shay had sent any cease and desist orders the Moxy's way. "Excuse me?"

"He's probably referring to Quinto and Rodgers," said Steele.

"Bingo," said Big D, flicking a finger at Shay. "The big guy and his too-cheery friend. It's hard to get into a rhythm when you keep getting interrupted and peppered with questions. It's distracting having those two snooping around."

I'd forgotten Shay had sent the pair back here. Hopefully they'd unearthed something of use. "Well, I'm sorry if our investigation into the *murder* of one of your friends is an inconvenience to you."

At least Big D had the decency to look sheepish. "Sorry. Chaz never talked to me much, but...you're right. To be fair, it's not entirely your pals' fault. Diamond keeps slipping off into the shadows to canoodle with his girlfriend."

A better segue had never been presented. "Speaking of girlfriends, we're trying to track down a bartender from Leopard Jane's. Fairy, big eyes, goes by the name of Crystal."

Big D looked at me like I was dense. "Uh...yeah. Who do you think Diamond's girlfriend is?"

Dennis might as well have smacked me over the head with the information. I glanced at Shay. "You know, I feel like I should've made that connection earlier."

"Don't worry," said Shay. "It only clicked for me when Dennis mentioned Diamond smooching his lady pal in the shadows."

Big D didn't let his confused expression go anywhere. "Huh?"

"A miscommunication," said Shay. "Where can we find Crystal and Diamond?"

Dennis pointed across the stage. "Somewhere on that side, I guess. The darker the corner, the better. Normally they hide out in the ready room, but, ah...we haven't cleaned it yet. It has a bit of an aroma."

I thanked Dennis and spearheaded our tracking effort, crossing the stage and diving into the backstage portions on the other side. Thankfully, despite the gloom it wasn't difficult to track our quarry. I simply followed the sounds of smooching and the occasional feminine giggle.

I found them in a dark corner as advertised, the presumed Crystal with her back to the wall and Diamond pinning her there—though not against her will judging by her pleasurable moans. Diamond buried his face in her neck, and he'd pushed her shirt up to her collar bone, his hands busy caressing her breadwinners.

I don't think they noticed me. I cleared my throat.

Diamond jumped back. Crystal eeked and pulled her shirt into place.

Diamond stammered and tried to collect himself. "Oh. Hey, brah. Brahs. I mean, uh... Detectives, ah..."

Shay apparently didn't feel like making introductions again. "Diamond, why don't you skedaddle back to the stage? Dennis is looking forlorn. Maybe you could continue practicing your tunes."

"Oh," he said, glancing at his girlfriend. "Well, actually, I was—"

"That's me being nice and telling you to get lost while we talk to Crystal," said Shay. "Got it?"

Diamond nodded, gave his girlfriend a longing look, and scooted.

Shay stepped forward. "Crystal, right?"

The young woman nodded, adjusting the airy white blouse she wore over a black checkered miniskirt. A single lock of dyed-black hair cut across her otherwise ash blonde bangs, and Jane hadn't lied about her eyes. They were big enough to dive into—pale golden-grey orbs that nearly matched her hair.

"I'm Steele, this is Daggers," said Shay. "We're with the police, investigating Chaz Willy Wilson's death."

Crystal left whatever feelings of embarrassment from being caught bare-chested at the door. "Oh my gosh, I know, right? How crazy is that? He was at Jane's just last night!"

"We understand you served him," I said.

"Yeah, right," said Crystal. "I usually do, him and all the other Cobra guys. It's how I met Diamond. He's so dreamy, isn't he?"

Shay neglected to weigh in. "So what can you tell us about last night, specifically?"

"Um...I'm not sure," said Crystal. "What do you mean?"

"We're trying to figure out what happened to Chaz," said Shay. "What led to his death. Part of that is figuring out where he went, who he saw, what he took part in. His band mates are too intoxicated to remember the events of last night."

Crystal nodded vigorously. "Gotcha. I understand. Well, let's see. Chaz and the other guys showed up at

Jane's at about...eleven, I'd say? They seemed pretty wasted, just like you said, even when they arrived. I mean, we probably shouldn't have served them, but Jane's not in the business of losing money, or so she always says. Anyway, they were all kind of rowdy. Chaz especially. He was, like...I don't know. In a mean mood, I guess?"

"What do you mean by that?" I asked.

Crystal swept her bangs to the side and out of her face. "He snapped a lot. Cursed a lot, too. He's not normally like that. He even got into a fight with B. B."

"He did?" said Shay. "What happened?"

"I don't know," said Crystal. "I couldn't hear anything. It was way too loud. And there weren't any fists or anything, just shoving. But I could tell they were upset."

That bit of knowledge felt noteworthy, so I took note of it. Literally. In my pad. "Jane said the band left together at around midnight. Any chance you know where?"

Crystal's brow furrowed. She looked as if she might hurt herself thinking. I got the impression she didn't practice the activity often.

She snapped her fingers. "Oh. I do remember. Sammy mentioned the Raccoon Ranch."

"The what now?"

"It's a brothel, down on Flatley with all the others," said Crystal.

The Raccoon Ranch? A brothel? Of course it was. "Do the Cobras go there often?"

"I...*think so?*" said Crystal.

"Given their lifestyle, I suppose we shouldn't be surprised," said Shay. "Do you have any idea if Chaz's wife, Heather, knew about his...*indiscretions?*"

"I don't really know," said Crystal. "I mean, it would be pretty hard for her not to. They were separated, I think. I assume she just accepted it, right?"

Shay glanced back toward the stage. When she spoke, her tone had softened. "What do you see in him, Crystal?"

"Who?" She scrunched her brow. "Oh. You mean Diamond? He's a sweetheart. Such a dreamer. I know he's not famous yet, but I have faith in him. He's got so much talent. I know he's going to strike it big one day, as soon as someone gives him his first break."

"He's using you," said Shay.

Crystal's eyes widened, if that was possible. "Excuse me?"

"You're behind on your rent," said Shay. "You shouldn't be with how much you're making. You're spending it on Diamond, aren't you? Supporting his lifestyle. You could do better."

Crystal crossed her arms. Her body temperature dropped ten degrees. "Diamond's going to be a star."

"Hey. Steele! Daggers!"

I turned at the sound of Quinto's hearty rumble to find the big man waving at us from the edge of the stage. We gave Crystal our thanks and joined him.

"Heard you'd arrived. Through the grapevine." Quinto shot a thumb toward Big D, who'd moved back to the drum set and was fiddling with the high-hat.

"Had a lead that led us back here," said Shay. "Diamond's girlfriend. How have you guys fared?"

I heard footsteps. Rodgers materialized from around the edge of the stage curtains. "As well as could be expected. Took a bunch of statements. Spent some time in the ready room looking for documentation, so don't blame us if we've acquired a certain camel-induced aroma. Some of the information we gathered might pay dividends down the road, but it hasn't yet. How about you? Filling in Chaz's timeline?"

"Slowly but steadily," I confirmed. "We've got him accounted for until midnight. I'm guessing our next stop will fill in the gap until his arrival at Heather's."

"Well, we're pretty much done here," said Quinto. "We could tag along, if you like."

I glanced at Shay. "You're the one with psychic knowledge. Are you sure this big lug doesn't have ESP?"

Quinto lifted an eyebrow.

"Our next stop is the Raccoon Ranch," explained Shay. "A brothel. Which I'm sure would be torturous for you to visit."

Rodgers elbowed Quinto in the ribs. "Sounds like a pair of someones need an escort. You know, to protect each other from their own worst instincts."

"You realize I'm the captain now, right?" said Shay.

"Right. Sorry," said Rodgers. "I'm trying a new equal opportunity snarkiness campaign. Just edit that in your head so I'm only disparaging Daggers."

I sighed. "No one puts any faith in me whatsoever. Come on, Quinto. Lead the way."

21

It wasn't that I thought Quinto knew how to get to the Raccoon Ranch because he frequented the joint. Far from it. Prior to his romance with Cairny, I'd assumed he'd been in a monogamous relationship with his work. Rather, I knew the guy had walked the beat with the Green Jackets before he'd joined the boys in blue. He'd made a point of telling us so the last time we ventured into the brothel district.

I spotted a few of the aforementioned Green Jackets as we rolled down Flatley in our rickshaws, partially to save time and partially to save our feet. The Green Jackets, so known for their olive-colored coats, consisted mostly of thick-headed skull crackers, former army types, and guys whose muscle mass outweighed their gray matter by a few orders of magnitude. Most of them carried truncheons, but not hidden like my own—rather in plain sight to discourage morons from trying to flee their financial obligations.

I didn't hold the Green Jackets in a particularly high regard, but at the same time, their presence made my life as a police officer easier. Without them, my brethren and I would have to spend far more time and resources patrolling the endless stretch of brothels on Flatley by ourselves, and while the Green Jackets contained their fair share of unsavory individuals, the consortium of whorehouses that paid for their operation enforced a strict policy of intolerance when it came to Jackets acting with excessive force or outside the boundaries of the law. Besides, they weren't all bad. Quinto was proof.

Our rickshaws clattered to a stop outside the Raccoon Ranch, an observation which I astutely based upon the enormous sign that hung outside the front reading 'The Raccoon Ranch.' I hopped off the handcart, helped Shay down, and paid the driver, then followed her inside as the bouncer held the door for us. Rodgers and Quinto performed a similar song and dance.

Inside, the brothel wasn't as nice as the last I'd visited in the course of our work, but neither was it a rat hole. Bleached wood and barbed wire ran around the perimeter of the first floor, pasted over an enormous wrap-around mural depicting a scene of rolling hills backed by snow-capped peaks and bright blue cloud-dotted skies. Clearly, the owners had run with the establishment's ranch motif, as evidenced not only by the wall art but also by the whiskey barrel tables, brown leather couches, and trophy animals adorning the floor. Between this place, our horse-themed lunch destination, and Leopard Jane's vaguely rustic flavor, I felt like the gods were trying to send me a message. Maybe I needed a vacation?

Shay snickered as she glanced around.

"Amused by the agrarian backdrop?" I asked.

"That's not it," said Shay. "I was simply reminded of the time we visited the other brothel, the 9's. Remember when that gigolo started grinding on you? Good gods, that was the funniest thing ever. It took all I had not to laugh out loud."

"Yes. Passion Faust," I grumbled. "How could I forget? Though I seem to remember you being more *enthused* by him than *amused*."

"What can I say? He was easy on the eyes."

Rodgers and Quinto joined us. The former took in the surroundings with wide eyes.

He whistled. "Wow."

"It's a themed bordello," said Quinto. "Not as crazy as some of them, if memory serves me right. So what's the plan?"

"We should split up," I said. "Shay and I can talk to the girls who work here. You guys take the staff. Try to figure out when the Yellow Cobras arrived, what they were up to, that sort of thing. Well...actually, I have a pretty good idea of what they were up to, but you know what I mean."

"Hold on there, cowboy," said Rodgers. "If memory serves me right, the last time we visited a brothel you and Steele talked to the prostitutes and Quinto and I were stuck gabbing with the security guards. How come the tables haven't turned?"

"You're upset about the last time?" I said. "Steele and I just talked about this. The prostitute we talked to turned out to be a guy. He was dancing and gyrating on me and everything. It wasn't a memorable experience."

"Oh, it was memorable," said Shay.

"That's immaterial," said Rodgers. "It's only fair to switch this time."

"You do realize you're married, right?" I said.

"Everyone here is in some form of relationship, am I right?" said Rodgers. "Besides, Quinto and I aren't animals. We're not going to jump the first floozy who walks by."

"Excuse me?" said a sultry voice. "Hi."

I turned and nearly lost control of my jaw muscles. "Oh, dear gods..."

While Rodgers and Quinto might not be animals, the woman standing behind us was trying her hardest to be. A black eye mask concealed part of her face, a narrow black tube top hid substantially less of her torso, and striped black and gray pants covered her from hip to ankle, though they were tight enough not to conceal much either. She also wore fake ears that poked up through her shoulder length brown hair. I wouldn't go so far as to say she actually resembled a raccoon, but she resembled what prepubescent boys with unhealthy obsessions with the outdoors *wished* raccoons looked like.

"Captain?" said Quinto. "I'm going to defer to you on this one. But you know I'm a man of principles, and from a perspective of fairness, I think Rodgers makes some *great* arguments."

"Ooh, a captain?" said the floozy. "Are you here for some role play? That sounds fun."

Poor girl. She'd be so disappointed when she found out Rodgers and Quinto weren't paying customers.

I turned to Steele, trying to give my eyes a reprieve from all the delectable bodies they'd had flaunted at them so far today. "Your call."

Shay looked at me, smiled, and gave Quinto a nod. "You two are up. Make sure you don't forget why we're actually here, otherwise you can be sure Cairny and Allison will hear about this. Daggers and I can handle the Ranch's less tempting constituents."

To their credit, both Rodgers and Quinto managed to express their enthusiasm without a single fist pump or cackle of glee.

Quinto placed his hand gently against the young woman's back. "Sorry about that, miss. If you could join us on the couch, perhaps? My friend and I have a few questions we'd like to ask you."

Rodgers and Quinto traipsed off in the direction of the nearest sofa. I glanced at my partner and shook my head. "You're enjoying being in a position of power way too much."

"What?" said Shay, still sporting her sly grin. "Someone needs to question her. Rodgers and Quinto had a point. It's only fair they get a shot."

"And would that issue of fairness still have reigned supreme if the harlot in question had been of the male variety, with chiseled features, perfectly coifed hair, and abdominal muscles like paver stones?"

Shay shrugged. "It depends. If he was dressed in a raccoon costume like that woman was, probably not."

I snorted.

Shay's smile melted away. "What? Don't tell me that outfit worked for you?"

"I mean… Well…it's *kind of* cute," I said. "You'd look good in it."

Shay raised both of her eyebrows. "Um…yeah. We're not quite at that point in our relationship yet."

I felt my cheeks warming. "*Right.* Well, I don't know about you, but I think it would be a great time to go question some waitstaff. Let's get to it!"

22

We headed first in the direction of the Raccoon Ranch's bar, because what would the day be without a fourth visit to an elongated piece of hardwood covered with beverage stains. There, hidden among the decorative horseshoes, rusted out wagon wheels, and coils of rope, we found another young woman manning the bottles. Unlike her coworkers disguised as raccoons, she wore a much more sensible outfit—a tiny tied-off flannel top and cutoff shorts with chaps. Perhaps Sammy Styles had stolen his pair from her. Of course, the Ranch probably only stocked women's sizes, but when had gender designations ever stopped rock musicians in their fashion choices?

We asked the bartender about Chaz, B. B., and the rest of the Cobras, but she told us she hadn't been in at the time, instead suggesting we try the bouncers who worked in twelve hour shifts. We thanked her and headed back out front in search of the guy who'd held the door open for us upon arrival. He was still there, and as we discovered, he'd been around during the Cobra's visit the night prior. However, he wasn't particularly interested in chatting, perhaps valuing his job security substantially higher than he did his sense of civic duty. With all the warmth of a snail on New Year's Eve, he told us to go bother his partner in crime, who he claimed we'd find in back of the Ranch taking a smoke break.

The back door squealed as I pushed it open, announcing our presence. There in the alley behind the Ranch, propped up against a nondescript brick wall that could've belonged to any number of other establishments, stood Sunny and Warm's bouncing partner. The guy lacked hair on the crown of his head but was hairy as all get out everywhere else, with a foot and a half long reddish brown beard and eyebrows that could entangle migrating birds. He resembled a pack horse, covered in leather and straps and with shoulders almost as wide as he was tall. Of course, he only stood about four feet six inches, but given his dwarven heritage, I bet he didn't feel too shabby about it.

The guy puffed on a wooden pipe. He dismissed us with his free hand as we stepped into the cool afternoon gloom. "Wrong door, folks. Head back around to the front."

"We're not here to get laid," I said. "Or...done getting laid, as the case may be. We're looking to talk to you."

"Something must be wrong with you, then," he said. "Nobody comes to the Raccoon Ranch to talk to old Jorbrick."

"Something *is* wrong with us," I said. "We took low-paying government jobs instead of something with more vacation days and better upside. But that's not why we're here."

Jorbrick furrowed his brow and puffed on his pipe, eyeing Steele. "Do you know what the hell he's talking about?"

"We're detectives," she replied. "With the NWPD. I'm Steele, he's Daggers. That's his version of a joke. Miraculously, they get funnier the more time you spend around him, which is sort of the inverse of the norm."

I gave her a smile. "Thanks."

"You guys got some ID?" asked Jorbrick.

"Do I have to show it?" I said. "We've interviewed so many people today I'm afraid I'm going to wear my wallet's leather out at the crease."

Jorbrick snorted and tipped his pipe at Shay. "You're right. That one made me chuckle. Fair enough. I'll take your claim at face value. What do you want?"

"Were you in last night?" asked Shay. "Around midnight?"

"Sure was," said Jorbrick. "That's right toward the end of my shift. Why? You here about those rock star dumbasses?"

"The Yellow Cobras?" asked Shay. "Yes. Did they come by the Ranch last night?"

"Sure did," said Jorbrick around the mouth of his pipe. "Bunch of pricks. Figuratively speaking, of course." The dwarf smiled and started to chuckle.

"Why is that funny?" I asked. "You know, other than the standard amusement factor of male genitalia."

Jorbrick pulled the pipe from his mouth and leaned forward off the wall. "Okay, so get this. Those rocker blockheads...what did you say their name was? The Yellow Cobras? Well they roll into the Ranch last night probably at a quarter after twelve. I'd seen them before. I wouldn't say they're regulars exactly, but they're not unknowns either."

"Hold on a second," I said. "Sorry to interrupt, but did all four of the band members arrive together? Chaz, B. B., Sammy, and Ritchie?"

"I don't know their names," said Jorbrick, "but yeah, there was four of them. Three humans, each with a different hair color, and the elf with the platinum blond locks. The girls inside recognized them right off the bat. So anyway, they're raring to go. Pick out their girls in short order and head upstairs to do their business. You'd figure everything was hunky-dory at that point, but fifteen minutes later, that's when the commotion started. Now this isn't my first rodeo. I knew exactly what to do. I hustled my squat ass up the stairs and busted into the room with the screaming coming from it. Now, I know what most of the girls at the Ranch sound like, and it wasn't any of them doing the cussing and yelling. Not most of it. It was that elf with the ridiculous hair."

"B. B.?" said Shay.

"Sure. B. B. Whatever. Well, he was pretty sore and was *this close* to taking it out on our girl Misty. Luckily we got to him before he did. But you'll never guess why the fool was so upset."

Jorbrick paused. I gave him a moment, but the dwarf was a master of suspense. "Um... Why?"

Jorbrick puffed on his pipe again. "Seriously...you're not even going to guess?"

I shrugged. "I don't know. Misty's secretly a man down below?"

Jorbrick laughed. "Hah! Yeah, the humor definitely gets better with more exposure. No, but that was a good guess. B. B. couldn't get it up."

"You mean..." Shay gestured to her groin area.

"Exactly," said Jorbrick. "Too hopped up on goofy pills, I guess. And as I said, he was *not* happy about it. So me and my partner Waternoose—he's the john at the front door—we drag that B. B. yahoo out of Misty's room and down the stairs, him still with his pants down."

"Bet that was fun," I said.

Jorbrick waved his pipe at me haphazardly. "I've seen almost as many dongs on this job as the girls inside have. I'm numb to it. Anyway, we're dragging the elf down the stairs, ready to toss his ass in the mud and tell him never to show his pretty boy face around here again when the other members of his band pour out of their rooms and run our way to figure out what the commotion is. I've seen this stunt before, so I disengage the elf to go cool the rest of the guys' heels, leaving B. B. to Waternoose. And so here I am, trying to keep a level head while the band mates are yelling and cussing at me, and wouldn't you know it, but the stupid elf gets an arm free and takes a pot shot at my pal."

"B. B. tried to punch Waternoose?" said Shay.

"Oh, he didn't try," said Jorbrick. "He succeeded. Didn't do much damage, mind you. Doped up, rail thin elves tend not to. But that was the straw that broke the camel's back. Waternoose took B. B. down to the ground. I turned to the rest of the rockers, ready to throw their asses to the floor just for being there, but despite them being high on who knows what, their fight or flight instincts still worked. They tore out of there like bats outta hell. I couldn't even get a hand on them. Could be I'm losing a step with all the years I've got on me. No matter. At least the girls got their pay and didn't have to do much for it."

"So, when you say Waternoose took B. B. down to the ground," said Shay, "did he seriously hurt him? Cut him up?"

Jorbrick puffed on his pipe and spoke around the mouthpiece. "*What?* No. Might've bruised his ribs a bit, but that's all. Just landed on him and tied his wrists together and maybe gave him a little knee in the gut for good measure."

"What about Ritchie?" I said. "You punch him in the face? Toss him in the mud?"

"Who?" said Jorbrick. "Never mind. Doesn't matter. I told you I didn't get a hand on any of the other three. They got away clean. Literally."

"And Chaz?" I said. "The one with the feathery blond hair? Did he seem...*off* in any way?"

Jorbrick shrugged and blew a smoke ring. "Beats me. Not like I hung out with the guy. Ask the girl he shacked up with. Not sure who that was. Maybe Cinnamon."

"And what happened to B. B.?" asked Shay. "After your partner hogtied him?"

"He had the Green Jackets pick him up," said Jorbrick. "They should've taken him to our lockup. We have one on site for drunks and rule breakers. They usually let the johns cool off and transfer them to you guys in the morning for processing. Based on your questions, I'm guessing that last part didn't happen."

"We found him elsewhere this morning," said Shay. "And with some mysterious wounds. Nothing to bother yourself over, though."

"Good," said Jorbrick with a smile. "'Cause I wasn't about to."

"Thanks for your help," I told the dwarf. "One last question before we go. When did this all end?"

"That's easy," said Jorbrick. "Waternoose hauled the elf off toward the lockup at about one, right at the end of our shift."

"Perfect. Daggers?" Shay nodded toward the door.

I responded in kind, holding the door open for her to head back in.

23

The door clanged shut behind us. I cast a glance down the hall, wondering which way led back to the bordello's main lobby. "Well, at least that clears a few things up. Now we can say with some certainty that Chaz, Ritchie, and Sammy went straight from here to Heather's. Chaz's limited time with a prostitute might explain his grabbiness at his wife's place. And we finally know what happened to B. B."

"Sort of," said Shay. "We know how we was separated from the rest of the group. We have no idea what happened to his chest or how he got out of jail. But we have a lead, which is better than nothing. Come on. Let's see if Rodgers and Quinto are behaving themselves."

We found the pair more or less where we'd left them, seated on one of the leather-wrapped couches smack dab in the middle of Raccoon Ranch, Nowhere. They'd been joined by a pair of additional hussies, one of them a skinny blonde and the other a plump elf half-breed. Both of them wore the same raccoon-inspired outfits we'd already been introduced to, but the half-elf pulled hers off better than the skinny blonde did, partially due to her darker hair but mostly due to the fullness of her tube top.

"Guys?" said Shay as we approached. "You about done?"

Quinto thanked the ladies and excused himself, pulling Rodgers along with him. "That was quick. You guys learn anything?"

I didn't think we'd been quite that speedy, but then again, time flies when you're ogling half-naked women. "The bouncer gave us a lead on B. B. DuPrat. Also filled some holes in our timeline. How about you two?"

"We found some success," said Rodgers, glancing back at the couch-bound ladies of the night. "We pulled back the mask on the events of last night, if you will."

I lifted an eyebrow. "If that's a raccoon metaphor, it's really forced."

"Hey, I *ear* you," he said with a smile. "Now if you'll shush, I can regale you with our *tail.*"

Steele eyed Quinto. "Did he ask any questions, or did he spend the entire time coming up with painful wordplay?"

"Knowing him he's upset he didn't manage to work 'stripes' in there somewhere," said Quinto.

"Not true," said Rodgers. "But I did fail to come up with a suitable pun involving *clause* and *claws.*"

"Guys..." said Steele.

"Right. Sorry," said Rodgers. "Regardless, we struck gold on two out of three. The thin blonde's name is Belinda. She shacked up with Sammy last night. The half-elf's name is Cinnamon. She was with Chaz."

"B. B. couldn't find his mojo, he started a ruckus, and everyone got involved," I said. "The bouncer already told us. Got anything new?"

Rodgers frowned. "First you disparage my puns, and then you won't even let me tell my story? It's rude, you know. Besides, how am I supposed to know what the bouncer told you?"

"Sorry," I said. "You're right. Go ahead. But assume we already know anything that occurred in B. B.'s room or in the hallway."

"Right. In that case...ah..." Rodgers snapped his fingers together a few times. "Quinto, help me out."

The big guy shook his head. "Puns or no, Allison isn't going to be happy to know a brothel got you so addled. Long story short, Chaz and Cinnamon didn't have sex. Not that they had a ton of time given B. B.'s disturbance, but given my knowledge of male anatomy and personal experience, I'd say that wasn't the limiting factor. Neither was a, ah...*physiological failure,* as with B. B. From Cinnamon's retelling of the experience, Chaz wasn't looking to make love to her, per se. Maybe at first, but he quickly starting pining for his ex-wife, Heather. Cinnamon said that sort of thing isn't uncommon—guys coming in more for emotional comfort than physical."

"So it's more or less what we already thought," said Steele. "Chaz came here. The environment stimulated him, or his thoughts at least, and sent him packing to Heather's afterwards. Given everything we've gathered since lunch, and adding to that Heather and Vance's testimony, we have a pretty good grasp of what everyone in Yellow Cobra was up to until about two in the morning."

"At which point we totally lose track of them," I said. "Except for B. B., of course. We lose track of him even earlier."

"But we know where he went," said Shay. "Or at least where he should've gone. He rendezvoused with the other members of Yellow Cobra at the Banks Hotel eventually. If we follow his lead, perhaps we'll unearth more clues."

"Might as well since we're already here," I said. "Rodgers. Quinto. You guys ready to go? And before you respond, do realize that any answer other than no will be relayed to your significant others in the most incriminating way possible."

Quinto snorted. "As if Cairny would trust you over me."

Rodgers pursed his lips.

"Not so with your belle?" I asked.

"Oh, no," said Rodgers. "Allison would never believe your lies either. But if she thought I was having too easy a time of it at work, she might threaten to take a long weekend away and leave me at home with the kids. I can't have that happen. Let's go."

We exited back through the front of the brothel, pausing to ask Waternoose for directions to the Green Jacket lockup. Turns out it was only a few blocks away, which both did and did not surprise me given the proximity of the brothels to each other and the sheer number of them on Flatley. With our rickshaws having disappeared and the air lacking its traditional midwinter bluster, we chose to walk, although I wondered about Shay's feet. Her choice of heels was a good one from a professionalism standpoint but a poor one from pretty much any other. At least we hadn't found ourselves going toe to toe with any belligerent ogres, doped-out drug dealers, or blood-sucking vampires—*yet*. Of course, if we did, Shay's shoes might come in handy. Staking a vampire was one of the most well-agreed upon methods of indisposing them, and heels were made of wood, weren't they? Or were those wedges?

I neglected to ask Shay about the construction of her shoes lest she take that as another unfounded assumption of mine regarding Chaz's murder. Instead, we talked about much more mundane things, like what sort of creature might be friends with a vampire and still have the fangs, claws, or bladed weaponry necessary to tear B. B.'s chest to shreds. Shay didn't care for that line of conversation either.

We skirted a large brown wagon someone had parked in the street—illegally, I might add—and the Green Jackets' lockup popped into view behind it. If the 5th Street Precinct had suffered from years of disrepair and then had an illegitimate lovechild with a single story brownstone, it might've looked something like the building in front of us, squat and featuring a mismatched façade of brick and stone. If the interior in any way resembled the exterior, then perhaps the drunks locked away inside welcomed their inevitable transfer to the nearest police station.

A couple of thick-necked Green Jackets stood in front of the doors, their legs planted at shoulder width and their arms crossed over their chests. The more talkative of the pair held up a hand as our group of four neared.

"Hold it right there, gang," he said. "Official Green Jacket business, here. Turn it around."

"Sorry, pal," I said. "City police trumps private every time." I pulled out my badge and flipped it for him to see. Sure enough, I noticed serious wear in the leather at the crease. I hated being right.

"Oh," said the guard, bringing his arm down. "Well, about time you showed up. To my knowledge, the night shift guys sent word your way about the escape, well...last night."

"The escape of B. B. DuPrat?" asked Shay. "Sorry. These things take time to investigate. Word only recently reached us."

The guard snorted. "Figures. Bureaucracy."

"I don't suppose you guys were here last night?" I asked.

The guard shook his head. "Nope. Everything we've heard is second hand. I can send word for the guards who were here though, if you need to talk to them."

"That would be great." I pointed at the door. "Is anyone in charge inside?"

The guard nodded. "Yeah. Sure. What was his name? Drogden, I think. He arrived a couple hours ago."

The Green Jackets had their own investigative team working on B. B.'s escape? I didn't realize they employed more than goons.

The guards didn't move, so I gestured toward the door again. "So...can we talk to him?"

"*Talk to him?*" The guard glanced to his partner, who frowned and shrugged in response. "Well, I mean...sure. I guess. Just, you know...be careful."

The guard pulled a key and unlocked the door. He cracked it, glanced inside, then pulled it open further and waved us in. I wasn't sure what all the cloak and dagger was about, or what the man's cryptic warning meant, but the creative half of my brain couldn't help but think this Drogden character might be an investigator of the paranormal kind.

Shay, Rodgers, Quinto, and I stepped into the lockup interior, which wasn't as sad and pathetic as the outside indicated. The front portion in which we stood held a few desks closely packed together. Beyond that, past a half-height wall, I noticed a maze of steel-barred cells, with halls sneaking around and behind them to provide access. All in all, there was probably space for thirty ne'er-do-wells, and that was without packing multiple idiots into the cells that had the space.

The door squealed shut behind us. I surveyed the premises. Drogden must've cast a spell of obfuscation, because I didn't see anyone who looked like they might fit that moniker, or anyone at all for that matter. Quinto didn't either, apparently.

"Hello?" he called out.

Quinto's big voice echoed around the room's many reflective surfaces. No one answered.

No *one.*

A bestial growl erupted from somewhere in the back. We all jumped.

My eyes widened. "What the *hell* was that?"

24

The inhuman growl sounded once again, and I felt the hairs on my arms prickle. I looked around, but I couldn't spot the source.

A scamper of feet. A flash of green somewhere in my peripheral vision. A rush of oncoming air.

I reached for Daisy and spun, but I wasn't quick enough. With my arm still in my jacket, the green form lunged from behind one of the workspaces and latched onto my arm, pulling me down behind the nearest desk.

I gurgled and fell, the ceiling spinning as I lost my balance. My attacker gave me no respite.

"Get down! All of ya," he hissed. "What in the world's wrong with ya?"

I finally managed to get eyes on him. Rather than a four foot ball of muscle, teeth, claws, and gangrene, he was a rather inconspicuous goblin, perfectly normal except for his attire. He wore a khaki shirt tucked into a pair of khaki shorts that ended at mid thigh. His long black hair had been pulled into a ponytail, and white socks rose from the mouths of his worn hiking boots, reaching to the top of his calves.

Steele, Rodgers and Quinto took cover behind the desk, Quinto as best he could given his size. I stared at the goblin. "And you are?"

"Name's Drogden," he said. "I'm with animal control. And what in the fiery, blazing pits of hell are ya doing here? I told those Green Jacket numbskulls to watch the door!"

"Animal control?" said Shay. "So that growl we heard..."

Drogden nodded. "The beast I've been trying to corral for the last two hours—till ya lot of tossers came in and riled him up with yer whoopin' and hollerin'!"

On cue, a bit of movement caught my eye. From past the half-height divider, I saw a brush of orange fur and the swish of a brown-tipped tail.

"*Beast?*" said Rodgers, eyes widening.

"Aye," said Drogden. "A fully mature Delovian prairie lion. Male. A majestic beast, if I do say so meself. Deserves to be set free not caged for people to gawk at, but I don't have any say in the matter. Can't leave him here, in any case."

"A lion?" said Quinto. "How the heck did a *lion* get in here?"

"Not sure," said Rodgers. "But I think we finally figured out what happened to B. B.'s chest—and what killed Chaz."

"Say what in the who, now?" sputtered Drogden. "Are ya saying this lion *ate a man?* Who the hell are ya, anyway?"

"We're detectives with the NWPD," said Steele. "And no, nobody was eaten. But someone was killed, possibly by a beast such as this one."

Or by a vampire, I thought to myself. *Or a were-lion.*

Drogden shook his head. "Ya had me scared there for a second. *Eatin' a man...*"

Something about what Drogden had said finally clicked. "Wait...you've been in here with that thing for *two hours?*"

"Well, that's the thing, ya see," said Drogden. "The beast's tame. Hasn't come at me except when I tried to catch 'im. I'd wager he's well fed, and not off the meat of a dead man, if ya catch me drift. Doesn't mean he's not a cagey son of a centaur. Almost had 'im cornered in one of the cells three times, but he bolted off each time afore I could get the door closed. Also chewed through one of me best catch poles." Drogden jerked a thumb toward the corner, where a wooden pole now ended in splinters.

I sat up a little. Somewhere in the back, I heard the lion growl again, but this time the sound didn't come across as quite so blood-curdling. Not that I suffered a sudden death wish to wrestle the thing, but if a four foot tall goblin in khaki shorts could withstand two hours in closed quarters with the animal, I figured I could manage not to die for a few minutes.

"So, how can we help?" asked Quinto.

"*Help?*" I said. "Back it up there, big fella. Have you forgotten we're homicide detectives? What in our training makes you think we're qualified to wrangle a savage beast from the plains of some gods-forsaken wasteland?"

"We've butted heads with worse," said Quinto, tapping his scarred forearm. "And by Drogden's admission, he's not so much a savage beast as a wily escape artist enjoying a taste of freedom. Besides, have you forgotten our creed? To protect and serve?"

"I always thought that was more of an either or," I said. "The beat cops protect, we serve. And even if we're supposed to do both, that doesn't mean the creed applies in all situations. What if there's a tsunami? Am I supposed to protect the public from that, too?"

Quinto ignored me and turned to Drogden. "You need help, I'm assuming."

Drogden narrowed an eye, surveying Quinto before he turned his peepers on the rest of us. "Well...you and the bellyacher are big, if nothin' else. And even though I doubt ya know the first thing about trappin', ya probably do work pretty well as a team if yer detectives. What the heck. Couldn't hurt. I'm down to me last catch pole, anyway."

Shay regarded Drogden with the same look she gave me when it was obvious she believed I hadn't thought things through. "I'm hoping you have some sort of plan?"

"Sure," said Drogden, hitching his khaki shorts even further up his thighs. "We'll try the same thing I was doing earlier, trying to force the beast into one of the holdin' cells and lock him up tight, but this time we'll have more people to use as a funnel."

"Perfect," I said. "So I'll play the part of a delicious, walking meat funnel. Got it."

"I ain't gonna throw ya out there slathered in steak sauce, ya dolt," said Drogden. "Strategery. That's the key. Now as ya can tell, the animal's sequestered amidst the cells. I've got one open in the middle of the nearest hall. If we can push 'im toward it, he'll have nowhere else to go once we catch him in a pincer. You two big-guns can push 'im from the right. The rest of ya follow me. I've only got one good catch pole left, but he's wary of me. He won't bother us."

"Which means he'll try to tear his way through Quinto and me," I said. "But hey, I'm sure if we ask nicely he'll let us go with a gentle mauling."

"Figure it out, will ya?" said Drogden. "There's furniture aplenty. Make a barricade or somethin'. Yer the one's who volunteered, in any case."

I was about to remind him I did no such thing, but Quinto clapped me on the shoulder. "Come on, Daggers. We'll improvise."

Not wanting to sound like any more of a Negative Nancy than I already had, I simply nodded. Drogden shimmied to the side and extracted his one remaining pole. He looked to Rodgers and Shay.

"Remember, fan out to my sides, but stay behind me. Ready?"

"Wait," I said.

The trio turned. I rummaged around in my jacket, found Daisy, and tossed her to Shay, who caught my truncheon with a deft hand.

"Take care of her," I said. "And yourself. Rodgers, you might want to snag one of those broken poles. Better than nothing."

Shay eyed my nightstick, knowing I wouldn't part with her lightly. "And you?"

"You heard Quinto. We'll play it by ear—and hopefully not lose one in the process."

Drogden didn't seem to think that was amusing. He popped his head up and scanned the cell areas. "Looks like he's on our end. We'll get 'im started. The open cell's on yer side. Don't waste time dawdlin'."

He waved to Shay and Rodgers, and they shuffled around the edge of the far desk. I turned to find Quinto had already moved to the far side of the room. He hefted a pair of wooden chairs in his massive mitts.

"Don't look at me like that," he said. "These are mine. Grab another one and head over here."

I picked up the nearest one and joined him. "I sure hope this is hardwood."

"Looks like oak," said Quinto. "We should be fine."

"Thanks. That's very comforting."

"Seriously," said Quinto. "We've taken on worse."

"Not intentionally," I said. "Not knowing it would be worse. And we got lucky to get out of a few of those scrapes alive, never mind unharmed."

"We agreed to help, and we'll do just that. Come on."

Quinto hefted his chairs and pushed through the door at his side. I channeled my inner ringmaster and followed him through, wishing I'd commandeered the whip we'd found tying Chaz to the tree and brought it with me.

Quinto crept down the hall with his two chairs held out legs first. I did the same, struggling under the weight of my single chair. Apparently, Quinto had the strength of an ox on steroids.

The big guy nodded to the side. "There's the cell."

It stood open, with the door swung all the way to the side. It didn't seem particularly appealing. "I know Drogden said he thought the lion had eaten recently, but I'd sure feel more comfortable with a few steaks to throw in there."

I noticed a flash of orange, and the sound of nails clicking off tile reached my ears. The lion had turned the corner and started to approach us, eyeing us with what seemed to me a mixture of curiosity and disdain.

By the gods, but the beast was big! At about two hundred pounds, I thought myself decently sized, but the animal must've easily doubled that. His head bobbed a good four to five feet off the ground, swaying as he walked.

"Quinto," I whispered. "I'm starting to regret my earlier decision."

Based on the big guy's tone of voice, he had, too. "Easy. Easy. Back away. Give him space."

Drogden, Rodgers, and Shay turned the corner, the animal control specialist looking far more confident than did our detective pals. Rodger's broken pole shook, and Shay gripped Daisy with enough strength to force the blood out of her fingers.

"That's a boy," said Drogden, keeping the pole before him and using it to herd the lion. "Good boy. No sudden movements now."

Based off the glance he shot our way, I think he meant us. As if I needed to be reminded...

The lion closed on our position, glancing back toward Drogden and his pole intermittently. He started to circle as he realized Drogden's plan. I still couldn't get over the beast's size.

The goblin gave us a nod, his pole extended to keep the lion at bay. "Go on. Give him a nudge."

"*What?*" I hissed. "Are you crazy?"

"Figuratively," said Drogden. "Come around the side. Try to coax him into the cell."

Quinto blocked the majority of the hallway with his double set of chairs, so of course the task fell to me. I swallowed hard and took a step forward, my chair wobbling.

"That's it," I said, cooing to the enormous lion and feeling like a walking piece of rehydrated human jerky. "That's the ticket. Just a little—"

The lion roared and spun, lashing out with a huge paw. My chair exploded into a cloud of splinters. Quinto bellowed and lunged to the side, his chairs held like oversized boxing gloves. The lion danced and spun, hopping inside the cell to avoid Quinto's oak-fisted dance. Drogden dove in, jabbing his pole behind the door and whipping it to the side. Quinto just managed to twirl out of the way as it clanged shut.

I sat there in the hallway, pieces of smashed chair littering my pants as I watched the lion circle the cell, separated from me only by steel bars and prayers. Sweat moistened my brow and underarms, the foul smelling kind that arose from stress as opposed to physical exertion. My heart thumped in my chest so loudly I feared it might hop up my throat and make a break for it.

I glanced at Drogden. Suddenly, I felt an immense amount of respect for the diminutive goblin, but rather than a statement of admiration or thanks, all I managed to squeak out was a simple, "I am *never* doing that again."

25

I leaned back in my chair, cooling my heels as I watched Drogden try to coerce the lion into doing his bidding. With Quinto's help, he'd moved a portable cage from the brown wagon out front all the way inside and up against the cell door. Now he tried in vain to coax the beast into the cage, but barring the magical appearance of a bale of catnip, I didn't think he'd have much success. The animal growled and paced, angry that he'd been tricked. He'd already ruined the last of the goblin's catch poles and turned the others into mangled stubs.

The front door squeaked, and I turned, expecting Shay. Rodgers and Quinto had already left for the precinct, whereas my half-elf partner had exited to chat with the Green Jackets outside—or so she'd claimed. In reality, I think she simply needed air. Not that I could blame her. The lion experience had been more harrowing than Drogden had led any of us to believe.

Instead of Shay, however, fate dealt me a different card. A new Green Jacket, to be specific—one with a thick black beard, sunken eyes, and a nose as broad as a barge. He held his body rigid, his shoulders square and tense as he stepped inside cautiously, casting his eyes from corner to corner as if searching for demons in the shadows.

"Howdy," I said, picking my feet off the desk and moving them to the ground.

"Hey."

He didn't bother to make eye contact, continuing his visual survey. Eventually he settled his eyes on Drogden, the cage, and its feline inhabitant. He peered at the medley for a moment before his shoulders finally relaxed.

"Oh, thank the gods," he said. "You've got that beast under control. You know, for a while after I woke up this afternoon, I thought it had been a bad dream. Would've made more sense that way, to be honest."

I gave the guy a nod. "I take it you're one of the Green Jackets who was here last night when the, ah...*incident* occurred."

"That's right," said the man. "Blanchard's the name. Caldwell outside sent word for me. Said there were cops here asking questions. That you?"

"That's right. I'm Jake Daggers. NWPD homicide."

"*Homicide?*" said Blanchard. "Holy crap. The lion *killed* someone? I mean, it's not that surprising. I'm shocked he didn't kill the guy we had in here last night. But still—someone's dead? Here?"

"Settle down, hotshot," I said. "Someone's dead, but not here. Elsewhere. And their death may or may not be directly related to the lion. Either way, that's for me to figure out. What I need from you is an explanation of what the heck happened last night, because right now I'm about as lost as a blind man wearing earplugs in the middle of a rainstorm."

"Sure," said Blanchard. "Uh...where do you want me to start?"

"Last night at about one o'clock, a drunk elf with a shock of platinum blond hair should've been delivered your way via one of the bouncers at the Raccoon Ranch. Name of B. B. DuPrat. Ring a bell?"

"The description does, sure," said Blanchard. "The name doesn't, but a lot of folks who get locked up here give us assumed names."

"What did he tell you he went by?" I asked.

"Dick Longflop."

I snorted, only managing to keep it together by the thinnest of margins. "Right. Let's start with him. What happened after he made it to your doorstep?"

The Green Jacket crossed to the nearest desk and rested his posterior against one of its corners. "At first? Not much. It'd been an exceptionally slow night. He was the first one we admitted. The only one, actually. 'Course he made up for the lull by cussing and screaming enough for five men, but he couldn't fight off the effects of the drugs and booze he'd swilled forever. I think he finally passed out about an hour later."

"And then?"

Blanchard sighed. "It was quiet until around four. That's the hardest part of the night to get through, even for career night-shifters like me. My partner and I were sitting right here in the front, probably dozing off like we usually do around that time. Then I remember hearing the door. It squeaks, you know."

"I've noticed."

"So I look up, blinking the sleep from my eyes, and the door's still open. Someone's holding it from the outside, can't see who. I hear a couple people arguing. I stand up and call out. 'Hello?' And then believe it or not, a giant lion saunters on in here like he owns the place—which I guess you can believe since the beast's still here."

I pulled my trusty pad out and took notes. "What happened next?"

"I freaked out," said Blanchard. "Flew back about five feet and shouted out a curse my mother wouldn't be proud of. My partner did the same. We just about fell over each other trying to get the hell out of here."

You ran out the door past the lion?

"Are you kidding? We busted through into the holding cells and hauled ass to the fire exit in back."

"Leaving B. B. in his cell," I said.

"Dude, don't get on my back over that," said Blanchard. "That was the last thing on my mind. He was in a cell, anyway. What was the lion going to do to him?"

I ignored the dig. "So you made it out back in one piece. What then?"

The man threw up his hands. "I don't know. We were in shock. My partner and I didn't know what to do. We threw some ideas around, but they all sounded crazy. After a few minutes, we settled upon locking the place down to make sure the beast didn't escape. I'd lost my keys in the commotion, but my partner had his, so we locked the back door and headed around front to do the same. Right as we exited the alley onto Flatley, we caught sight of three guys running into an alley across the street. Two new guys holding the elf with the blonde hair between them."

I looked up from my pad. "Can you describe these two individuals?"

"I don't know, man," said the guard. "It was late. I was wired with adrenaline. I barely got a look at them before they disappeared."

"I don't need to know their weights down to the pound, or how many moles each one had on their left ass cheek. Anything would help."

Blanchard scrunched his brow. "I want to say one was skinny, with black hair. The other had...braids, maybe? Or a single braid?"

"There wasn't a fourth? One with feathery blond locks?"

"I only saw the three."

I tapped the pencil against the lined paper in my pad. "I don't suppose you went after them?"

Blanchard shook his head. "No. Maybe I should've. It all happened so fast though. I was totally caught off guard. I mean, *a lion*? Really?"

The door squeaked, and Steele stepped in. I held up a finger in her direction. "One more thing and I'll let you go, Blanchard. After the trio ran off, what did you do? Not head back inside, of course."

"No, man," he said. "That was all she wrote. We locked the place up, went to report it, and went home. Heck, I'm not paid enough to do more."

"Okay. Thanks. You mind letting me have a word with my partner?" I pointed toward the door.

"You bet." Blanchard nodded to me, then Shay, then made his exit.

Shay took the man's spot at the edge of the desk. "Learn anything?"

"More or less." I gave her the cheat sheet version.

She chewed on her lip, taking it all in. She didn't immediately respond.

"Something on your mind?" I asked.

She shook her head. "I don't think Rodgers was right."

"Oh, he's always wrong," I said offhandedly. "But what specific comment are we talking about this time?"

"I don't think the lion killed Chaz."

"Because he didn't arrive with Ritchie and Sammy to break B. B. out?" I offered.

"Not necessarily," said Shay. "I don't put a ton of faith in the eyewitness testimony of a man who went from asleep to confused to terrified over the course of a few seconds. Besides, he admitted he barely got a look at the escapees. Chaz might've been leading the charge, already in the alley by the time Blanchard got a glance at them."

"But you don't think he was here, do you?"

"No," said Shay. "I mean, it's possible. Not likely, given the testimony, but if he was, he certainly wasn't murdered here. I took a look around outside. I didn't see any evidence of blood in the surrounding alleys or on building walls. No camel prints in the mud, either. And I'm sure you'd agree with me that if Chaz had his throat torn here, there'd be blood everywhere."

"The lion could've lapped it up."

"I suppose he *could've*," said Shay, "but we're talking about a *lot* of blood. Lions aren't that meticulous, as far as I know. Especially not ones that have already been fed, as Drogden suggested. And I don't know if you noticed, but there are a few droplets of blood here and there. I'd say they're consistent with B. B.'s wound, not Chaz's."

I hadn't noticed the droplets. "I was simply playing devil's advocate. I don't think Chaz was murdered here either. It doesn't have that distinctive camel smell."

Shay tapped her fingers against the desk and sighed. "The good news is we have one more entry into our timeline of last night's events. The bad news is it doesn't seem to involve Chaz."

"I know," I said. "It's almost as if, following his trip to Club Midnight, Chaz just...*disappeared into the night.*"

Shay frowned. "Don't start with me. Not unless you have evidence to support your theory."

"Do gut feelings count as evidence?"

Shay shook her head. "Come on. Let's get back to the precinct. With any luck, it won't have caught fire in our absence."

26

Shay proved to be right in the most literal sense of her wishes, but it turned out her fears were well founded. As we walked into the lobby of the precinct, we once again found a crowd loitering around her new office.

"I swear, problems never piled up this quickly when the bulldog was around," I said, glancing at the mob.

"You sure about that?" said Shay. "Maybe you never noticed because you were only concerned about the Captain coming to chew on your hide. You only approached him when you needed something."

"That's not true," I said. "I invited him out to drinks. Once. I think."

Shay took a deep breath. "No sense delaying the inevitable. Let's see what's resulting in the end of humanity this time."

We walked toward the crowd, who hadn't yet realized we'd entered the arena. It didn't take them long to figure it out. One of the amassed fighters said something and pointed our way, causing the whole group to straighten, turn, and peer at us like a gang of meerkats.

The one closest to us, a clean-shaven bluecoat with a square jaw, held up a finger as we approached. "Ah, Captain. There you are. Look, I—"

The officers and detectives behind him drowned him out as they all simultaneously voiced their own concerns.

"Captain, I have a—"

"Listen, here! There's a four-thirty five—"

"Out of my way, all of you. I need to—"

"Stop. *Stop!*" said Shay, lifting a hand. "Let me in my office first. And one at a time, please! You're officers of the law, not town criers."

Everyone piped down—almost. The square-jawed bluecoat didn't seem to get the message. "But Captain, this is urgent. I—"

"You just moved into last place," said Shay as she reached the door and opened it. "Better learn to listen the first time. The rest of you, line up. Let's hear it."

While the other members of the police force had already quieted, now even the muttering faded away.

I blinked. I'd always known Shay harbored a ferocious spirit animal within her—perhaps a tiger or a badger—but I hadn't expected to see her release it so quickly, especially after the morning's complaints hurled at her under similar circumstances. Clearly she'd taken her own advice to heart, and based on the line of her jaw and the steely glint in her eyes, she wasn't faking it.

Steele retreated to her desk, leaned against the edge, and eyed the assembled masses. She pointed to the guy more or less in front, a diminutive dark-skinned fellow who I think worked on the second floor.

"You," she said. "You look familiar, but I apologize, I don't remember your name."

"Ortiz, ma'am," said the man. "Burglary."

"Great. Ortiz," said Shay. "Nice to meet you. What do you need?"

He held up a sheaf of papers. "I have a warrant request for an ongoing case involving a guy who's been suspected of art theft."

"Well, that's easy," said Shay. "Leave it with me. I'll take a look at it and sign it as soon as I'm able. Next."

Ortiz stepped forward, gave the papers to Shay, and headed out. Shay set them down and pointed out the next guy. "You. Wormwood, right? Let's hear it."

The detective nodded. "That's right. I guess maybe my situation's not as urgent as everyone else's, so..."

"Make it quick, then," said Steele.

"Okay," he said. "Well, before the old Captain retired, he'd promised me a meeting to discuss a fraud case I'm working on. We've got a trio of possible suspects, but only enough resources to focus on one at a time. We were going to figure out which one made the most sense to tackle first."

"Well, obviously I'm not the old captain," said Shay. "Nor am I familiar with the case. Write me a summary. I'll take a look at it and schedule a meeting if you want one. Or you can simply make a recommendation. You know the case better than anyone, right?"

"Ah...right," said Wormwood. "Perfect. I'll do that."

"Next."

One of the two remaining bluecoats stepped up—not the one with the square jaw. "Captain. Got a four thirty-five in progress."

"In plain verbiage, please," said Shay.

"A fire," said the officer. "A church of some sort down on 1st. A suspected arson."

"Then what are you talking to me for?" said Shay. "Alert the fire department if you haven't already. Get the arson team down there yesterday. Seriously, this isn't hard. Come on."

The officer ran off, looking rather sheepish, leaving only the original, defiant bluecoat.

"Thanks for being patient," said Shay. "Now, what's the problem?"

The man's square jaw seemed abnormally tight, but other than the facial tic he held his annoyance in check. "As I was trying to tell you earlier, we have a bit of a situation. An escaped suspect."

"From our precinct?" asked Shay. "How did that happen?"

"Not from the precinct, specifically," said the officer. "The man was being transferred to the courthouse. Thugs hit the transport. Broke him free. Managed to get away."

"What was the man suspected of?"

"A number of things," said the officer. "Drug trafficking. Racketeering. Intimidation."

"So, non-violent crimes, ostensibly," said Steele. "Daggers? A little help?"

I lounged by the door, taking it all in. At her summons, I stood straighter and quickly engaged my gray matter. "Well...first thing is to put out an APB, but that's obvious. Then gather the patrol officers from the beat where the bust took place. Have them canvas the surrounding neighborhoods. Also notify the detective team who brought the suspect here in the first place. They should know his haunts. Might make the manhunt easier."

My partner turned captain pointed at me. "What he said. Good enough for now?"

The officer nodded. "Yes, ma'am."

He about-faced and exited the office. I stayed at my post by the door, listening as his footsteps faded into the muted hum of the pit. Steele similarly kept guard at her desk, though her shoulders sagged and some of the tension drained from her face.

I waited until Shay made eye contact and gave her a nod. "Nicely done."

"Thanks," said Shay. "I was trying to channel my inner Captain Armstrong. Did it work?"

"Well, you didn't curse enough, and some of those folks left the office with a glimmer of hope that you might actually care about people at a personal level, but other than that? You bet."

Shay snorted, the corner of her lip lifting. "I'll work on that. It's draining though, keeping up that façade. I don't know how the Captain did it."

"Maybe it wasn't a façade. Or perhaps he had a bit of medusa blood somewhere in his lineage, and after so many years on the job, the squishy bits had all turned to stone. You know—except for his jowls."

Shay's smile grew. "You never quit, do you Daggers?"

"Seriously, though," I said, approaching the desk. "You handled that exceptionally. I didn't have to step in at all—mostly because you asked me to step in, but that's what delegation is all about. I'd bet you could do this full time if you wanted."

"Please," said Shay. "We both know that's not happening. Not that I'd *want* to be a captain full time after today. I'm not sure what you saw in this position, to be honest."

"I admired it from afar," I said. "Now that I'm closer, I have to admit I'm rethinking my career aspiration."

A knock sounded at the door. We turned to find a twelve-year old runner standing outside the frame.

He looked confused. "Uh...is the captain in?"

"That's me," said Shay.

The kid lifted an eyebrow.

"Don't look so surprised," I said. "The city's making quick strides in gender equality. What's the message?"

"Right. Sorry." The youth popped over and produced a slip of paper from his pocket. "This is from a guy over at Club Midnight. Name of Vance Ichabod Mortensen."

"*Ichabod Mortensen?*" I said. "How did we never think to ask for his full name? I've never heard a more stereotypical name for a vampire."

"*Vampire?*" said the kid.

"Don't mind him. He's got an overactive imagination." Shay grabbed the slip of paper and opened it. She followed that with snap of her fingers. "Bingo! We've got an address for Jefferson Torment. Come on, Daggers. Time to move."

27

knocked on the door and waited. After a moment, I heard a rustle, followed by the clack of a latch. The door opened about an inch, a chain connecting it and the door frame at face height. From through the crack, an eye stared at us, pale amber in color. Though I assumed the eye belonged to a face, I couldn't be sure. New Welwic is a strange town.

"Yeah?"

"Are you Jefferson Torment?" I asked.

"Who's asking?"

Steele stood at my right shoulder. The eye shifted from me to her and back.

"We're with the police department," said Shay. "Mind opening the door?"

"What? Huh-uh," said the voice. "No way. I didn't do anything. Wrong guy."

"We're not here to arrest you," I said. "We're here to talk about a friend of yours. Chaz Willy Wilson. Name ring a bell?"

The eye narrowed. "Yes... What about him?"

Torment didn't have to talk to us without a warrant on our parts. I figured the truth might set his lips free. "He's dead."

"*What?*" said the voice. "Hold on."

The door closed, I heard the clink of the door chain, and it reopened. In its wake stood a tall man, dark of skin and with dreadlocks that reached almost to his navel. He wore a black leather vest without a shirt underneath it, showcasing an assortment of tattoos across his arms and chest. He even sported some on his hands, neck, and one at the corner of his right eye, that of a miniature skull. Baggy black pants hung from his hips, studded with silver rivets and with an assortment of thin chains hanging from the pockets.

"Did you say Chaz Willy Wilson is *dead?*"

"You're Jefferson Torment, correct?" I said.

The man nodded. "Yeah. Seriously, what happened to Chaz?"

"We were hoping you might be able to help us figure that out," said Shay. "Mind letting us in?"

"Uh...yeah, sure," said Jefferson. "Just watch out for the kittens."

"*Kittens?*" Based on Jefferson's black leather vest, chains, and body art, cat breeding seemed an unlikely hobby for him. Still, some of the toughest looking dudes on the planet turned out to be softies inside. One need look no further than Quinto.

Torment waved us in. "Here, uh...follow me. We can talk over here."

By 'over here,' Jefferson meant his living room, but given that his apartment wasn't very large, it served multiple purposes: living room based on the couch—a carbon copy of the stuffed, knobby-kneed ones we'd seen at Club Midnight, dining room based on the circular table and chairs, library based on the bookshelves, and combined cat sanctuary and *sheer hell* based on the dozens of furry puffballs that roamed the premises. Well, maybe not dozens—but at least ten.

I gagged a little as I entered the room, but honestly, I was surprised the smell wasn't worse. Given my own apartment's history of feline intrusion, my nose was more than attuned to the animals' distinctive aroma. Jefferson must've meticulously refreshed his litter box, which I found at odds with his apparent bachelorhood. Perhaps a secret live-in girlfriend hid in the back hallways.

Shay and I took a seat on the couch, which was about as comfortable as a moss-covered rock. Mewling white, black, and brown hellions circled my ankles as Jefferson pulled up a chair. "So...you're serious, then? Chaz is dead? What happened?"

"We're not entirely sure," said Shay. "We found him in Rucker Park this morning tied to a tree. We're tracking his movements from last night. We understand you guys met at Club Midnight?"

"That's right," said Jefferson. "I'm pretty much a regular. Chaz visited more infrequently, but I'd say he popped by a couple times a month. Maybe more."

I glanced around the room as Shay and Jefferson talked. Though on first glance it seemed cheerier and sunnier than anywhere in Club Midnight's shadow-soaked depths, on closer inspection Jefferson had outfitted it in similar ways. It went beyond the couch, which clearly he'd chosen for aesthetic purposes. I noticed a number of interesting trinkets on the bookshelves, from finely-spun glass spider webs to antique inkwells and elaborate candelabras. A collection of small animal skulls had been scattered among the knickknacks—hopefully not those of his deceased feline friends—and though my eyes weren't quite hawkish enough to read all the spines of the books, a few titles caught my eye, *Death of the Succubus* and *Daemonologie* among them.

"Vance said he saw you and Chaz talking last night," I said. "You mind if I ask about what?"

"Oh, the usual," said Jefferson. "Life, death, the hereafter. Love and pain. Chaz seemed pretty bent out of shape in that department, but then again he was really screwed up. Not sure what drugs he'd taken before he popped by the club, but they'd messed with him something fierce. Oh, and we talked about the supernatural. You know. Vampires."

I glanced at Shay. "*Vampires?*"

"Yeah," said Torment, not getting that I hadn't directed that particular comment at him. "We talked about vampires all the time. Myths and legends. Their habits and haunts. Whether vampirism is a disease or a curse or something else entirely. He was *really* into vampire lore. That's how we met. The first time I saw him at Club Midnight, he was hanging out in the corner by himself—which isn't particularly odd, but he didn't look much like the Midnight type, if you catch my drift. But the book he was reading—*The Revenant*, I think?—a super hardcore vampire text. We got to talking. Hit it off right away."

I shooed a cat that considering turning my leg into either an impromptu scratching post or a urine sponge.

"And this interest of yours in vampires. Is it more theoretical in nature, or is there an experimental component?"

Jefferson's brow furrowed. "I don't follow."

"Do you or did Chaz know any vampires?" I asked. "Real ones. Living ones—or undead ones, however you want to define them."

"Uh...you serious?" said Jefferson. "I'm not sure how to answer that. I mean, I've never had one come up to me and flash me their teeth. Chicks have told me they're vampires at Club Midnight before, but that's a come on. The real deal, though? There might be some, even regulars at the club, but if so, they keep a tight lid on their operations. As I would if I were one. Seriously, read some vampire history. Their ilk hasn't been treated well over the centuries."

To her credit, Steele didn't dismiss our current supernatural tangent. "Vance said he saw you leave the club last night with Chaz's band mates Sammy and Ritchie. Was anyone else with you? Did you meet anyone along the way?"

Torment's eyes widened. "Wait. Back up a few steps. Are you saying what I think you're saying? Was Chaz murdered...by a *vampire?*"

His tone of voice would've been more ominous if it hadn't been punctuated at the tail end by a pathetic mewl.

"*I'm* certainly not saying that," said Shay, glancing toward a kitten napping on her shoe. "It's an unlikely possibility, but one we're entertaining. Please answer the question."

Jefferson shook his head. "No. It was just us."

"And where did you go?"

"Dragon Tattoo. It's a parlor fifteen minutes down the street from the club. Chaz had always admired my ink and figured he'd finally take the plunge." Torment showed off his arm as some sort of evidence of the statement's veracity.

I lost some of the air from my sails. "Let me guess. An ankh? On his chest?"

"That's the one," said Torment, flicking a finger my way. "Kind of basic if you ask me, but hey, for a tattoo virgin? Not a terrible first piece. It was something to work around. I mean, you know...before he died."

"So to confirm," said Shay. "You travelled to the tattoo parlor alongside Chaz, Ritchie, and Sammy. Somewhere around two o'clock. Is that correct?"

"Spot on," said Torment.

"And then?"

The heavily-inked one shrugged. "Beats me. I hooked Chaz up with my artist, helped him figure out what he was getting and where, and headed back to the club. I've gotten a hundred tats. I don't need to sit around and watch someone else get one."

"So you don't know what Chaz and his band mates did afterwards?" asked Shay.

"Nope," said Jefferson. "Sorry."

Shay sighed. "Figures. Thanks for taking the time to talk to us. If nothing else, it puts us a step closer to figuring out what happened to Chaz."

Steele gave me a nod and stood. I followed suit, as did Jefferson.

"So...Chaz," said Torment. "Killed by a vampire? Really? He didn't turn?"

Shay rolled her eyes. "I'm not dealing with this. Daggers, you take it. I'll hail a rickshaw downstairs."

Shay clopped away on her high heels. Jefferson waited for my answer with bated breath. I couldn't let him down.

"Let's put it this way," I said. "I've put werewolves behind bars, tussled with zombies, and avoided getting killed by more kinds of mages than there are colors in a rainbow. I don't know who or what killed Chaz yet...but the supernatural explanation is looking increasingly likely."

28

Shay and I trudged back inside the precinct, marched into the captain's office, and collapsed in the chairs in front of the desk. Thankfully, no officers had set up picket lines in the hall this time, so we were able to put our weary posteriors to rest. Good thing, too, because neither Shay nor I were in any sort of mood to deal with additional bureaucratic incompetence.

"Well, that was useless," I said.

Shay nodded. "You'd think *one* of Chaz, Ritchie, or Sammy would've mentioned something to the artist at Dragon Tattoo about their plans for after leaving the shop, but no. Apparently they were even less chatty last night than they were after we found them this morning—unless the tattoo artist intentionally misled us. Think we should bring him in?"

I shook my head. "Don't get me wrong, I got an off vibe from him too, but my impression was that he was living in his own world. It's possible Chaz or one of the others mentioned something and he didn't process it. It's an artist thing, I think."

"Unfortunately, it leaves us back up the proverbial foul-smelling creek with no paddle," said Shay. "We still have no idea what happened to Chaz after about two thirty, we don't know how he got separated from the others or when, and we have no idea how the lion fits into the picture."

"Speaking of which, we'll have to track down Quinto," I said. "He was supposed to look into the circus angle on that camel. The lion probably came from the same place."

Shay tapped her fingers on her armrest and stared at the wall, pursing her lips the whole time. The way she sank into the chair, the way her shoulders sagged, and the vacant look in her eyes gave proof to her exhaustion. She'd said she'd barely slept last night. What time was it now? Three in the afternoon? Four?

"You doing okay?" I asked.

She looked up. "Huh? Yeah, I'm fine. I just wish we had more concrete leads." She tapped her fingers on the armrest some more and glanced at my jacket. "Have you been taking detailed notes?"

"Sure," I said. "Want to see them?"

"Yes, but not page by page. Rather all together."

"You want me to grab the cork board?"

Shay smiled. "You read my mind."

"Give me a sec."

I stood and exited the office, walking over to the storage closet in the corner. There, I pulled out our trusty board. I made sure to snag some loose sheets of paper, push pins, and red yarn before I wheeled the contraption into Steele's office.

I positioned it in front of the chairs and dumped the supplies on her desk. "You want to read out notes from my journal or put stuff on the board?"

Shay shrugged. "I'd rather melt into this chair, but your handwriting isn't the cleanest. You should probably read."

I held a hand in her way as she started to rise. "It's not that bad. You stay seated. I'll work the pins and yarn."

I extracted my notepad, cracked it to the start of the case notes, and handed it to Shay. "Let's start with the timeline. I remember the first entry. The Cobras leave the Moxy at ten o'clock and head to the lavish home of the four-hundred year old Billy Charles." I wrote out the times and locations and pinned them on the board. "What's next?"

Shay peered into my book, squinting. She flipped back and forth, making sure to get the notes from our various stops. "Let's see. The boys take an unhealthy concoction of drugs at Charles' and head to Leopard Jane's. Time is about ten forty-five. They get to Jane's, drink and party, being served by Crystal until their departure at around a quarter to twelve."

I scribbled on slips of paper quickly. "Go ahead. I'll keep up and pin them all at the end."

"Alright," said Shay. "After that, the entire Yellow Cobra crew heads to The Raccoon Ranch. Arrival time about a quarter after midnight. They only stayed for half an hour before they were kicked out due to B. B.'s impotence and antics. He's taken into custody, escorted to the lockup, and the rest of the band members escape. From there, they head to Heather's apartment, and since they arrived at one fifteen or so, they probably couldn't have gotten into much trouble in the meantime."

Shay paused. My pencil hand flew. "Go on."

"Oh, it's not you," she said. "Just making sure I had this right. Chaz assaults Heather, Sammy and Ritchie pry him off her, and the trio head to Club Midnight, where I presume Chaz moped about his romantic situation. They arrive at two in the morning, give or take a few minutes, and meet up with Jefferson Torment. He leads them to Dragon Tattoo at maybe a quarter after two. Chaz gets a simple piece of ink, and they all leave the shop together in the two forty-five to three o'clock range. And...that's all we've got."

My right hand ached from so much speedy writing, but I pushed through. "That's not everything. We pick back up with Sammy and Ritchie at the Green Jackets' lockup at four."

"Well, right," said Shay. "They pop by, unleash a lion, somehow manage to free B. B. from his cell— maybe using the keys that guard Blanchard claims to have lost—and hightail it out of there. All told that doesn't take more than a few minutes."

I took a deep breath and exhaled as I released the pencil. I gathered the slips of paper and arranged them in order on the board using the pins. "Okay. Here's our timeline, including the places our cast of characters visited. We've got a gap between three and four and, unfortunately, a big one right in our time of death window from four until the point we found Chaz in the park. Now for the next part. Suspects. Who've you got?"

"Well, first and foremost has to be Diamond Drummond," said Shay. "By his own admission, his relationship with Chaz was strained. Chaz hired him as a roadie, but it's obvious Diamond's ambitions are higher. When Benson mentioned he should start practicing, his face lit up. If he killed Chaz, he must've known replacing him in Yellow Cobra would be a possibility given his looks and skills, all of which makes me think that if he's our guy, he's not nearly as dumb as he pretends to be."

I nodded. "Sure. And his buddy Dennis could be an accomplice. We'll have to check with Rodgers and Quinto to see if they found any firm alibis for the pair during their investigation. Also, I think Heather's an obvious suspect. Being attacked by an abusive estranged husband? That could incite some passions, to put it mildly. Not to mention she inherits his wealth, whatever that happens to be. Perhaps it isn't much, but if Chaz is the Yellow Cobra songwriter, she'd inherit his intellectual property as well as his material goods."

"All of the Yellow Cobra members have to be suspects at this point," said Shay. "Given our current understanding, they may all have had opportunities to kill Chaz, although we're not sure if any of them had a motive. Initially, it would seem they had financial incentives *not* to, but there may have been other mitigating factors. Crystal mentioned bickering between Chaz and B. B., and Billy Charles hinted that he thought B. B. might be better off starting his own band rather than sticking with Chaz in Yellow Cobra."

"Possible," I said. "But we need more firm motives. And since we're throwing out people who we have strong suspicions about, let's not forget the Cobra's manager, Benson Forsythe."

Shay lifted an eyebrow. "What motive would he have? Chaz was his primary source of income."

I started to write all the names down on slips of paper. "As I think I already mentioned, perhaps he saw Chaz as too combustible and planned to promote Diamond all along. Or he thought Yellow Cobra could survive on B. B.'s personality alone. Or he's a vampire and couldn't help himself."

Shay rolled her eyes. "Right... Let's get them on the board. And try to match each individual with their location using the string."

I glanced at the ball of red yarn. "You sure about that? That's a lot of potential combinations. I think we might need multiple colors."

"You're probably right," said Shay. "Were there others in the supply closet?"

A knock sounded at the door. Shay and I both turned. Cairny stood there.

"Hey guys," she said. "Got a minute?"

"Sure," said Shay. "What's up?"

"I've been studying Chaz's corpse all day, and I'm confident about a few more of the details surrounding his death. Want to take a look?"

More clues? You bet we were interested.

29

Shay's heels clicked on the stone as we took the stairs into the dungeon. Once again I shivered upon hitting the bottom despite the fact that the temperature couldn't have been more than a few degrees cooler than in the pit. My repeated reaction to the space couldn't simply have been a response to what it held, could it? Perhaps there was a scientific reason for my shivering. Humidity, maybe? I bet Cairny could provide clues if I pushed her on the subject.

"So, Shay," said Cairny as we entered the main examination room. "Can I ask you a question before we get started?"

"You bet," she said. "Shoot."

"I stopped by to say hi to Quinto," said Cairny. "Supposedly he and Rodgers had gotten back from doing some legwork with you. I swear I caught a hint of perfume on him. Not his usual musk. Something more flowery."

I suppressed a smile. "What's the matter? Don't trust him?"

Cairny shot me an inscrutable glance. "Of course I do. But it wasn't simply the perfume. There was glitter on his coat. Rodgers sported it too, not to mention the aroma. But neither of you seem to, which is why I'm confused."

"Cairny," said Shay with a broad smile. "I'm impressed. Picking up small details like that? I must be rubbing off on you."

Cairny returned the smile. "You're not the only one who benefits from our chats. But that doesn't answer my question. What were Quinto and Rodgers up to?"

"He didn't tell you?"

Cairny shook her head. "He skirted the issue."

I snorted. "That goofball. You'd think he'd know honesty is the best policy."

Shay waved a hand. "You have nothing to worry about, Cairny. We visited a brothel during the investigation. Quinto and Rodgers got revenge for being relegated to interrogating the bouncers and cooks the last time we made a trip to one of those places. I promise you your beau didn't misbehave. He stayed in the lobby the whole time."

We'd reached the exam table. Chaz's cold body graced its face, a blanket pulled up to his midsection.

Cairny took up position on the opposite side of the table from us. "I figured it was something like that. I don't know why he wouldn't tell me. Seems silly not to."

Shay lifted a brow. "You're not concerned about him wandering off, are you?"

Cairny shrugged. "I don't know. Not really. But I like him. Quite a lot, actually. I don't want anything to drive a wedge between us."

"Cairny, I guarantee you you're the prettiest, most intelligent woman he's ever dated," I said. "Before he mustered up the courage to ask you out, most of his dates involved a bottle of beer, an extra large bag of fried corn chips, and a box of old case files. He's not going anywhere. Now you mentioned you had more information regarding Chaz's death?"

"Sorry," she said. "You're right. First things first, I've determined Chaz died from blood loss following his neck injury."

I glanced at the gaping wound in question. It hadn't gotten any prettier. "I thought we'd already established that. You said so yourself."

"Technically, I don't think I did," said Cairny. "I intimated it was his cause of death and gave you grief over not coming to that conclusion yourself. But it's a moot point. Though I found copious quantities of narcotics and other drugs in his system, it was his neck wound that killed him, of that I'm sure."

"I could ask how you determined that exactly, but I have a feeling it would go over my head," I said. "So that's good, right? He died the way we thought he died. What else can you tell us? Did you determine how he obtained the wound?"

"In that, I'm confident in my original diagnosis," Cairny said. "Teeth. The tearing pattern of the flesh confirms it."

"And I don't suppose you know what sort of teeth inflicted the wound?" I asked. "Were they human? Animal? Perhaps a lion's?"

"*A lion?*"

"We found one," I said. "Don't ask."

Our midnight-haired coroner paused and chewed on her lower lip.

"Well?" I said after a pause.

"I'm thinking." Cairny stared at the wound. Eventually, she shook her head. "No, I don't believe so."

"Good," said Shay. "That matches our reasoning, but out of curiosity, why would you say so?"

"Well, I'm no zoologist," said Cairny, "but to my knowledge, lions are big."

"I can attest to that..." I said, recalling the beast at the lockup.

"Big mouths, big teeth," continued Cairny. "The size of the wound isn't right. An adolescent lion, maybe, but not a fully grown one. Although I suspect the type of teeth that caused the wound might be similar in structure."

Shay lifted a brow. "What do you mean by that?"

Cairny pointed to the gashes in Chaz's neck, specifically to the sides. "See these two tears? They were caused by canines—the teeth, not dogs. Whatever bit Mr. Wilson possessed ferocious fangs."

"*Fangs?*" I said.

"Don't start, Daggers," said Shay.

Cairny crossed her arms and tilted her head at me. "Is he still sold on his vampire theory?"

"Is there a reason I shouldn't be?" I said. "So far, every piece of forensic evidence you've cited is screaming cape-clad, nightwalking bloodsucker."

"Not everything," said Cairny. "While the bite marks are roughly the size of a human mouth, they're a little too narrow, and the evidence indicates the attacker possessed fangs on both the upper and lower dental arch, which—correct me if I'm wrong, Daggers—doesn't match existing vampire lore. And that's not all. There's a more interesting tidbit I brought you down here to share."

"Being?" asked Shay.

Cairny crossed to another table, picked up a glass cell culture dish, and brought it over. "Do you remember this substance?"

I glanced inside the dish. Translucent flakes dusted the inside of the glass.

"The gross film that was all over him," I said. "What about it?"

Cairny smiled. "I think I figured out what it is. Took a lot of time under a microscope trying different likely combinations, but the flaky translucent nature gave me some clues. The fact that it created a film made me think it had to contain a protein, perhaps enzymes. My first thought after I convinced myself about the neck wound was, what if it's saliva? Mixed with something, certainly, otherwise it wouldn't create a film. Something brown, given the color."

"Hold on a sec," I said. "*Saliva?* And you're *sure* a lion wasn't involved?"

"I already told you, I think the wound is too small," said Cairny. "Besides, wouldn't a lion that savaged a man's throat do more damage? Eat him, even? A single bite to the neck seems unlikely."

"But you have other evidence to support your conclusion, don't you?" said Shay.

Cairny nodded. "I tested a number of *brown pastes,* should we say. Don't ask. It's as unglamorous as it sounds. I mixed each with a bit of my own saliva and dried them. Eventually I found a substance that produced a film of roughly the same color and consistency as this one."

Cairny eyed us. We waited.

"Well," I said. "Go on. The suspense is killing us."

Our coroner's smile spread. "I think this film is a mixture of saliva...and *peanut butter.*"

I blinked. If I wore glasses, I would've taken them off and rubbed at the spot where they hung on my nose. "Come again?"

"Or any kind of nut butter, really," said Cairny. "Almond butter, cashew butter. They all have the requisite protein content, so I imagine they'd behave similarly."

"But...this stuff was all over him, correct?" I said.

"Mostly," said Cairny. "It wasn't under his clothes, but I found traces on his face, hands, chest, and arms."

"So we're supposed to believe...what exactly?" I said. "That a pack of stray dogs licked him to death after a freak nut butter accident?"

Cairny's brow furrowed. "No. I already told you, it was the neck wound that killed him."

Despite the interpersonal strides she'd made, Cairny still struggled with sarcasm.

I turned to Shay. "Are you making any sense of this?"

My partner shook her head. "Not yet. We need to think this through. Cairny? Thanks for the update. Let us know if you stumble across anything else."

"Sure," she said. "Though it wasn't really a stumble. It was heck of a lot of work testing those saliva combinations. I'm *still* parched."

I almost told her that she should've forced Quinto to spit into a bucket for her, but that was both gross and I didn't want to pull her back into a conversation about her significant other. Instead, I thanked her and ushered Shay toward the stairs, her cryptic analysis weighing heavily on my mind.

30

"Okay, so how about this," I said as I paced back and forth across Shay's new office. "Chaz's obsession with vampires started long ago, correct? We're not entirely sure when, but it's been an ongoing fascination at least since his penning of "Creatures of the Night." Probably a ways before. According to Vance, Chaz wrote the song following an encounter with a real vampire. What if we assume, at least for the moment, that both Vance and Chaz were telling the truth."

Shay sat in her desk chair, leaning back and resting her head against one of her hands. She took a deep breath and let it out slowly. "Alright. Fine. I'm stretching my creative muscles. Let's assume that. And?"

""Creatures of the Night" toes the allegorical line between a romantic encounter and that of a more insidious one," I said. "So let's take our assumption one step further. What if Chaz's encounter with a vampire not only occurred but served as the basis for his ballad? What if he was trying to warn people through song?"

"About what?" said Shay. "Heather being a vampire?"

"No," I said. "She came to the precinct in the middle of the day. Besides, I don't think they'd met when he wrote the song. I'm talking about the person who sent her our way. Benson Forsythe."

Shay didn't seem to even possess the strength to shake her head. "You keep beating that horse, not noticing it's dead. And by the way, Chaz's trips to the brothel and his wife's apartment seem to indicate he wouldn't have had any interest in a romantic relationship with Benson."

"And I don't think one existed," I said. "The romantic nature of the song must've been used to hide Benson's assault. The real encounter between the two was probably far less passionate. Think about it, though. We've already talked about the women in Benson's office, the ones who might've been enthralled. We've talked about his inexplicable magnetism. What if he used that on Chaz? To get him in the band and keep him there? Perhaps Benson recognized Chaz's talent and forced him through supernatural means to comply, to front his band and rake in fame and fortune for Benson in return."

Shay sighed. "You realize this doesn't provide Forsythe with a motive for murder, don't you?"

"Of course it does," I said. "We know Chaz was obsessed with the supernatural. Read about it. Talked to others about it. Perhaps there was a reason. Perhaps he was trying to find a way to break Benson's control over him so he could forge his own fortune. Maybe he *did* find a way and used it, or threatened to. Benson couldn't have that, could he? So he killed Chaz to keep

Yellow Cobra intact, knowing he could go to Diamond as a fill in, or simply eliminate Chaz entirely and promote B. B. as the face of the band."

"And the peanut butter?"

I stopped pacing. "I'm, ah...still working on that."

"Face it," said Shay, her head resting against her hand. "We suffer from an abundance of suspects and a distinct lack of verifiable motives. Until we start whittling suspects out of our pool with alibis or assign them more concrete motivations, we're not going to get any closer to solving this thing—and that's before Cairny's bizarre revelation."

"You think she could be wrong?" I asked. "I mean, I know we trust her, but *really?*"

Shay yawned. "Everyone makes mistakes, but Cairny's track record has earned her the benefit of the doubt."

Shay remained in her chair, her eyelids falling and her breathing slow. Some might say she looked peaceful. I knew the truth of it.

I mentally kicked myself for putting her in such a state. True, I wasn't the one who'd named her interim captain, a position she was sorely unprepared for in terms of experience if not intellect or leadership potential. But I *had* stormed out last night after hearing the news—the night, mind you, that had followed our first day as an intimate couple. How stupid could I have been? I was beyond lucky she was so understanding of the reasons leading to my frustration, but there wasn't a doubt in my mind my childish actions had contributed to her sleepless night. And here I was, pushing her to relentlessly pursue the case, filling her ears with my unfounded theories, all while her body screamed for a good night's rest.

"Shay," I said softly.

No response.

Louder this time. "Shay?"

Her eyes snapped open. "Yes? I'm listening."

"You can go home, you know. Get some rest. Quinto, Rodgers, and I can handle this. I mean, given the insane circumstances of the murder, it doesn't look as if the killer is going to strike again any time soon."

Shay blinked and shook her head. "No. I'm fine. Really."

I approached her and pulled her signature move, sitting on the corner of her desk. "Look, I know you're trying to set a good example on your first day as captain, but there's no sense in killing yourself. It's okay to be vulnerable, to show a little weakness now and then. That's one of the reasons you surround yourself with people who care for you and who you trust, so they can lift you up and carry you when you fall down."

Shay lifted an eyebrow. "Are you suggesting I'm going to fall asleep on my feet?"

"I was speaking metaphorically."

My partner gave me a sidelong glance. "That's a surprisingly enlightened point of view, and not one I'd particularly expected to hear from you."

"Are you kidding?" I said. "If anyone should know about vulnerability and the value of friendship, it's me. I've been down the other road. I know where it takes you. Trust me, you don't want to travel that path. Not that you're anywhere close, but still."

Shay nodded slowly. "I...appreciate your concern, Daggers. I really do. If I feel like I can't keep going, I promise I'll let you know. I won't fight it, but for now I'm doing okay. I just need to stay focused. Why don't you snag Rodgers and Quinto? I've got a few last ideas to pursue before we call it a day."

I hoped she was being sincere with me. Even though I wouldn't mind carrying her home and tucking her into bed, I'd rather it didn't come to that. "You got it."

I left and did a little searching. Rodgers I found in the break room, snagging a cup of coffee. Luckily, he had a bead on Quinto, who we found in the form office rustling through the bins in search of obscure documents. Honestly, I'm not sure why he bothered. Shay was captain now. Didn't he know he could postpone all paperwork until the police chief installed a permanent boss? Or at least I think that's how the crony system worked...

We all headed back to Shay's office. To her credit, she was still awake, peering at the contents of the cork board.

"Hey, Steele," said Rodgers. "Daggers said you wanted a word with us?"

She looked away from the board. "Ah. Good. I've got some ideas for avenues to pursue. Rodgers, you first. You said you're familiar with Yellow Cobra, right?"

The sunny, blonde-haired detective shrugged. "Familiar in the sense that Allison dragged me to a few of their concerts back in the day."

"I was hoping you might be able to tell me about the history of the band," said Shay. "Specifically about their origins, when B. B. and Chaz first started it up. It might shed light on possible motives for Chaz's murder."

"It might," agreed Rodgers, "but unfortunately I don't think I'm the man for that job. I don't know their story that well. Allison might, to be honest, but even she didn't start following them until they got popular. Although..."

Steele lifted an eyebrow. "Although, what?"

"Well, Allison used to subscribe to a rock magazine," said Rodgers. "*Shablam.* I remember seeing it on her coffee table when we were dating. I seem to recall articles about Yellow Cobra. The magazine's locally based, I think. I bet if I popped over to their offices, someone could give me a behind the curtains glimpse into the band and their past."

"Perfect," said Shay. "Get on it quick, then. Who knows when they'll close up shop for the night."

Rodgers nodded and headed out.

"And me, boss?" said Quinto.

Shay grimaced. "Don't call me that. I told you, it makes me feel weird. First of all, I need to know if you managed to track down that circus, the Minestrone Brothers."

Quinto shook his head. "Sorry. I looked into it, but the records I was able to find showed those guys went out of business years ago. So either they've managed to bring the band back together, so to speak, or something fishy is going on."

Shay stroked her chin. "Dang. I was hoping that avenue would prove fruitful. Oh, well. For you, I'm afraid I have a more mundane task. I need you to run background checks on everyone. Diamond and Dennis from the Moxy, Benson Forsythe, Heather Cleary-Wilson, and the three remaining Cobras. Maybe something from one of their pasts will stick out. Combined with whatever information Rodgers digs up, it might give us a suspect to narrow in on."

Quinto smiled. "Don't worry. I'm used to doing the mundane jobs. It's sort of my wheelhouse."

"Thanks," said Shay.

"But what about you two?" asked Quinto. "Got any hot leads? Or do you plan to kick back and relax? Honestly, it might not be a bad idea. You're looking worn out, Steele."

"Not really the best way to phrase that," I said. "But I already brought up the issue. She says she's good to go. I'll keep an eye on her."

Shay smirked at me. "You always do. But we won't be staying. I have one more place I want to visit."

Was that a dig at my less-than-stealthy ogling? I did enjoy watching her walk but usually from the backside. Last I checked she didn't have eyes in the back of her head.

"Where to then?" I couldn't think of any stops we'd neglected to make.

"One of the first places we probably should've gone after finding Chaz tied to the tree with that whip," said Shay, standing. "Tommy Llama's."

31

As our rickshaw pulled up outside Tommy Llama's, a few things immediately caught my eye. First, Tommy, or whoever owned the place, had an unhealthy obsession with the titular animal. A huge pokerwork art piece of a llama, burned into a five foot wide slice of redwood that must've weighed close to a ton, hung over the entrance, but that wasn't all. The words 'Tommy' and 'Llama' in the store's sign had been styled to look like standing and sleeping llamas, respectively, and a taxidermied version of the beast in question stood in one of the shop windows, tongue sticking out between his teeth as if sneering at onlookers.

The shop had also seen better days. It wasn't weathered or dilapidated, per se, but the entire right side of the establishment had been boarded up with plywood. Glass shards littered the ground outside, and a sign had been affixed to the boards reading, 'Please, pardon our dust!,' which didn't seem like the most accurate of warnings given the glass.

I hopped off the rickshaw, helping Shay down before opening the front door. A chime sounded as we entered, and I absorbed the interior. Shelves filled with boots of all shapes and sizes covered the walls. Clothing racks dotted the floor, filled with flannel shirts and leather jackets, heavy-duty denim pants and light-brown suede coats with frilled edges. I spotted at least a hundred hats suitable for ranch hands, and glossy, polished wood covered every square foot of the floor, walls, and ceiling.

A big boisterous voice called out from our right. "Howdy there, folks!"

I turned to find a broad-shouldered, heavy set man approaching from the direction of the sales counters. A wide, chocolate brown suede hat sat on top of his head, and a long, grey-tinged horseshoe moustache dripped from his lip. He wore the best duds his store had to offer, including a pair of shiny scaled boots made from the skin of a snake or armadillo.

"Welcome to Tommy Llama's Exotic Leathers and Apparel," he said. "I'm the man, the legend, Tommy Llama. Can I help you find something in particular? Maybe a fox fur coat or a pair of crocodile skin boots for the missus? They'll be a whole lot more comfortable than them man stompers she's got on now, not to mention a dang sight more attractive, if you don't mind my saying."

I thought about coming to the defense of Shay's fashion choices, but I got distracted by the enormous rearing creature behind the man. "Is that a bear?"

Tommy turned to the mounted beast, who stood near the cash registers with his paws lifted in the air, claws out and razor sharp. Each mitt could've covered my face with room to spare.

"Better believe it," said Tommy. "That there's Walter. Ever been to the Koldash Nature Preserve north of the city? Well, Walter's the largest brown bear ever caught within a hundred miles of it, or so my guide told me when I speared him. Also caught me a chamois, a musk ox, and a fully-mature cougar." He pointed out the beasts' locations in the store as he rattled them off. "Shot that last one right between the eyes with a crossbow. You a hunter?"

"Um...not in the sense you are, I think."

"You a small game man, then?" said Tommy. "That's a shame. No real sport in rabbits and possums, if you ask me. Not a problem, though. We're all in it for the same reasons, am I right?"

Tommy gave me a wink, and I furrowed my brow. What reasons was he referring to, exactly? The desire to strip animals of their skins for fun and profit? A feral love of the hunt? Or perhaps simply the opportunity to lord his youthful exploits over customers too nice to tell him to shut up and go away.

"But enough talk," said Tommy. "You're here to buy, and I'm here to help? What can I do for you?"

"We're not here to purchase anything, Mr. Llama," said Shay. "We're from the police department."

The man's mask of friendship disintegrated. "It's Tommy. Mr. Llama was my father. But why didn't you say you were cops? Explains your ridiculous getups."

I glanced at Shay. She responded with a lips-pressed-together look of mirth, though whether over the comment regarding our clothes or his last name I couldn't tell.

"Well," said Llama. "Go on. You know where the break-in happened. Take a look. File your vandalism report. Not like it's going to do me any good. At least I have insurance."

"Sorry. *Vandalism report?*" said Shay.

"Oh, for gods sakes," said Tommy. "Yes. The vandalism report. I sent word about the break-in when I first arrived this morning. Honestly, I'm pretty miffed it took you an entire day to arrive. What kind of schedules do you idiots keep, anyway?"

"Pretty tight ones," I said. "We've had a lot on our plates today. And believe it or not, we're not here to file a report."

Tommy blinked. His eyes widened, and he shook his head. "You're *not?* Then what the hell *are* you here for? No. This is ridiculous. I won't stand for the police relegating my concerns to gumpish flunkies. I'm going to need you to send over a superior officer for me to give them a piece of my mind."

I clenched my jaw, but through sheer force of will I managed not to punch the guy. "I'm a senior detective, *Llama.* If you want to talk to my superior, she's standing beside me. *Captain* Shay Steele."

Steele somehow managed to remain pleasant in the face of his boorish nature and simmering sexism. "It's alright, Tommy. I'll be happy to take the report while we're here. Daggers?"

Shay held out a hand. It didn't seem like an opportune moment for a high five, so I stretched my brain muscles, reached into my jacket, and handed her my notepad and pencil.

Shay cracked it open to a fresh page. "Time of incident?"

"I'm not sure," said Tommy. "Sometime before I arrived this morning."

"And when was that?"

"Eight forty-five, maybe? Before nine for sure."

"Who came into your store?" asked Shay.

"How would I know?" said Tommy. "I wasn't here."

"So you wouldn't know what occurred inside your store either, then, would you?"

"Of course not."

Shay looked up from the notepad. "This isn't much of a report so far, Mr. Llama. Do you have anything *useful* for me to put in here?"

"Well, of course I do," he said. "Whoever busted in here broke all three windows on the right hand side of my store. And they stole a number of my wares. Chaps, a whip, and vambraces, at least."

His mention of chaps made me think of Sammy. Suddenly I no longer suspected he acquired them from the Raccoon Ranch.

"Sorry, *vambraces?*" I said.

"Forearm armor," said Tommy. "You know, like bracers?"

"Is that standard attire for handling lions?" asked Shay.

"*Lions?*" said Tommy. "What do lions have to do with anything?"

"I'll ask the questions, thank you." Shay turned toward the area with the broken windows. "I'm assuming you had the boards put in today? Did you clean the area adjacent to the break-in at all?"

"We swept up as much of the glass as we could," he said. "Didn't want customers getting their shoes all cut up."

"So just sweeping then?" asked Shay. "No mopping?"

"No," said Llama. "Does it matter?"

With Steele, details of that nature always mattered. I gave her a nod. "What are you getting at?"

"No mud. No blood," said Shay. "That means B. B. wasn't here. If Ritchie was, it was before he encountered his friend the mud pit. I'd wager Chaz and the others came here in search of a whip to tame the lion, which explains how the whip got into Chaz's attacker's possession."

"Ritchie? Chaz? Who are these people?" said Tommy. "Do you have a lead on the vandals?"

"Ding, ding," said Shay. "We have a winner!"

"We probably would've caught the guys already if not for our *lax schedules*," I said.

The heavyset store proprietor at least had the dignity to put his hole digging shovel to the side for a moment.

Shay handed me the notepad. "I think that'll be all, Mr. Llama. Unless you have anything else to add?"

Llama shook his head. "Uh...no. That's about it."

I tucked the pad away. "I have one last question for you, if you don't mind."

"Um...sure, I guess," he said.

"You're a sportsman," I said. "Bears. Mountain lions. Things with big, sharp teeth. You ever hunt game of a more...*supernatural* nature?"

Shay sighed. "Not this again. I'll be outside."

She turned and headed toward the exit, leaving me standing there with a goofy look on my face and a finger in the air.

Llama peered at me sideways, his eyes narrowed. "*Supernatural?* You mean like centaurs or something? What do you take me for, a barbarian?"

I could tell I wasn't going to get anything of use out of the man, so I gave him a more pleasant goodbye than he deserved and followed Steele out the door.

32

found my partner leaning against the bricks outside Tommy Llama's. Her body sagged, her posture resembled that of a sloth, and she seemed to be putting forth a herculean effort simply to keep her eyelids halfway open.

"How about I make you a deal?" I said.

Her eyes snapped open. "What was that?"

"I said, how about I make you a deal? I'll agree to stop bringing up the vampire angle if you agree to go home and get some rest."

Shay narrowed an eye, on purpose this time. "Doesn't sound like much of a deal. If I'm not around, how would I know you'd stick to your end of the bargain?"

"You'd have to trust me," I said. "I'm a man of my word. Of course, I tend to speak in intentionally vague ways. Gives me more wiggle room in these sorts of situations. I blame it on all the lawyers I've dealt with over the last decade."

Steele straightened. "I'm fine."

"Don't lie to me," I said. "You're exhausted. You're practically falling asleep standing against this wall. That's something only narcoleptics and emergency room doctors are proficient at. Besides, I made a promise to Quinto to take care of you. I wouldn't want to let the big guy down."

A smile spread across Shay's lips. "And I take it Quinto's concern is your primary motivating factor?"

"I'm on the job, so I'm blaming it on him, but I think you know otherwise."

Shay tucked her smile away for future use. "I'm touched, Daggers, but I'm telling you, I'll be fine. Really."

I lifted an eyebrow. Mine were big and bushy, not like Steele's sleek narrow ones, so the effect wasn't as neat as when she pulled the move, but it got my point across.

"Okay," said Shay. "I'll admit I could use a boost. Another coffee. Strong stuff, preferably. I'll suffer through the taste if it gives me back the pep in my step."

I glanced up and down the street. I pointed. "That looks like a bodega. Pop 'n Shop. I'd wager they have coffee. Might not be the best quality, but sometimes these mom and pop stores surprise. I'd bet they have snacks, too."

We started walking. Shay gave me a dubious look. "Snacks? I thought I'd helped wean you off those."

"You have, as should be obvious from my physique," I said, patting my midsection. "I haven't eaten a kolache in weeks, thanks in part to my failed attempt at the coffee cart this morning. That said, between all this walking and thinking, I'm ready to wolf down a chimera, conservation status be damned. You need coffee? I need food."

Shay shrugged. "Well, you know me. Under normal circumstances, I'd prefer we sit down and have a decent meal, but I don't see any restaurants nearby, and without a quick hit of caffeine, I might not last until we find one. Maybe the Pop 'n Shop will have something...*edible.*"

"That's the spirit." I reached the front and held open the door, which dinged upon my pull. "After you."

Shay walked in, and I followed. Racks of goods—some fresh, but most preserved—formed a trio of aisles in the center of the diminutive store. A dull eyed orc, with grayish green waxy skin, pointed ears that stuck through a tuft of curly black hair, and a fat lower lip, nodded as we entered. Behind him, a coffee pot bubbled merrily. To his side on the front counter sat a pair of warming pans.

Shay approached the guy. "Hi. Can I get a coffee? As large as you sell. And with plenty of cream and sugar."

The orc nodded, responding in a deep voice. "You got it."

"Well, I see your aversion to snacks isn't calorie based," I said, joining her.

"I told you, I need a perk."

The orc spoke over his shoulder as he poured coffee into a tall waxed paperboard cup. "How about you?"

"What's in the pans?" I asked.

"Sausages on the right, pretzels on the left," said the orc, turning back with a full cup.

I pursed my lips. "How old are they?"

"Made the sausages fresh this morning," he said. "Couple of drunks cleaned us out last night. Pretzels are fresh, too. Mostly."

That last bit didn't inspire a lot of confidence, and I had my doubts about the sausages. "Do you make anything on demand?"

The orc nodded to a vat of hot oil by the wall. "I can fry churros. Only takes a minute."

"Ooh, fried sugary dough," I said. "I'll take two."

The orc moved to the fryer. Shay gave me another look. I shot it down.

"Don't give me that. You're the one with double sugar and cream in her coffee."

"And it's only barely palatable," said Shay, grimacing as she tasted it. "I still think we could do better on food, though. Now that I have *this,* anyway."

"Yeah, well, we don't have time for that, do we? Have to get back to the case."

"*We do?*" said Shay. "Because unless Rodgers or Quinto dug something up, I'm not sure what our next avenue to pursue is right now."

She'd seen right through my churro-inspired bluff. I improvised. "What are you talking about? There's plenty to pursue."

Shay wasn't about to let me off that easy. "Like?"

"Ah...well. Let's see. Consider this. We have no reason to think it wasn't the Yellow Cobras who broke into Tommy Llama's last night. They stole a whip and one of his pairs of chaps, we presume. We don't know exactly what time they broke in—probably between three and four if our timeline is right—but the gods know there's not a lot of people out at that time of night. The Cobras must've been quite a sight to behold. Drunk rock stars with eyeliner and big hair, geared out in leather chaps and forearm bracers and a whip, parading around with a lion in a cage drawn by a camel. Surely someone around here saw something, and if they did, that's a sight they'd remember. You, clerk, at the churro station. Are you guys open twenty-fours hours?"

The orc turned, lifting up the basket with my churros to let them drain. "Ah...yes."

"And I don't suppose you were in last night?" I said. "Late? Between three and four?"

"Uh...yes, actually."

"Daggers, you've got it wrong," said Shay. "Yes, at some point the Cobras must've come into possession of the camel and the lion, but not when they broke into Tommy's. They were still snagging their gear at that point."

"Maybe, maybe not," I said. "Could be they jacked the camel for fun, tried to snag the lion, realized they couldn't, and came to Tommy's for protection. Clerk? You see any circus animals go by last night?"

The orc dusted my churros with cinnamon sugar, popped them in a paper bag, and returned our way. "Well...no, but—those guys you mentioned came in here, I think."

"Wait...*really?*" I said.

The orc nodded, tossing my churros on the counter. "Two drunk guys? One of them had big hair, the other had chaps and a whip. You said between three and four, right? I think they came in about three fifteen, three thirty."

Suddenly, Shay seemed very awake, and I doubted it was from the coffee. "Two men? Not three? You say one had big hair? Was it black? What did the other look like?"

The orc blinked, blitzed by the number of questions. "Uh...that's right. Two. Poofy black hair on the first. The other had brown braids and a bandana. He was the one with the leather chaps and the whip."

Shay eyed me. "That means Sammy and Ritchie lost Chaz sometime between two thirty and three thirty."

"Interesting." I nodded to the clerk. "Did the pair buy anything?"

"You think I let them use the bathroom at three thirty out of kindness?"

"They stopped for a pee break?" I asked.

"Metaphor," said the orc. "They bought stuff. A bunch of items."

"Like what?" I asked.

The guy gave us a sidelong look. "You're cops, right?"

Shay and I produced our badges at the same time.

"Alright," said the orc, holding up his hands. "Just asking. First off, they bought a ton of sausages—they're the ones who cleaned out the warming pan. I forget everything else they bought. Let me check the ledger."

"*Sausages?*" said Shay. "I bet that's why the lion wasn't so hungry this afternoon."

He rummaged under the counter and produced the ledger in question. "Okay, let's see. They bought all the sausages we had on hand. Fifteen, to be specific. Two fifths of vodka. A bag of pork rinds. Some fried corn chips. Two packages of beef jerky—"

"Someone had the munchies..." I muttered.

The orc kept going. "A loaf of bread. A jar of peanut butter, and another of jam."

"Hold on," said Shay. *"Peanut butter?"*

The orc didn't understand her tone. "Yeah. You know. For sandwiches?"

Shay turned to me. "Well, that answers one question. The follow up is, how did the peanut butter get on Chaz? Who killed him? When did he reunite with Sammy and Ritchie, and how did he get separated in the first place? And, of course, where the heck did the lion and camel come from?"

The clerk lifted a finger and pointed it toward the door. "Did you check the zoo? It's only a ten minute walk away."

"No, these animals came from a circus, not a..." I paused as the words churned through my brain. "Wait...the zoo's only ten minutes from here?"

The clerk nodded.

I turned to Shay. "But what about the bridle?"

"It's only ten minutes," said Shay. "Can't hurt to check."

"Rodger that," I said. "Buddy? Thanks a bunch."

I paid the orc for our pick-me-ups, gave him a hefty tip, and hoofed it out the front.

33

The sun hovered over the horizon as we reached the gates to the New Welwic Zoo, sending its weakened winter rays glancing across a thirty foot wide orange and green sign that hung above the ticket sales kiosks. Statues of bears, flamingos, and gorillas sprouted from the concrete in front, their bronze surfaces long since tarnished into scaly green eyesores. Reliefs of a variety of beasts shared space with the zoo's name on the wide sign. The carvings had fared better than the statues, but only by a razor's edge, their green paint peeling and the wood underneath worn.

Despite winter's grip and the time of day, I'd expected to find at least a handful of other park goers at the entrance, but reality squashed my expectations. Rope hung between posts in front, and none of the kiosks burned bright with lantern light. A young woman with long brown hair held in a braid, wearing green khakis and a matching long-sleeved shirt, stood at the edge of the rope barrier, however. We approached her.

"Excuse me," I asked. "Is the park open?"

"Sorry, folks," she said. "It's too late today. Besides, we had vandals break in overnight. They let some of the animals loose, and we're still cleaning up the mess. Try again tomorrow."

"Tomorrow's not going to do, I'm afraid. I'm Detective Daggers. This is Captain Steele. We're with the NWPD." I dug out my badge and flipped it open. The crease hung on by a thread. I hoped it would make it through the end of the day. At least I knew the new captain wouldn't give me a hard time about replacing it.

"Oh, you're here," said the young woman. "Excellent. I imagine you'll want to talk to head zookeeper Pope, then?"

"About the vandalism?" I said. "You bet. Is she in?"

The young woman lifted both of her eyebrows. "Are you kidding? After last night? Where else would she be? Though she's been up since well before dawn. I don't know how pleasant she'll be."

"Well, she won't be the only one, then," said Shay, lifting her coffee cup. "Mind finding her for us?"

"You bet. Here. Come around the rope. I'll let you wait by the kiosks."

The young zoo hand unlatched one of the rope sections and waved us through. After she'd escorted us to the ticket counters, she took off in search of her superior.

I leaned against one of them and peered toward the zoo proper. An exotic blend of vegetation flourished within, deciduous trees without leaves, evergreens with, and a number of more tropical looking specimens that stubbornly hung onto their leaves despite the New Welwic winter, probably confused out of their tiny tree-minds and kept alive only by the prayers and dark magic of the zookeeper. Melodic bird calls rang out from within the foliage, probably from colorful avian species who wished they'd never been brought here in the first place.

I turned to Shay. "You ever visited this place?"

She shook her head. "No, but I'd heard about it. I knew it existed."

"How did we not think to come here first?" I asked. "I mean, the camel and the Minestrone Brothers bridle, sure. But after the lion?"

"Circuses have lions, too," said Shay. "Don't beat yourself up over it. For all we know, the Cobras *did* steal the camel from a circus. Those boys got around last night, that's for sure."

I picked up a map from a dispenser adjacent to the ticket booths and unfolded it. It took me a little searching, but eventually I found what I was looking for. The zoo did, in fact, have a camel enclosure, hidden in the back among what it considered its desert landscape. A lion enclosure sat not too far from that in the zoo's savannah section, which I supposed made sense, both from a terminology standpoint and from the fact that savannahs were essentially deserts with grass.

I heard footsteps. I lifted my head to find a short elf woman approaching, busty and thick in a way most elven women weren't. Her green khaki shirt stretched tightly over her bosom, as did her similarly shaded pants over her thighs. Her long blonde hair, held in a tight braid, flicked from side to side as she walked, much like the tail of one of the many beasts in her menagerie. She was cute, although a polar opposite of

Shay. Except for her compact stature and pointed ears, she reminded me of my ex-wife Nicole. Thankfully, that resemblance no longer induced in me a sense of wistful desire.

"Officers," she said as she neared. "I'm glad you've finally arrived. I'm the head zookeeper, Azalea Pope. You got my message?"

I folded the map and tucked it away in a jacket pocket. "Ah...*message?*"

"Yes," she said. "About the break-in? I dropped by the local precinct this morning and filed a report."

"Which precinct was this?" asked Shay.

"The nearest one," said Azalea. "On Mackinaw Street."

Shay looked at me. I shrugged.

Shay sighed. "I'm sorry, Ms. Pope. You're the second individual we've dealt with today who's tried to notify us about an overnight break-in only to have the word not relayed to us in a timely fashion. Looks like I'll need to have a word with the captain at the Mackinaw Street precinct to make sure it doesn't happen again."

I thought about making a snide remark about the efficiency of local government, but the point seemed self-evident. Besides, it didn't cast me in a good light, despite the fact that I was working my tail off on a case—for once.

"I'm sorry, too, Ms. Pope," I said, though I didn't feel quite as remorseful as I suspect Shay did. "I'm Daggers, and this is Steele. We're with the 5th Street Precinct, investigating a crime tightly related to your vandalism incident. Honestly, we didn't know you'd suffered a break-in until we lucked upon a witness who overheard us talking about your lion."

"King Geoffrey?" said Azalea. "Oh, by the gods! I hope he's okay."

It took me a second to process that. "You mean your lion? He's fine. Last I checked animal control was trying to coax him into a kennel at a lockup on Flatley. We also have a camel in custody, which I assume is yours, although we found it wearing a bridle from a circus act known as the Minestrone Brothers."

"The camel was a rescue," said Azalea, nodding. "We took custody of it when that circus went out of business. The bridle and a bunch of other gear came with it as a package deal. What about the other animals, though?"

"*Other* animals?" said Shay.

"Yes," said Azalea, nodding. "The otters? Baboons, capybaras, and pygmy deer?"

"Those are *all* missing?" I asked.

"To some extent or other, yes," said Azalea. "Many of them are still loose in the park, hiding in other enclosures, but I know some of them managed to escape our perimeter. Of course, by your surprise, I'm guessing I've answered my own question."

Shay shook her head. "Again, I'm sorry. We'll file another report once we reach the precinct. Contact Mackinaw Street and open communications with animal control. In the meantime, would you mind showing us the scene of the crime, so to speak? And walk us though what you know of the incident?"

"Sure, I can do that," said the stocky elf. "It's getting late, and I've about had it with diving into bushes and coaxing deer off of sharp rocks. Follow me. I'll show you what happened—or at least everything I've discovered."

Azalea turned and headed off at a brisk pace, leaving us with no choice but to bring up the rear.

34

"Well, here we are," said Azalea. "This is where the racket started. This is what got me up at a quarter to five and what's kept me racing around the park ever since."

I looked around. We stood in the middle of an intersection of gravel-paved paths. Behind me, separated from the path by a chest height wall and a chasm fifteen feet deep, stretched an enclosure filled with knee-high golden grass, a fair amount of dirt, and the occasional scraggly tree. On the other side of the path, greenery thrived to a much greater degree. Thick bushes and shrubs packed a smaller pen, one with a less imposing waist-high wall topped with a latticed fence. I heard the babbling of a brook and the occasional bit of squeaky chatter coming from within the foliage. Further down the path, I spotted a number of two story wire mesh cages I presumed were for birds.

"I'm sorry," I said, still gazing at the various enclosures. "What am I looking at?"

"The scene of the crime," said the zookeeper matter-of-factly.

I tried not to look confused, but I'm pretty sure I failed. "You're going to have to be more explicit, I'm afraid."

Steele nudged me. "Daggers, can I see that park map?"

I dug it out of my pocket as Azalea began to explain herself.

"Behind you is the tail end of our savannah exhibit," she said. "We keep the pygmy deer and the baboons in there because they get along well. Usually we try to fit at least two or three different species into a single enclosure. Not only does it help us cram more animals into the same amount of space, driving down operating costs, but we find a lot of the animals like it. They end up befriending each other, if you can believe it. Not necessarily the baboons and deer, but the capybaras and otters in the marshy river enclosure behind me are the best of friends. Of course, I get the feeling otters could befriend just about any animal."

"Except large predators, I assume."

Azalea smiled. "You'd be surprised. Seriously, they can charm *anyone*. Assuming they're well fed."

Shay peered at the map. "What about the camel and lion exhibits? They don't seem to be in this area."

The zookeeper shook her head. "They're farther up the path, in the northeast corner of the park."

I understood what Shay hinted at. Azalea had indicated the animals in this area had escaped, and yet it was the camel and lion who we'd come across, animals that weren't in the same vicinity. So why had the nearby beasts been let loose? A distraction, perhaps?

"Why don't you tell us exactly what happened last night?" I asked.

Azalea nodded. "Like I said, it started just shy of five in the morning, or at least that's when I heard the ruckus. I have a cabin on the property. It's not the most glamorous lifestyle, getting up at all hours of the night to treat sick iguanas or help zebus give birth, but what can I say? It's a labor of love."

"*Zebus?*" I said.

"A kind of cow," explained Azalea. "Anyway, I heard all sorts of shrieks and whoops and hollers, some of which sounded human, so I threw on clothes and ran out here as fast as I could. Well, by the time I arrived, all hell had broken loose. Someone had opened up both of the enclosures on either side of us, and darn it if those mischievous baboons hadn't already invaded the capybara and otter pen. At least the ones who'd gone in there were mostly contained. It was the others who gave me real trouble, mostly because whoever had opened the enclosure had dumped a bunch of junk food all over the place. When I found them, the baboons were tearing open bags of chips and fighting over them, whooping and shouting the whole time."

Somewhere from deep within the trees, a cry sounded, a cross between a deep throated shout and a woofy bark.

"See?" said Azalea. "I still haven't been able to track them all down. It's like they know I'm talking about them and they're sitting in the trees, laughing it up."

I turned to Shay. "That was the same cry we heard in Rucker Park this morning."

"Yes," she said, folding up the park map. "And apparently it doesn't belong to a fang-toothed demon with camel feet. Imagine that."

"They made it all the way to Rucker Park?" said Azalea. "Oh, gods... How in the world am I going to lure them back?"

"We'll notify animal control," said Shay. "They have a wily goblin trapper on their squad who's not too shabby at his job. He'll help you. I don't suppose you saw who broke in and opened the cages, though?"

Azalea shook her head. "Sorry. They must've taken off right before I arrived. There were still chips and beef jerky everywhere. Baboons are feisty, and they'll scarf down anything. If they'd had more than a few minutes, they would've eaten every last scrap of food left behind, including the peanut butter I found two of them fighting over."

Shay and I exchanged glances. "Come again?"

"They must've stolen it from the vandals," said Azalea, "but I was able to confiscate the jar before they opened it. Saved it, too. No sense wasting a full jar. I can use it for treats. Not for the baboons though. They certainly haven't earned it..." The zookeeper scowled.

"Wait...so the jar was unopened?" asked Steele.

"That's right. Still had that pressure-sealed top. Not that it mattered to the baboons. They can smell right through the glass. Makes them go crazy. Probably would've smashed it with a rock if I hadn't been there to scare them away." Azalea narrowed her eyes. "Why are you so interested, anyway?"

"Don't worry about that." Shay tapped the folded park map upon her palm and looked up the path. "So those cages over there. Those are bat enclosures?"

Azalea nodded. "That's right. One of them is, anyway. Mostly fruit bats, but we have some rat-tailed ones and flying foxes, as well."

"Wait...what?" I snatched the map from Shay and opened it. Sure enough, it stated the obvious right there in a fun, family-oriented font. How had I missed it?

"I don't suppose anyone broke into that enclosure, as well?" said Shay.

"Funny you should ask," said Azalea, her eyes still narrow. "The cage door was shut but unlatched this morning. I wondered if we'd forgotten to close it properly or if it had been the vandals. Either way, as far as I can tell by a head count, none of the bats escaped, despite the fact that they're nocturnal. If someone went in there overnight, I can't explain how none of them got away."

"Did you find a large quantity of blood in the bat enclosure?" asked Shay.

"*Blood?*" said Azalea. "No. Should I have?"

"Not necessarily," said Shay. "What about in the camel enclosure? Or anywhere else on the property?"

"Goodness, no," said the zookeeper. "Now you're making me worried. I thought the people who'd broken in were simple vandals, but now you're implying they're...what? Twisted animal torturers?"

I folded the map and returned it to my jacket. "We already told you, your lion and camel are fine. I assume the rest of the animals are too, though the baboon lost in Rucker Park might have to watch his back for dope heads and muggers. It's the vandals themselves who didn't fare too well." I pointed in the direction of the bat cages. "Did you find anything in the cage when you looked this morning? Items of clothing, more snacks, footprints, anything that might help us identify who was here overnight?"

"Can't say that I did," said Azalea.

"And in this area?" I asked. "Anything?"

"Just the snack foods."

I looked at Shay. We stood in silence for a moment. My partner chewed on her lip. Eventually, she broke the silence.

"Thanks for your help, Ms. Pope. We'll see ourselves out, and I'll make sure to address the issue with the Mackinaw Street Precinct and send word to animal control."

Azalea nodded and gave us a perfunctory return thanks. We turned and headed back toward the front gates, the path's gravel crunching underfoot.

Shay waited until we'd cleared out of the zoo-keeper's earshot to speak. "So, Daggers, you're my go-to source for crazy theories. Normally I'm dismissive of them, but I feel like I could use one right about now."

I snorted. "Me too."

"So you have nothing for me?"

We locked eyes. "Oh, I'm pretty sure we're on the same page about the implications of Zookeeper Pope's testimony. But with that said...I have no idea what any of it means. And I certainly don't know who killed Chaz or why."

35

We trudged back into the captain's office at the precinct and collapsed into our chairs. Steele spread over hers like cheese on a burger. I'd like to pretend I sat up straight, my back a steel rod and my mind crisp as a fresh leaf of lettuce, but I'd only be fooling myself. Thoughts, clues, and theories packed my mind like cotton balls in a jar, ready to pop all over the place at the slightest release of pressure. My knees and legs felt weak from the miles I'd put on them, and my feet hurt. Of course, I was smart enough not to mention that fact, not with Shay wearing heels and likely feeling as if the hot winds of hell itself coursed through her toes.

"You know," I said. "Could be that wearing heels is a good idea now that you're captain. Get your toes callused."

Shay shot me a confused glance. "What?"

I realized that despite her initial claims of psychic ability, she couldn't actually read my thoughts, at least not more than your garden variety 'wants sex, needs a beer and a sandwich' variety."

"Sorry," I said. "I was thinking about your high heels and how your feet must feel, and that got me to thinking about callused toes and how they might be useful when you need to put your foot up someone's ass. Metaphorically speaking, of course. Trust me, it was more amusing in my mind..."

"I'd hope so, because it wasn't at all outside it." Shay rearranged herself on her cushions and glared at the cork board.

"Not even a smirk?" I said. "This case must be wearing on you more than I thought. Or it was a terrible joke. Both valid possibilities."

Shay's face softened. "Don't take it personally. I get snappy when I'm tired. I think the coffee's wearing off."

It probably would've even if Shay hadn't spent the majority of the night creating a circular groove in her apartment's floor. The sun had set on our way back to the station, before we'd even left the zoo. The clock in the corner read six fifty-five.

"Let's face it," I said. "It's time to go home and get some rest. And I don't just mean you. Me too. We can pick this up tomorrow."

Shay considered my words. Her lips twisted. She seemed on the verge of agreeing when once again a knock sounded at the door.

We both turned. Rodgers stood outside the frame, his knuckles poised at the side of the wood. He sported one of his trademark toothy white smiles, but it faded as he set eyes on Shay.

"Steele? Dang, you look..."

Shay gave him a second. "Look what?"

"Um...nothing," said Rodgers. "Just remembering words of wisdom I've learned from my marriage. Got a minute?"

"Why not. Have a seat." She nodded to the empty chair in front of her desk.

"Great," said Rodgers, taking the proffered chair. "Remember how you sent me to that music magazine to investigate Yellow Cobra's past? *Shablam?*"

"We remember," I said. "And to be honest, you basically volunteered to go."

"Whatever," he said. "The point is I found a reporter who covered Yellow Cobra since their inception, and he was able to shed light on their interpersonal relationships."

Shay didn't look terribly interested, but she made a perfunctory effort. "Go on."

"Well, first and foremost, the band's been rife with infighting for years, almost since the beginning," said Rodgers. "According to the journalist I talked to, Chaz was a firebrand. Always mouthing off. Always trying to shine brightest in the spotlight. Always taking credit for the band's successes, whether he deserved the praise or not."

"So," I said. "That's typical diva behavior. Not exactly unexpected for the frontman of a rock band, and not particularly different than the reports we've already heard."

"True," said Rodgers, "but what we didn't know was how close Yellow Cobra had come to falling apart. According to the reporter, everyone butted heads with him at some point or another. Twice Chaz threatened to scuttle the band if everyone didn't get in line and follow his creative direction, and on another occasion, B. B. threatened to leave but ultimately stayed after Chaz threatened to blackball him."

I sat up a little straighter. Hadn't Billy Charles mentioned something about B. B. wanting to strike out on his own? Or rather, that he *should*.

"What exactly do you mean scuttle the band?" I asked. "And blackball how?"

"Blackball in the traditional sense," said Rodgers. "He claimed he'd use his influence in the rock sphere to make sure B. B. never got another gig if he left. But as far as scuttling the band, apparently Chaz was the founding member, and the deal he signed with Benson Forsythe didn't surrender his rights. He wrote the songs, owned the copyrights, and owned the rights to the band's name and likeness. So, for example, if the other guys in the band wanted to strike out on their own, Chaz would've had the legal right to pick a bunch of scrubs off the street and keep performing under the Yellow Cobra name."

Shay perked. "But I'm guessing if he died, that would no longer be the case."

Rodgers smiled. "The journalist didn't know. That's for a lawyer with a copy of his intellectual property agreement to decide, but in most cases? Yes."

"Which gives B. B. a motive for murder," I said. "As well as Benson Forsythe. More so than we already suspected."

Thankfully, Shay didn't bring up my supernatural suspicions about the band manager. "Forsythe? How so?"

"For the reasons we already discussed," I said. "He was losing money, stuck in a contract with Chaz with no way out. With a new frontman at the helm, and the Yellow Cobra name and brand intact? It could give the man a new lease on life."

I heard heavy footsteps, followed by a deep voice. "Hey, look. It's a party."

Quinto had joined us at the door, a sheaf of papers in his oversized mitts.

Shay waved him in. "It is now. What do you have?"

Quinto lifted the papers and approached the desk. "Your suggestion turned out to be spot on. We should've gone after the low hanging fruit first, but all the crazy elements of this case got us distracted, I guess. I dug in the archives, running background checks on all the major parties on your board. And wouldn't you know it? A couple of them stuck out."

All evidence of exhaustion had left Shay. She sat up like the proverbial rod to which her name alluded. "Who?"

"Diamond, or should I say Mickey Drummond," said Quinto, peering at the sheets. "He has priors for blackmail and extortion. Served two years. And wouldn't you know it, but his pal Dennis served four years for assault and battery."

"A big guy like him?" I said. "I'm shocked."

"Hey now," said Quinto. "We're not all bad."

"He wore a skull and crossbones t-shirt, though," I said. "Kind of a giveaway."

"And that's not all," said Quinto. "I just received news from a runner. Yellow Cobra? They're playing a show tonight."

"And I think we all know who's singing and playing rhythm guitar," said Shay.

I eyed her. She shot me and Quinto a glance. The big guy gave me and her a nod. Rodgers seemed upset at being excluded.

"So...what does this mean?" Rodgers said. "Diamond and Dennis did it?"

"I'm not entirely sure," said Shay. "But I'd wager my lunch money the pair was involved, probably with another member of Yellow Cobra or its management. And lucky for us, they're all getting together in one spot. I say we head back to the Moxy, gather up the lot of them, and put this thing to bed."

The metaphor might've not been the choicest given our collective exhaustion, but her sentiment was well taken. I had my suspicions about who'd been involved, but I needed to put their feet to the fire, drug overdoses or alibis be damned. Only then might we finally get some answers.

36

A crowd had assembled outside the Moxy's exterior, mostly held in check by movable posts strung together with rope. A pair of bouncers—Dennis not among them—had herded the assembled masses into some semblance of a line. The patrons shuffled forward, eager to hand the bouncers their cash and be let inside. Among them I saw an overabundance of young ladies, some with wild hairstyles and brightly-colored locks, others with studded leather jackets and tight denim pants. Some even rocked homemade apparel with Yellow Cobra patches and embroidery. As I skirted them, heading toward the side door with Steele, Rodgers and Quinto beside me, I overheard snippets of conversation.

"A special showing? Can you believe it? Normally they only perform a few nights a week."

"Two nights. But I overheard the band has big news to announce. Maybe another international tour?"

"Not what I heard. Rumor has it they booted Chaz from the band."

Gasps.

"Not Chaz! They can't replace him!"

"That's not what I heard. Someone told me he left of his own accord. He's going to start a new band. Green Panther."

"You're all wrong. I heard he got drunk last night and quit. Now he's groveling trying to make his way back, but the rest of the band won't let him. Not like they need him. B. B.'s my favorite. He's the *real* creative spark."

I left the argument of who was better than who in my wake and cracked the side door. With the sun having set, the club's interior no longer seemed so dark and oppressive, but a low roar emanated from inside. Cigarette smoke wafted into my nostrils, as did hints of other burnable herbs and cured plants of questionable legality.

I nodded toward the stairs. "Let's check the ready room."

We headed down the steps to the door with the gold star affixed to it. I tested the handle and found it amenable to my touch.

"Freeze!" I said as it swung open. "NWPD. Hands in the—"

I stopped in mid-phrase, realizing the quartet of floozies with fluffed up hair who lounged across the sofas inside weren't particularly impressed with my vocal ferocity. They peered at me with glazed eyes, mildly confused and unfazed by the lingering smell of camel droppings and the implications thereof. I know I wouldn't have sat on those couches, not after having seen what the camel had done to them.

"Say..." the one closest to me said as she puffed on a cigarette. "You're not with the band."

The one on the end noticed me, as I did her. Thankfully, or not depending on one's viewpoint, her shirt actually covered her breasts this time.

"Hey," said Crystal, swiping her mostly blonde bangs out from in front of her face. "You're the detectives from earlier. You ever figure out what happened to Chaz?"

Shay wasn't in the mood for any crap, literally or figuratively, I imagined. "Where is everyone, Crystal?"

"Who?" she said. "You mean the band? They're already on stage. Well, behind the stage, I think. You know...getting ready?"

"What about Diamond?" asked Shay.

Crystal's face lit up. "Didn't you hear? He's taking over for Chaz. He's finally getting his big break!"

Or taking it, I thought. "And his buddy, Big D?"

The light left Crystal. "I don't know. Up around the stage, too, I guess."

One of the floozies on the couch blew out a long puff of smoke and eyed Rodgers. "Hi there, cutie. You like to rock?"

Rodgers gulped. "I'm having flashbacks to when I met Allison. Get me out of here, Quinto."

Quinto shook his head and muttered under his breath. "Lucky bastard..."

Shay pointed a finger at Crystal. "Stay here. Don't get in the way."

"Get in the way of what?" she said, but we'd already turned and headed back the way we'd came. We left Quinto by the side door, in part because he'd better hold the exit in the event that Big D tried to make a break for it, but also because his rock quarry-like face was better equipped to rebuff the groupies' attempted affections.

Rodgers, Steele, and I wormed our way through the side halls toward the front of the club, pushing past patrons who'd jammed the spaces in hopes of finding a spot for quiet conversation. As we walked, I heard the occasional twang of a guitar or cymbal crash over the crowd noise.

After much effort and mumbled apologies, we forced our way into the music hall proper. Seemingly the instant we did so, a hush fell over the crowd. I turned my eyes toward the stage to see the Yellow Cobra guys, Sammy, Ritchie, and B. B., the latter in a frilly long sleeve shirt that hid his mauled chest, walk onstage to wild applause. With them strutted Diamond, outfitted in a bejeweled black leather vest that matched his stage name in sparkle if not value. They all headed straight to their instruments, Ritchie diving behind his drum set and the others snagging their guitars.

"Thank you!" shouted B. B., waving at the crowd. "Thanks for coming! We are...Yellow Cobra!"

With that simply announcement, the band attacked their instruments. A cool catchy melody swept over the arena. "Creatures of the Night," I quickly realized by the lyrics. Diamond sang.

I turned to Steele, speaking in a voice loud enough for her and Rodgers to hear me but hopefully not so loud as to upset the surrounding patrons. "Well, we arrived at about the worst possible time."

"No kidding," she said. "I don't know how happy these folks would be to have us end their show prematurely—and that's assuming we could even reach the stage right now."

A piqued voice rose above the crowd from the direction of the entrance. "Excuse me. Sorry. Make way. Coming through."

The masses parted, and Phillips squirted through the void.

"There you are," he said. "Boy, am I glad to find you by the door. I wasn't looking forward to fighting my way through the crowd in search of you."

The poor guy looked disheveled. I gave him a nod. "Phillips, what's going on? Shouldn't you be at home by now? Don't tell me they've got you working overtime?"

"You guys aren't the only ones burning the candle at both ends," he said. "Don't worry. I volunteered. But that's not why I'm here. Earlier today, while you were gone, we received a message from the Mackinaw Street Precinct. Something about a stolen transportation cage and a bunch of missing animals from the New Welwic Zoo. We added it to the alert board at the station for the patrol cops to be aware of."

"Gods be praised, the system works," I said.

"Sort of," said Shay. "Nobody went to talk to Zookeeper Pope, and we weren't alerted about it even though Quinto had already brought a camel back to the station. Is that really why you're here, Phillips?"

He nodded. "A couple of bluecoats found the cart and sent word. I knew you'd want to be alerted straight away."

"Because you heard Daggers and Steele visited the zoo," said Rodgers. "Thoughtful, if a little excessive."

"Uh...no, sir."

"*No?*" I said. "Then why in the world are you here?"

"Well, because of the cart," said Phillips. "But I didn't know you'd gone to the zoo. Rather, the beat cops said they found a large quantity of blood at the scene. You're homicide detectives. I figured it was the right call."

Shay slapped me on the arm. "You hear that? Sounds like we finally found our crime scene. Way to go, Phillips!"

The young bluecoat smiled. "Thanks, Captain."

I massaged my arm and frowned. "Yeah, thanks. Finally some good timing to counteract the bad. You up for more overtime pay, Phillips?"

"What do you have in mind, sir?"

"Stay here. Check out the show," I said. "But watch the door. Make sure none of the Cobras weasel their way out. Quinto's guarding the back, so that's covered. Rodgers? Maybe you can locate Benson? I want to make sure he doesn't slink off, either."

"And I'm guessing you and Steele are off to see the lion cart?" he said.

"You're as sharp as a tack, my friend."

"Figures," he said. "But I'll do it. And not only because I might be able to brag to Allison that I got to see the last Yellow Cobra concert."

"That's the ticket," I said. "Steele?"

She gave me a nod. We got the address from Phillips and pushed our way back out through the front.

37

Phillip's address wasn't quite as accurate as I'd hoped, but Shay and I found the spot anyway thanks to the lanterns the beat cops had set up at the scene. They shone like beacons of curiosity, their light spilling from the mouth of an alley tucked between two mottled brown brick buildings, one shuttered and with a 'For Lease' sign hanging over the door and the other a warehouse of some sort.

A light snowfall had started to fall, though the air remained too warm for it to stick. Certainly, the flakes hadn't impacted the bluecoat at the foot of the alley. He stood there, impervious to their assault as he plucked something from a small brown bag and stuffed it in his mouth.

We approached the man, a middle-aged guy with broad shoulders and a brown beard that grew thicker around his neck than it did over his face. He eyed us, but didn't move to stop us. His legs might as well have sprouted roots.

"You those detectives?" He stuffed more of the bag's contents into his mouth.

I eyed the bag. What was it? Chewing tobacco? "Daggers and Steele. That's us. This the alley with the cart?"

The officer turned and spat. Remnants of sunflower seeds spewed from his lips. It wasn't quite as disgusting as a spray of brown, nicotine-soaked saliva would've been, but it was close.

"This is it," he said. "Go on in. Have a look. We tried not to touch anything. I know how persnickety you lot are about your crime scenes."

Between the man's word choice and his clear disdain for our presence, I gathered he didn't have any career aspirations beyond his position. Good thing, too. A spittoon wouldn't match the station's décor.

"Just a sec." Shay pointed toward the alley interior. "When did you find this?"

The officer shrugged. "I don't know. Hour. Hour and a half ago."

"While on your beat?" asked Shay.

The guy nodded. More sunflower seeds went into his mouth.

"Was anyone here?" asked Shay.

"Nope." The seeds gave his voice a warbled texture.

I nodded toward the lanterns. "Come on." The 'this guy's useless' was implied.

I led the way into the alley, skirting a stack of trash loosely piled against the bricks on the left-hand side. Unfortunately, my route took me straight into a trap. Mud squelched as it met my boots, squishing and rising over my soles.

"Oh, and watch for the mud," called Officer Spittle-face.

I ground my teeth. "Thanks."

A drain pipe ran down the edge of the warehouse, spilling its contents behind the pile of trash. The warmer than normal temperatures must've melted whatever snow lingered on the roof and sent it pouring into the alley. I pulled my foot from the mud with a wet smack and scraped it against the bricks to clean it.

Shay picked her way around the trouble spot. "Better you than me, given our footwear. I owe you one."

"That's me," I said. "The proverbial guinea pig. Just push me in the way of any wild animals, stray fists, or crumbling masonry. I'll be fine."

I banged my boot against the bricks a couple more times and danced along the edge of the structure toward the cart, brightly illuminated by the pair of lanterns Officer Spittleface had mounted on stakes at the scene. The cart itself, marked on the sides with the words 'Live Animal Transport,' stood about six and a half feet tall and was mounted on two enormous wooden wheels with a hitch assembly hanging from the front. I spotted a few long leather straps that looked as if they were meant for attaching the thing to a horse, but I imagine they could've just as easily been used with a camel.

Shay had already moved to the backside of the cart. She peered into the iron-banded box and gagged. "Ugh. Jake, come look at this."

I did as she asked. As I skirted the corner, I got a whiff of what had wrinkled her nose—a sour, metallic tang of blood mixed with a potent musk reminiscent of the zoo's worst offerings. I plucked one of the lanterns from its post and held it into the cart's cavity. Sure enough, a dark, sticky substance coated the floor, as well as parts of the sides and ceiling. Because of the darkness and mud, I couldn't tell how much of the stuff had spilled outside the enclosure, but I could tell it wasn't blood alone that coated the inside of the cart. Copious amounts of hair had been sprinkled into the mixture. The cart's walls also appeared to be heavily scratched, but whether the damage was new or old, I couldn't tell.

I returned the lantern to its stake. "Well, unless multiple people were murdered in New Welwic Zoo transport wagons last night, I'd say we found our cart."

"Agreed," said Shay. "Why don't you check the front? See if there are any clues we might've missed. I'll do the same here in back."

"Clues *you* might've missed?" I said. "I can try, but I'll probably fail."

Despite her exhaustion, that brought a smile to her lips. I skirted back around the edge of the cart, keeping my feet close to the shuttered building and out of the muck. I cast my gaze around, more slowly this time.

"You noticed the mud, of course," I said.

Shay's voice drifted around the side of the wagon. "I would've had a hard time missing it thanks to your own squishy encounter."

"So you noticed the tracks, then," I said. "The mud, well...*muddied* them, for lack of a better word, but they seem to be about the same size and shape as the camel footprints we found in Rucker Park this morning."

Shay hummed some sort of agreement.

I glanced toward the pile of trash. "Did you notice the garbage? Some of it's been knocked out of the cans. I can't imagine it was deposited that way to being with."

"Daggers?" said Shay. "Come look at this."

I turned around and found Shay kneeling at the side of the alley. A few loose pieces of trash inhabited her side as well: stray sheets of newspaper, cigarette butts, an old shoe, and bits of rotting foodstuffs, mostly. Shay held something else in her hand, though.

"What's that?" I asked.

Shay stood and turned. "An empty jar. Well, mostly empty. There's a little something left at the bottom. Could be mud, but I think it's...peanut butter."

I blinked. "That's...*odd*."

"Is it?" said Shay. "The zookeeper said she found baboons fighting over a jar near the animal enclosures last night."

"Yes, but she also said the baboons weren't able to get it open. That she confiscated the jar. And the bodega owner who pointed us in the zoo's direction said he sold the Cobras *a* jar of peanut butter. As in singular, not plural."

"Maybe he misremembered," said Shay.

"He checked the ledger," I said. "I doubt he'd have marked it down wrong. Sales are that orc's livelihood. He wouldn't make that sort of mistake often."

"What are you saying?" said Shay. "That the orc from the bodega is in on this somehow?"

I shook my head, but I'd already retreated into the depths of my mind. There *was* an explanation that made sense. Sort of.

"Well, I don't know what to tell you," said Shay. "We can bring this to Cairny, but I'm pretty sure this is pea-nut butter. Certainly I'm not going to taste—hey, where are you going?"

I'd started to drift toward the far end of the alley, the one opposite from where we'd entered. "I've got an idea. Follow me."

38

I made it to the street and peered down its darkened lengths. The neighborhood we'd entered wasn't particularly busy given the hour, but lights nonetheless shined from beneath the eaves of a few shops. I squinted as I tried to make out the signs above them. One featured a picture of a shoe and a pie and the name The Cheery Cobbler. Another sign read Qwik Wicks, which sounded more my speed, but the picture next to the name made me think the place was a candle shop rather than a convenience store owned by a guy with a lisp and a poor grasp of punctuation. I did eventually spot the place I'd hoped I would—a small freestanding building by the name of Go Go Grocery.

Shay joined me at the mouth of the alley. "Daggers?"

"Come on," I said, tilting my head toward the shop. "Let me do the talking."

A few quick steps brought me to the door. I pulled it open, hearing the shopkeeper's bell ring out. Lights burned bright within, showcasing the store's assorted snacks, groceries, and household goods, all set on racks much like they'd been at the Pop 'n Shop bodega.

A gnome with a long pipe in hand, wearing a velvet nightcap in addition to a set of purple pajamas, sat on a stool behind the front counter.

I approached him. "Hey, pops. Got a question for you."

"*Pops?*" he said. "I'll have you know I'm sixteen, you old fart."

"Tell it to the wrinkles on your face." I took out my badge. "Either way, if you're telling the truth, you shouldn't be smoking. Or violating occupational workplace standards."

"Whoa, whoa," said the gnome, putting down the pipe. "I don't want any trouble. This is a family business. My dad owns it. We're not breaking any age-related hiring rules."

"Good," I said, returning my badge to my jacket. "Now tell me. Someone came in last night. Probably between four thirty and six thirty. Bought a jar of peanut butter. Who was it?"

"*What?*" The gnome looked at me like I'd lost it. Maybe I had.

"Last night. Peanut butter. Four thirty. Six thirty. *Who?*"

I heard Shay's voice from behind me. "Daggers... Calm down."

The poor gnome blinked. "Dude, I don't know. I don't work the night shift. My pops does."

"I need to talk to him. Now. Where is he?"

"Upstairs in the loft," said the gnome. "We rent the whole building. But he might be asleep. He doesn't take over until ten."

I looked around. A door to the side of the counter beckoned. "Those the stairs?"

"Yeah," said the gnome. "But you can't go barging in there. That's our home."

Shay stood behind me. In addition to being calmer and more level-headed than I was, she was also captain now. She didn't make the rules, but she enforced them. Punished the stubborn jackasses who barged into people's apartments without warrants and excluded the evidence said knuckleheads gathered. Somehow I suspected she wouldn't cut me any slack due to our relationship, not even in exchange for sexual favors—especially because the favors usually flowed in the other direction.

"Look," I told the gnome. "What was your name?"

"Gniddgnissario."

"Okay, Nidnis... Nidni... Can I call you Nid?"

The kid nodded.

"Here's the deal, Nid," I said. "I'm a homicide detective. My partner Steele is, too. Someone was murdered in an alley around the corner from here last night. I think they came in and purchased something from your grocery. I have to get a description. It could break our case wide open. So unless your old man's in a coma, I'm going to need you to take me to him to see what he knows. Steele can guard the door, make sure nobody makes off with anything. Is that okay with you?"

"Uh...yeah. Sure. I guess." He hopped off the stool and landed lightly on his feet. "Come with me."

He led me up the stairs, which thankfully were sized for normal people—Nid had said they rented the building, after all. At the second floor landing, we stopped in front of another door. I had to reign in my desire to kick the thing down while Nid produced a key, which he inserted into a secondary lock installed at knee level.

The lock clacked, he pushed the door open, and ushered me in. The smell of cooked beet greens and bacon greeted me, as did the whistling of a tea kettle and the shrieking of a teeny, tiny baby gnome. The gnome lass who held the babe stared at me as I entered, as did an assortment of six or seven other gnomes of indeterminate ages, all of them seated at a diner table roughly the size of my coffee table at home.

Suddenly I felt overjoyed that I hadn't barged in like a rampaging bull. Given that I dealt with murderers for a living, it was easy to forget most people in the city had families and were simply trying to get by.

"Uh, mom? Dad?" said Nid. "This is officer...Daggers, was it? With the police. He needs to talk to dad."

"Detective, actually," I said. "But it's okay."

One of the gnomes—to my eyes neither discernibly younger or older than any of the others—stood and skirted the table. "Yes? Can I help you?"

I felt the weight of over a dozen small eyes on me, burrowing into me with a mixture of anger and fear. Was it my size? It wasn't that I was a police officer, was it?

"Ah...sorry to interrupt your dinner," I said. "Or breakfast, for you anyway. Whichever. I just need to ask you about last night. A man came into your store. I'm guessing between four-thirty and six-thirty. He bought peanut butter. Am I right?"

"Yeah," said the father gnome. "That's right. He didn't look too good. Was all muddy and had a welt on his face. I had to get the mop out after he left."

I didn't need to ask the next question, but I did anyway, just to be sure. "His hair. Describe it for me."

"It was black. Curly. He had a lot of it."

I suppressed a fist pump. "Thanks. That's all I needed. You guys have a wonderful dinner."

I turned and raced down the stairs where I found Steele still standing by the door. I shot her a grin. "It was Ritchie."

She lifted an eyebrow. "The gnome upstairs identified him?"

I nodded. "He fell into the mud outside. He came here and purchased a second jar of peanut butter. He's the one who killed Chaz."

Shay's brow furrowed. "Okay, I'm with you so far. But...*why*? And not just why, but how? What the heck happened out there?"

I rubbed my hands together. "I'm not sure, but it's high time we found out."

39

My badge—still somehow attached to the rest of my black leather wallet—got me past the bouncer at the Moxy's front door. Inside, I found the situation largely unchanged from when I'd left it. A dense crowd packed the club's main floor, bouncing and gyrating along with the music. The Yellow Cobra quartet, with Diamond having replaced Chaz, continued to rock, though they'd all developed a sheen of sweat thanks to the bright lights, the heat of the huddled masses, and their own exertions.

I found Phillips and Rodgers standing against the wall near the front door. I waved and closed on them, with Shay at my side.

"Guys," I said. "Give us an update."

"I talked to Benson," Rodgers said over the crowd. "Made myself explicit about his required participation in our stunt. He's in his office. He won't try anything. Phillips and I've been here by the front the rest of the time, and Quinto hasn't shifted from his post at the back—at least he hadn't the last time I checked. Those groupies are persistent."

"That's not all. We sent for backup." Phillips pointed out a pair of bluecoats, one by the bar and another at the base of the crowd, near the hallway toward the back. "There's another with Detective Quinto. They arrived maybe ten minutes ago. Good timing, for you two as well. This is the Cobra's encore. They came back onstage a couple minutes before you popped in."

"Perfect," I said. "When this song's over, I want everyone to move. Rodgers, you head to Benson's office and snag him. Phillips, you'll help Steele, Quinto, and the rest of us wrangle the Cobras. I want all of them. B. B., Sammy, Ritchie, Diamond, and Dennis. And hopefully we can send a team to snag Billy Charles. I'll want to talk to him, too."

Rodgers looked to Steele. "That good with you?"

She nodded, which reminded me I should be letting her take the lead now. Then again, her being captain didn't necessarily mean she wanted to dictate the course of our investigations. Perhaps she preferred for me to take charge in those scenarios, or she felt comfortable wrestling the reins from me if I happened to deviate from the strategy she would've suggested. Or she valued my fragile male ego and knew I liked to boss people around every now and then.

"What about you guys?" said Rodgers. "Find anything?"

I nodded. "Ritchie did it."

"Seriously?" said Rodgers. "What happened?"

"We'll explain it later," said Shay. "Or rather, I hope Ritchie or one of the others will, because right now we're pretty clueless about how or why it happened. But we'll get there."

The music intensified, a crescendo of wailing guitars, thumping drums, and ringing cymbals, all with Diamond's warbling voice carrying over the rest of it. With a resounding cymbal crash, it died, and B. B. called out. "Thank you! Thank you! Good night!"

The Cobras waved, bowed, and exited toward the back of the stage.

"That's our cue," I said. "Let's move. Phillips? Can you notify Quinto?"

"You bet." He motioned to the officers at the sides of the club, both of whom were thankfully paying attention. They nodded and started to close on the stage as Phillips worked his way into the back hallway. Rodgers headed toward the stairs to snag the band manager while Steele and I pushed our way through the crowd.

I led the way, feeling like a fish swimming upstream, but eventually I reached the elevated platform. A decent mob still gathered there, chatting, sipping on their beers, and dancing to the ghost echoes of the music. I pushed through them, too, and mounted the stage. From there I headed stage left, knowing the route to the ready room lay that way.

My hunch paid off. We intercepted the Cobras as they reached the side door, where Quinto and a bluecoat had stopped the bunch as a precautionary measure. Shay and I blocked their escape from behind, as did the pair of bluecoats who'd come with us, and Phillips came from up the hall to catch them in a pincer move.

I caught the beginnings of an argument as we arrived.

"What do you mean we need to come back with you to the police station?" said B. B., his cheeks red and sweat dripping down his brow. "We were already there this morning. I told you, we don't know what the hell happened to Chaz. Besides, we just finished a show. This is *sooooo* not the time."

"Look," said Quinto. "I know that, but unfortunately you're all needed for additional questioning. I'd think you'd be willing to help us find the man who murdered your friend and band mate even if it inconvenienced you. You *would*, wouldn't you?"

B. B. complained but in a way that professed his innocence. Sammy shook his head. Diamond looked around dumbly, though to be fair, it was roughly the same look he'd given us earlier in the day. Big D clapped him on the shoulder and said something in his ear. I didn't like his posture.

"Don't even think about it, big guy," I said, calling out to him.

Dennis looked up.

"Yeah, you," I said, pointing at him. "Whatever it is, drop it."

I scanned the crowd one more time. *Damn...*

"Guys?" I said. "Where's Ritchie?"

My question spurred a number of glances in all directions.

"Seriously? Somebody? Where is he?"

Sammy took up the call. "Man, I don't know. I think he exited to the other side of the stage or something."

I locked eyes with Quinto. "Handle this, okay? Steele. With me."

I took off back the way we'd come, Shay hot on my heels. I crossed the stage and exited to the right this time, back into the maze of curtains and pulleys and dark corners in which we'd earlier found Diamond hard at work groping Crystal. This time, however, the corners seemed darker and much less full of roadie hands caressing fairy breasts.

"Ritchie?" I called out. No answer. *Damn.*

"He couldn't have gotten out, could he?" said Shay. "We've got the exits covered, unless he somehow managed to sneak back around to the front or out a window—not that I'm sure there are any of those."

I refused to believe it. "How did he know we'd come after him? Did he see us in the crowd?"

"You want to split up?" asked Shay.

I shook my head. "Stick with me. Keep looking."

I plunged onward into more hallways filled with crates of empty beer bottles, stacks of old flyers, and assorted rigging elements. The halls only darkened I progressed. I nearly tripped over a length of coiled rope, and I knee-capped myself on an old discarded bass drum.

The more I searched, the more my despair grew. We couldn't have lost him. We simply couldn't have. There was no way he could've escaped our net. Not unless...

We turned a corner. There, at the end of a hall, I spotted motion. My eyes had adjusted, but only enough to get a general gist of what was going on.

I noticed a dark figure. A man, with dark hair. Ritchie.

More motion. A pained moan. Ritchie leaned over. He had someone at the wall, his face at their neck.

Cold dread filled my veins. I leapt forward, ripping Daisy from my jacket but knowing it wouldn't be enough to fend him off. I cried out.

"Nooooo!!!"

Ritchie pulled back, his teeth flashing in the darkness, but normal, neither elongated nor dripping with blood.

The figure behind him moved, one with wavy blond hair and a denim jacket over a black crop top. She blinked and looked at me.

I blinked back. "Heather?"

"Uh...detective?" she said. "What are you doing here?

The answer to that was simple. What *she* was doing there, on the other hand, was a much more interesting question—but one I had a good feeling I knew the answer to. And as I ran through the possibilities in my head, one thing was clear.

The case suddenly made a whole lot more sense.

40

gripped the door handle and twisted, pushing into the interrogation room. We'd placed Ritchie in the nice-by-comparison upstairs unit, though by the looks of things, the sterile, empty room, bright lights, and shiny metal table at which he'd been seated hadn't buoyed his spirits. Sweat dripped from his brow, leaving a trail of nervous energy that disappeared into his puffy black mane before eventually reappearing as stains underneath his armpits.

He looked up as Shay and I crossed through the door and joined him at the metal table. For a moment, a glimmer of hope shone in his eyes. The glimmer wavered, however, as he laid eyes on a brown paper bag I held in my right hand.

"Hey, detectives," he said. "When am I going to be able to leave? I already came here with you guys this morning. I've told you everything I know."

I took a seat in one of the metal folding chairs that faced the table, placing the bag on the table's edge. Its top sagged slightly to one side, neatly creased.

Shay took the seat next to me. "About that, Ritchie. Detective Daggers and I were hoping to go over the events of last night with you one more time."

"Again?" said Ritchie. "Come on. Seriously. I told you. After last night's concert, I went with Chaz, B. B., and Sammy to Billy Charles' place. We partied, drank, and took some drugs. I'm not sure what, but they hit me like a ton of bricks. Knocked me out cold, or at least I thought they did. Next thing I remember was waking up at the Banks with you two, your friend, and that hotel lady standing over me. That's it. That's all I've got."

Shay eyed him coolly. "So you wouldn't remember anything that might help us understand how Chaz ended up dead with his throat torn open in the middle of Rucker Park then, would you?"

"I'm telling you, *no*," said Ritchie. "Trust me, I'm devastated over it. Crushed. I've been on an emotional rollercoaster all day. First, I feel like it's a joke, then I get depressed, then angry. I'm all over the place. I don't know what to think."

"You seemed to have your thoughts pretty well in place as you fondled Chaz's ex-wife in the back of the Moxy," I said.

"Heather?" Ritchie stammered. "No. I mean...we were both upset. You know. Over Chaz. Things happen when you get emotional like that."

"You can drop the act," said Shay. "We talked to B. B. and Billy Charles."

Ritchie blinked in the bright lantern light. Another bead of sweat dripped down a previously established trail. "Excuse me?"

"We spoke to both of them," Steele said. "Billy admitted he hadn't told us the full story about what happened last night. He said he and Chaz got into an argument that ultimately resulted in you guys leaving the party. Remember that?"

Ritchie didn't say anything.

"Right," said Shay. "Anyway, according to Billy, Chaz went on a bit of a tirade. Insulted him to his face. Called him a quote 'two-bit hack' and 'former has-been with more wrinkles than a pair of elephant testicles.' Sammy took Chaz's side and, apparently, you and B. B. sided with Billy. That alone isn't a big deal. Chaz went off the rails often, we now understand, but Billy wasn't in much of a mood for it last night, especially after he'd gone out of his way to throw a party for you guys on your one year anniversary at the Moxy. So before you all split, he made sure to slip some extra powerful drugs into Chaz and Sammy's stash, drugs which *you* happened to be holding."

"I...don't remember that," said Ritchie.

"We think maybe you do," I said. "As we mentioned, we talked to B. B. again, too. We know you were smashed. You were all ingesting an assortment of drugs and alcohol from the moment you left the Moxy until the wee hours of the morning, or so we assume. But only Chaz and Sammy got the toxic cocktail of tranquilizers and anxiety meds. You and B. B. didn't. As a result, you might remember *some* of what happened. B. B. did. He admitted he recalled getting locked up on Flatley, and he remembered the lion and that you went back to the zoo afterwards."

Ritchie's eyes widened. More sweat beaded at his brow. His gaze quickly shifted between Steele and me. "Guys, I'm telling you. I'm being honest. I don't know what happened last night! *I swear!*"

"Don't lie to us, Ritchie. We found the lion transport cart. I tracked you to the Go Go Grocery, and the owner identified you." I reached for the bag, opened it, and produced the mostly empty jar within. "We found the peanut butter."

Ritchie's eyes widened even more. He froze, but the effect only lasted a second. Without warning, he covered his face and burst into tears.

I glanced at Shay, my eyebrows raised. I'd broken men, made them cry before in interrogations—but never with a mostly empty jar of nut butter.

"It...it was an accident," sobbed Ritchie. "Gods, I didn't mean to kill him. He was just being such an asshole, and I thought I'd teach him a lesson. Make him crap his pants. Served him right for being such a prick. But then I opened the door, and...gods, there was so much blood! *Damn it...*"

"So you *do* remember what happened last night," said Steele.

Ritchie nodded. "Not everything. Some of it. Enough."

"Then tell us what you *do* remember," I said. "You can skip the very beginning. Billy's place, Leopard Jane's, the Raccoon Ranch. What happened after B. B. got arrested by the Green Jackets, when you, Chaz, and Sammy split?"

Ritchie rubbed his eyes, trying to stem the tide of tears. "We, ah...went to Heather's. Chaz insisted. I think he was upset about being kicked out of the Ranch. Maybe he really needed to get off. The drugs can do that to you sometimes. Anyway, at Heather's, he got aggressive. Handsy. Tried to force himself on Heather, and seeing that? Man, it just... I..."

Ritchie clenched his jaw and curled his hand into a tight fist. His nostrils flared, and he squeezed out another tear.

Shay leaned forward, picking up on the same cues I had. "How long have you had feelings for Heather, Ritchie?"

The first unclenched, as did his jaw. "A long time. We dated, once or twice. Years ago, before she and Chaz hooked up. We were never a thing, but I always hoped, especially once she and Chaz split. But...she still had feelings for him, you know?"

I nodded. I'd guessed something along those lines, though I hadn't suspected they'd ever dated. "So you pulled Chaz off Heather. What then?"

Ritchie shook his head and held it in his hands. "We went to that goth joint, Club Midnight. Chaz was in a hell of a mood. Depressed because of Heather, angry about B. B. and the Ranch, out of his mind and hallucinating from the drugs. Then that friend of his comes by, some guy with a bunch of tattoos."

"Jefferson Torment," said Shay.

"Yeah, him," said Ritchie. "They start talking about vampires because supernatural creatures are Chaz's favorite thing in the world, I guess. Chaz was admiring the guy's new ink when suddenly he says screw it, I want one. So we followed the guy to a tattoo shop and

Chaz gets a vampire symbol on his chest, because of course he does."

"An ankh," I said. "Right. And that's where we lose you guys. So what exactly happened after that?"

Ritchie took a deep breath, his voice firming. "The whole time he was getting a tattoo, Sammy and I were trying to figure out how we could bust B. B. out. Sammy thought we needed to recruit an army and charge the place, but he was high as a kite. Then Chaz finished with his tat and since he's on this vampire high, he says all we need is a single vampire to help us—his 'brethren' he called them—because they have super-human strength or psychic powers or something. And he says he knows where to find them."

"The zoo," said Steele.

Ritchie nodded. "Yeah. He drags us there and over to a cage full of bats. He busts in and starts asking them for help. Pleading his case. And they get really agitated. Start flying and whipping around him like crazy. Spooky stuff. And then, suddenly, Chaz just passed out. Collapsed on the floor of the bat enclosure. That's when the bats quieted back down."

"And how Chaz undoubtedly got covered in bat crap," I told Shay.

"Anyway," continued Ritchie, "while we're there, Sammy has this idea. We can steal some bloodthirsty animal and unleash it on the lockup to scare everyone away, then we can bust B. B. out. So he finds the lion pen, and he's about to break in there when I stop him. I mean, the lion would've eaten him whole! So I con-vince him to head back out, and we break into a nearby store and steal some leather armor and stuff. We buy some sausages for the lion and snacks for us, too. And then, back at the zoo, we find this cart and manage to get the lion inside by piling all the sausages in there. But then we need a way to move the cart, so we steal this really cool camel and have him drag the cart over to the jail for us."

"And we know what happened there," I said. "But how did you get the lion in the lockup without getting hurt?"

"Dude, I don't know," said Ritchie. "I blacked out during that part. I just remember helping B. B. out of there, and he's been mauled by the lion, and there was blood. It was scary. But we made it out alive, and then we had to take the camel and the cart back to the zoo. Plus we had to get Chaz out of there. So we head back to the zoo, but when we arrive, Chaz isn't in the bat cage anymore. That's when we find him wandering out of one of the other animal enclosures, and all hell breaks loose!"

"What happened?" asked Shay.

"I don't know," said Ritchie. "I guess Chaz let a bunch of the animals loose. But they all started attacking us. There were these little deer with tiny horns and these huge hairy hamster things with big buck teeth."

"Capybaras," I said.

"Yeah, whatever," said Ritchie. "It was a scene out of a nightmare. And then the damn baboons showed up, barking and shouting and going after whatever snacks we had left. And of course I was the one holding everything!"

"So what did you do?" asked Shay.

"I got rid of everything," said Ritchie. "Threw it wherever I could. I think I tossed the beef jerky and bread into the cart and the other stuff out in the open. Probably three baboons dove into the cart after the food, and I locked them in there as quick as I could to keep them from coming back out. The others were fighting over the peanut butter and chips. Sammy and B. B. had already bolted, and I was about to too, but then here comes dumbass Chaz, whooping and hollering like the baboons. He jumps on the camel, freaking it out, and it takes off. I only just managed to hop onto the back of the cart before it tore out of there. The poor animal was so freaked out he ran for a good fifteen minutes, all while Chaz rode him like a bull and I clung onto the back of the cart for dear life."

"And that's how you found yourself in that alley?" I asked.

Ritchie nodded again. "Chaz finally got him under control and reined him in. I tried to calm the poor beast, but Chaz was all jacked from the experience. Got his blood pumping, I guess. Kept talking about how it made him feel alive, like a man. And then...he mentioned Heather again. He had this wild look on his face. And...I knew what he was planning. I knew it. I couldn't let that sick asshole do anything to hurt her. So I turned to him, and I... I said..."

Ritchie hesitated.

"Go on," I said. "If you want us to put a positive spin on your case to the DA, you'd better tell us the truth."

Ritchie swallowed hard. "I told him...if he ever touched Heather again, I'd kill him. But I swear to the gods I didn't mean it. I just couldn't have him hurt her.

Not like that. Not that it mattered. Chaz turned red as a beet. Told me it was none of my damned business and that he'd do whatever the hell he pleased. And I...well, I took a swing at him. I missed, though. He didn't. Nailed me right in the cheek." Ritchie pointed to his black eye.

"And he knocked you into the mud," said Shay.

"That's right," said Ritchie. "Didn't last long after that, though. He screamed at me, telling me I was done, out of the band, right before he passed out again and fell into a pile of trash at the end of the alley."

"So how does the peanut butter fit into all this?" I asked.

Ritchie held his head and started to cry again. I blinked. The peanut butter was two for two this interrogation.

"I don't know, man," he said, sobbing. "I wasn't thinking straight. All I know is I was angry. No. *Furious.* How dare that asshole throw me out of the band? And to think he could take advantage of Heather? *Are you kidding me?* What a self-absorbed prick. So I sat there in the mud, just staring at Chaz in the trash, listening to those damn baboons going at it in the cart, and I got this crazy idea."

"To slather your band mate in peanut butter and feed him to the baboons," said Shay.

"No, not *feed him,*" said Ritchie. "It was a prank to teach that bastard a lesson. See how he liked it to wake up and find some stranger on top of him, terrifying him. Except instead of a person it would be a trio of baboons. But I swear, I had no idea the animals would kill him! I thought they'd lick the peanut butter off him and maybe scratch him up a bit if he fought back."

"But they did kill him," I said.

The sobbing continued. "I got scared when I didn't hear anything from Chaz for fifteen minutes. I opened up the cart, and the baboons bolted. That's when I saw all the blood. Gods, there was so much of it..."

"And let me guess," said Steele. "You saw the neck wound. Chaz had been on a vampire high all night, and you figured, maybe I can frame this as a vampire murder? So you threw Chaz on the camel's back, took him to the park, and tied him up to a tree using the whip you'd stolen from Tommy Llama's leather shop."

Ritchie nodded. He didn't make eye contact, and he spoke in a low voice. "I swear, I didn't mean to kill him. It was supposed to be a joke..."

I rapped my fingers on the table's cool metal surface, eyeing Ritchie the whole time. His slumped posture, his tears, his resignation. It all spoke to his truthfulness, despite the disbelief his story inspired.

"Well, Ritchie," I said. "I have some good news for you."

He looked up, his eyes wet and shimmering. "Yes?"

"Heather's safe now," I said. "Chaz will never hurt her again. Thanks to you. You, however, could be going away for a very long time."

Ritchie hung his head and begun to cry again. I clapped Steele on the shoulder, and we both rose and headed for the door.

41

The door clicked shut behind us, and Steele and I began our trek back to our desks. The halls echoed our footsteps, as most of the beat cops and detectives had long since headed home for the night.

"Well, that went surprisingly well," said Shay.

"I know," I said. "I didn't expect to get such a detailed testimony considering the amount of drugs and booze he wolfed down last night. And who ever thought peanut butter would be considered a murder weapon?"

Shay snickered. "You really think he's going to go to prison for an extended period of time?"

I shrugged. "Depends on where the prosecution decides to take it. Best case scenario for him, they charge him with reckless endangerment. Worst case would be manslaughter, I think. But even if he doesn't get convicted of murder, those are serious charges. He'll be behind bars for a while."

"At least Heather will be happy," said Shay. "She'll inherit Chaz's fortune."

"However large or small that may be," I said. "I'm guessing she might be disappointed in the amount. Although, who knows? She might be more devastated by Ritchie's conviction if that backstage canoodling at the Moxy was any indication."

"She can pay him visits," said Shay. "Just not conjugal ones."

"Because they're not married?"

"Because those aren't allowed in real life."

We found Rodgers and Quinto, along with Cairny, at their desks outside Steele's new office, the trio chatting up a storm and laughing intermittently.

"Hey guys," said Shay. "What are you doing here? Don't tell me you're still interrogating suspects."

"What?" said Rodgers. "Oh, no. We're not working. But we felt we'd set a bad precedent heading home before you did, especially given your sleep struggles last night. Besides, we were curious about how it would go with Ritchie."

Quinto gave Steele a nod. "How are you holding up, by the way?"

"I'm upright, somehow," said Shay. "But I'm on my last legs, so I'll make it quick. Ritchie confessed. He killed Chaz, but it wasn't murder. That's on the baboons. Still, this is probably the first time in recorded history that peanut butter killed a man through means other than choking or obesity."

Our detective and coroner pals stared at us with questioning faces.

"We'll explain tomorrow," I said. "You can probably fill in the details for yourselves. Whatever you imagine won't be crazier than the truth. But Steele's right. It's high time we turned in."

"Fair enough," said Cairny, as the assembled masses grabbed their jackets. "But before you leave, Daggers, I wanted to let you know. I performed a physical on Mr. Forsythe, one that included a thorough examination of his teeth, and though I can't make the claim with one hundred percent certainty, it's my opinion as a medical professional that he's not nor ever has been a vampire."

Quinto gave Cairny a look. "And how thorough was this physical, exactly?"

She elbowed him in the ribs. "Get your mind out of the gutter. Besides, I touch dead people for a living. You're worried about me touching a living one?"

Quinto chuckled. He, Rodgers, and Cairny all said their goodbyes, including another round of congratulations for Shay, before heading for the front door. Shay walked into her office, snagged her overcoat off a rack, and joined me in heading toward the exit.

"So..." she said. "Anytime you're ready, feel free to congratulate me for being right this whole time."

"About what?" I said.

"Occam's razor? The simplest explanation is almost always the correct one. I totally called it."

"*Simplest?*" I sputtered. "You call what happened simple? Vampires would've provided a much more sensible explanation for the day's events."

"Speaking of which, you really had Cairny check Benson Forsythe for signs of vampirism?"

"Why not?" I said. "She was here. Her investigation into Chaz was complete. Might as well put a bow on that line of thought."

Shay laughed and shook her head. "You know, it's amazing to me how after you'd drawn the connection between the peanut butter and the baboons, and even after Cairny admitted that baboon teeth could've been responsible for Chaz's wound, you still held out hope that a vampire did it."

"Hope is a strong word. I simply wanted to eliminate the option. Besides, you forget there are a few things baboons and peanut butter can't explain about the case."

Shay cracked open the door and held it for me as we stepped outside. "Such as?"

"Benson's odd magnetism," I said. "His power over those drug-addled women. And Chaz's own connection to the bats. Tell me, if he wasn't a vampire or vampiric thrall of some sort, how did he get the bats to fly around him while he was in the cage? Why didn't they escape? And why did they only settle down when he passed out?"

"I don't know," said Shay. "Dumb luck?"

I tilted my head. "You of all people know that's not a thing. Not in our line of work."

"And vampires are?"

I smiled. "Could be. If we happen across another murder of Chaz's nature, I'll certainly entertain the idea—so long as the stiff's not covered in butter or jam or honey or something of that nature."

We paused on the precinct's front steps, the darkened night air finally bringing with it a bit of a chill.

"So, uh, Jake," said Shay. "I know it's been a long day, and I'm not in the mood for long, emotional discussions, but other than your apology this morning, we haven't had a chance to discuss our relationship."

My stomach froze with dread, but I managed to push past the icy obstacle and compose myself anyway. "Look. Shay... I meant everything I said this morning, about your intelligence, your tenacity, your leadership ability. I thought you'd make an excellent interim captain, and after seeing you on the job today, I know you will. You already are."

Shay smiled. "Thank you, Jake. That means a lot. But I was talking about our, you know...*real* relationship. In some ways it seems like a forgotten past, but at the same time, our magical night together on the *Prodigious* was only two nights ago."

"Right." I swallowed and cleared my throat. "And you were, perhaps, ah...looking to relive it?"

Shay lifted an eyebrow. "You're feeling forward, aren't you? To be honest, yes, but not tonight. That's sort of my point. I'm a dead woman walking right now. I'm amazed I'm still on my feet."

"Right," I said, feeling simultaneously disappointed and relieved. "Can I walk you home, at least?"

"*Walk?* Are you kidding. I'm taking a rickshaw. Seriously. I'm done."

"Well, at least you finally admitted it."

Shay smirked. "As I said I would."

"Of course," I said. "You're a woman of honor, as well as beauty, intelligence, and...well, there are too many adjectives to list. The point is, I guess this is where I say good night."

"Hold on, now," said Shay. "I didn't say you weren't welcome at my place. I simply said I wasn't getting frisky. There's a difference."

I stood there for a moment as the hamster that worked the wheel in my brain took a break, probably looking like a doofus the whole time.

"Daggers?"

"Right," I said, snapping out of it. "Just working through the implications of that. I'd love to come over. Though perhaps I should drop by my place first and grab a fresh set of clothes. Maybe a few."

"Whoa there, cowboy. Now you're getting presumptuous. This is a one night offer. No exchanges, refunds, or returns. Or at least, that's the current policy."

"Works for me," I said. "I'm the master of punishingly slow relationships. To me, this feels like riding a racehorse. Or a race camel, as today's events have proven is a thing."

Shay chuckled and shook her head. I leaned over the steps, looking for a rickshaw, but none appeared. As I stood there, Shay snuck in and wrapped an arm around my midsection. I kept one arm free to hail a cab and reciprocated the hug with my other. Though the night's chill had finally intensified, it was more than her physical proximity that filled me with warmth.

I smiled, and so did she. Together, we stood on the steps, pressed against each other as we waited for a ride.

ABOUT THE AUTHOR

Alex P. Berg is a mystery, fantasy, and science fiction author, a scientist, and a heavy metal aficionado. Connect with him at www.alexpberg.com. If you'd like to be notified when new books are released, please sign up for his mailing list on his website. You will only be contacted when new books come out, your address will never be shared, and you can unsubscribe at any time.

Word of mouth is critical to author success. If you enjoyed this novel, please consider leaving a positive review on Amazon. Even if it's only a line or two, it would be a *huge* help. Thanks!